FORGOTTEN
TRAIL

Also available by Claire Kells

The National Parks Mystery Series

An Unforgiving Place
Vanishing Edge

FORGOTTEN TRAIL

A NATIONAL PARKS MYSTERY

CLAIRE KELLS

CROOKED
LANE

NEW YORK

Copyright © 2023 by Kathleen Coggshall

Published in the United States by Crooked Lane Books, an imprint of The Quick Brown Fox & Company LLC.

Crooked Lane Books and its logo are trademarks of The Quick Brown Fox & Company LLC.

Library of Congress Catalog-in-Publication data available upon request.

ISBN (hardcover): 978-1-63910-526-7
ISBN (ebook): 978-1-63910-527-4

Cover design by Nicole Lecht

Printed in the United States.

www.crookedlanebooks.com

Crooked Lane Books
34 West 27th St., 10th Floor
New York, NY 10001

First Edition: November 2023

10 9 8 7 6 5 4 3 2 1

For my family

THE CALL CAME in, not from a park ranger, but from the newly minted manager of the Pinnacles Grand Hotel, a man named James Dunaway. His voice reminded me of a weatherman's: his tone formal, his words crisp and polished.

Also, like a weatherman, he had bad news: not a spate of rain in the forecast, but something worse. Something that made his surefooted voice tremble ever so slightly.

One of his guests was dead.

"I'm sorry, can you repeat that?" I asked Dunaway, as a man in board shorts flopped into the lane next to me. I was in a pool, of all places, and the lifeguard seemed displeased with my attempt to have a serious conversation with someone on the phone while mostly submerged. The morning rush made for a chaotic scene in this sunny corner of Burlingame, California.

". . . certainly dead . . ." came the caller's next attempt.

The splashing next to me drowned out Dunaway's voice. "I didn't catch that—you said someone found a dead body in your hotel?"

"Yes," he said. "Housekeeping found the body early this morning."

"Did you call the police?"

There was a brief but noticeable pause. "Yes, of course."

"Are they there?"

Dunaway cleared his throat. "The local police department sent one officer, but she's insisting this isn't her jurisdiction. A park ranger gave me your number."

I lifted my goggles off my face and sighed. "My personal number?"

"Well, yes, I assume so. You're Special Agent Felicity Harland, correct? With the Investigative Services Branch?" He had been in such a hurry to tell me his emergency that I hadn't had the chance to introduce myself.

"Yes," I said. "I'm with ISB."

"And you're covering Pinnacles National Park?"

I had to think for a minute. Somewhere in the back of my mind, I recalled an email that had gone out to all ISB agents a few months ago about a new hotel opening within the boundary of Pinnacles National Park, which meant we might have to deal with incidents there. There were, in fact, a number of hotels in the US on national park lands, but most of them were historical sites: stately, magnificent spectacles that attracted a different type of tourist than the ones who tended to venture deep into the parks themselves.

So, yes, there was *that* email, but then there was the other email from two days ago, informing me that I'd be covering a random assortment of small national parks in California for the next couple of weeks, should any park rangers require our investigative assistance. While I hoped someday to get a permanent assignment somewhere, that day hadn't come yet. I was still the low man on the totem pole. Or woman, as it were.

"Yes," I said, ruing the fact that my investigative partner was off in Sequoia at the moment, assisting the National Park Service as the fall season hurtled to a close. The massive snowstorm headed for the Sierras couldn't come fast enough.

As for me, I was used to taking calls at the worst possible moment—in a pool, on a mountain, cramped into a bush plane. *So much for trying to squeeze in a workout before heading up to the FBI field office in San Francisco.* When it came to crimes in the wilderness, convenience wasn't much of a consideration.

I held my phone above the water while curious swimmers looked on. The empty evidence bag next to my swim gear kept my phone dry, but it also kept people out of my lane. For the most part, I was fine with circle swimmers, but after dealing with my share of lane hogs and flailing breaststrokers, I'd decided to up my game with evidence bags.

"When can you be here?" Dunaway asked. "I assume you're local?"

"No, sir. Not at the moment."

"Well," he muttered. "That's unfortunate. I would appreciate it if you could get here as quickly as possible. We could really use your assistance."

Dunaway possessed the bland accent of a Californian, but it almost felt like he was making up for that fact by using diction that I'd only ever heard on network television. I chalked it up to nerves. People said and did all kinds of things when they were nervous.

"Well, usually a park ranger or the local police contact us after a preliminary investigation suggests that a crime has occurred," I said. "Has there *been* a preliminary investigation?"

A woman in a faded Speedo leaped over my head into my lane, having assumed that my workout was over. I really didn't want to get out of the pool, though. It was only a little after seven-thirty AM, the late October sunshine sparkling on the water. I wasn't looking forward to spending the rest of my day indoors. Ray Eskill, my superior at ISB, had put me on a task force to tackle cold cases from national parks dating back to 1872, when Yellowstone was established. It was quite the project; I had a whole stack of case files in the trunk of my rental car. Among them was an unsolved double murder in Pinnacles Monument—now Pinnacles National Park, as of 2013. *I guess this was meant to be*, I thought ruefully.

Dunaway was getting antsy. "Ma'am—er, Agent—here's the thing . . . my hotel opened less than a week ago. We haven't even had our grand opening ceremony yet—which, by the way, is on the schedule for next weekend. I'm still learning the ropes here, trying to get things off on the right foot. I would appreciate your discretion."

"Yes, but . . . has a crime occurred?"

He cleared his throat. "It has."

I planned to come right back around to the whole nature of this "crime," but for now, Dunaway and I had to hammer out some logistics. A big part of my job as an ISB agent was to work out the details before we devoted time and resources to an hours-long trek into a wilderness area. "And this hotel of yours is located *in* the park, correct?"

"Yes. The vast majority of our guests park near the Chaparral Trailhead at the west entrance; from there, it's a two-mile hike south on the Juniper Canyon Trail to the hotel trail. It's another two and a half miles from there to get to our property."

Four-and-a-half miles? That changed the game quite a bit. I'd have to pack a change of clothes and at least two liters of water. It wasn't often that the powers that be called in a chopper to help me process a scene, but I wondered if Ray would decide to give the FBI a heads-up on this one. A murder at the Pinnacles Grand was sure to get some publicity, and I might not be able to handle a pack of journalists and overeager tourists angling for a view.

Turning away from the phone for a moment, Dunaway offered a cheery hello to someone in the background: a curious hotel guest, probably. I could tell by his voice that he was working hard to keep up the façade.

"When can you get here?" he asked.

"I'm about thirty minutes south of San Francisco at the moment, so . . ." I glanced at the clock above the trash can. "A couple hours, at least." I palmed the deck and pushed myself out of the pool. These days, pain was mostly a distant memory. My shoulder had healed up nicely from the bullet fired into it fourteen months ago, and even my back, badly broken on a trek in the Australian outback several years ago now, rarely gave me trouble anymore. The only slight discomfort I felt was in my neck thanks to a pancake pillow and a rock-hard mattress at last night's Comfort Inn. There were other wounds, too, the kind that required mending of a different sort, but I tried not to think about those.

"I just want to avoid the FBI coming in here brandishing guns and egos in our first week of operation," Dunaway said. "The hotel's investors want a smooth opening."

"I'm sure they do." I took off my swim cap and grabbed my towel off the bleachers. I tilted my face toward the sky, squinting into the morning light, and relished the sun's balmy warmth on my wet skin. With my eyes closed, I could almost imagine myself standing on the shore of an alpine lake somewhere, not on a concrete pool deck a half mile from one of the busiest freeways in the United States. I immediately thought of my partner, Ferdinand "Hux" Huxley, who probably *was* standing on the shore of an alpine lake somewhere.

"How soon can you get here?" Dunaway asked, as politely as possible.

"Mr. Dunaway, I don't even know what I'm dealing with here. I've got to brief my partner, and assuming he's reachable, we should be there at noon, best case. Depends on traffic and the difficulty of that four-mile-plus hike."

There was a pause as Dunaway processed what must have sounded to him like an undesirable timeline. "What should I do with the body?" he asked.

Ah, yes, more logistics. The Pinnacles Grand hotel manager was no park ranger, that was for sure; he sounded every bit like the proprietor of a luxury hotel whose reputation was on the line. "I assume you made sure the victim is deceased?" I asked.

"Yes, well . . . it's obvious." He coughed into his hand.

"How obvious?"

"He's stiff, ma'am." Dunaway exhaled evenly. "He's dead."

"Then do nothing until we get there," I said. "Absolutely nothing."

"Yes, but . . ." He trailed off.

"But what?"

"But won't it start to smell?"

I couldn't help but crack a wry smile; everyone was always worried about the stench. "Where is the body currently?" I asked, sensing the lifeguard's eyes on me. *Yup, this is a weird conversation to be having poolside, but that's how it's got to be.*

"On the floor."

"Where, though? In a guest room? Outside by the pool? In the lobby?"

"In one of our cliffside suites."

I decided not to waste time by asking questions that would answer themselves once I arrived on the scene, but still, the impulse was there. "Turn the AC in the room way down, but keep the fan off," I said. "And don't touch anything. Don't let anyone come or go. Best practice is to put some bright-colored tape on the door so people stay away."

"I'm not doing anything to draw attention to this situation," he said. "I'll stand outside the room and wait for you to get here."

I understood his perspective—nosy hotel guests roaming the grounds, their cell phones at the ready for a social media blast—but he and I were coming at this situation from two completely different angles. Dunaway was determined to put his hotel's best foot forward despite the dead body in one of his hotel rooms, while I was mostly concerned with preserving the crime scene—assuming this *was* a crime scene.

"Like I said, it could be a while." I put my towel around my waist and stuffed my gear into my swim bag. I looked out at the pool, at the random assortment of half-naked humans making their way through the water. "One other question, Mr. Dunaway."

"Yes?"

"Are your guests safe?"

"Pardon?"

"If you or the officer suspect a crime has been committed, then it sounds like a killer must have passed through your hotel in the last few hours or so. Have you talked to the officer about this? Because it might be worth calling in some backup—"

"No, no—it's not that kind of situation."

Dunaway's answer startled me a little bit, in that his lack of alarm told me that he already seemed to have an idea of what happened. If that was the case, I might not have to fly down the 101 at rush hour. Hell, I might even have time to grab a coffee on my way out of town.

"What do you mean by that?" I asked.

"The person who, um—who killed him. She's here."

"The suspect is *there*? With you?"

"Well, I'm no detective, but it looks pretty cut-and-dry to me." He cleared his throat. "Don't worry, ma'am. The officer reassured me that everyone here is perfectly safe."

Now *there* was a line I'd heard before. It didn't make me feel better, not in the least.

"Can you tell me who—"

Dunaway cussed under his breath—not at me, clearly, but I could hear the stress in his voice as he dealt with someone asking about an unaccounted-for employee. "I'm sorry," he said. "I have to go. Ask for me when you arrive, and my staff will direct you."

Before I could ask him any more questions about the suspect that some local police offer had in custody, he hung up. I checked my watch.

It was time to get on the road and call Hux.

CHAPTER

2

WHILE MAKING MY hasty exit from the pool complex, I tried Hux on his satellite phone, but he didn't answer. No surprise there; my tirelessly eager partner always liked to get an early start, especially when setting off from his cabin in Sequoia National Park. Most days, he was on the trail by four AM, ready to tackle a long day in the Sierras.

Hux didn't mind the early mornings like I did: the darkness, the cold, the eerie silence that preceded the wilderness's ambient chaos. He trusted himself in the worst of conditions, which was something I couldn't say for myself.

That said, Hux towered over me by a foot and outweighed me by a hundred pounds, so he had the edge on me physically. He also had military experience and a tracker's mind. He'd dealt with terrorists, land mines, bombs, and wars during his multiple tours as a Navy SEAL. He had battle scars that made me feel a little self-conscious about the titanium rod in my back and the surgical hardware in my shoulder, although both were earned in their own way. To his credit, though, Hux saw me as his equal—or, rather, his superior. He still had another year of training to go before he met the qualifications for special agent.

For now, however, I just needed him to answer his phone. I redialed the number for his Iridium, an indestructible piece of modern technology that he carried with him. It wasn't a foolproof way of contacting him; these types of phones relied on the positioning of the satellite to pick up a signal. Hux was always on the move and he moved fast, which meant that if you didn't get him on the first try, you just waited a few minutes and tried again.

After another attempt, the connection went through. He picked up on the second ring. "Harland," he said, jovial as ever. I could hear the smile in his voice, even though he sounded uncharacteristically out of breath. "You're awake at this hour? Is it your birthday or something?"

I glanced at my watch. It was 7:37 AM.

"I've been up for hours, actually." Well, *hours* was a stretch. I'd gotten out of bed at six fifteen, brushed my teeth, inhaled a granola bar, and pulled on a swimsuit before driving in a bleary-eyed haze down the 101 to the pool.

"That's a lie."

I couldn't help but laugh. "It might be. Now, look—please tell me you aren't a hundred miles off the grid right now."

"No, ma'am," he said, which made me feel old, even though we were less than five years apart in age. "I was just leaving the ranger's station."

Under more relaxed circumstances, I'd ask him what business he had at the ranger's station, but I always tried to respect the fact that sat phones had limited battery life. For that reason, and to spare Hux my feeble attempt at chitchat, I said, "Okay, here's the thing. I know you're pulling double duty down there while the good weather holds, but I just got a call from a hotel manager in Pinnacles National Park."

"Pinnacles, huh?" Hux was breathing normally again. I guessed he'd been climbing some steep terrain and had found a place to stop. "Didn't they just build a brand new hotel up there?"

"The Pinnacles Grand," I said. "You're familiar with it?"

"I read about it in the NPS newsletter," he said.

"Oh—well. That's pretty nerdy."

He laughed. "I guess I'm the only one who reads that thing?"

"I wouldn't say that. Ray's a fan."

"I'm not sure that makes me feel better."

I dropped my keys opening the door to my ugly-as-sin Hyundai rental and bent over to grab them, acutely aware of the chap in his tennis get-up watching me from across the parking lot.

"Anyway, I'm on my way up there now," I said, wrestling with my towel. "Any chance you can get yourself to Pinnacles later today?"

"Shouldn't be a problem; the chief knows my ISB duties come first. I just need to swing by the cabin to grab a few things, and I'll be on my way."

"Great." I was tempted to tell Hux not to rush, but the truth was, he couldn't afford to take his time. Such was the nature of the job.

As if reading my mind, or at least the note of anxiety in my voice, he said, "I should be on the road by oh-eight-hundred. Anything I should know before I get there?"

"It's a hike-in lodge situation. Park at the Chaparral Trailhead and you'll see the signs."

"How long's the hike?"

"Four and a half miles."

He whistled. "I love a challenge."

"This could definitely be that. See you soon." The call ended, which made me feel terribly alone for some reason, even though I knew Hux would be meeting me in a few hours. Maybe it was the tennis player ogling at me from across the parking lot. He flashed me a smile, which I returned with a feeling of grim obligation. His gaze swept my body in one shameless appraisal.

Ugh.

"Beautiful day, eh?" he remarked.

"Can't complain," I said with a grunt.

Before he could strike up a conversation that was going to end badly, I put my damp towel on the front seat and climbed in. Even though California wasn't home, I'd grown to like the mild weather, especially the sunny autumn months. The traffic bothered me, but I understood it. A climate like this tended to attract the masses.

I shoved my bare feet into my flip-flops and powered on the ignition. It didn't exactly start like a dream, but it wasn't a total clunker, either. I'd been behind the wheel of worse. My phone vibrated with another incoming call as I was pulling out of the parking lot onto a quiet residential street with mature trees. I reached for my phone and somehow managed to drop it in that sinister crevice between the console and the seat. After bypassing an old french fry and some other life forms I tried not to think about, I got ahold of my phone while it was still ringing. The caller was from an unknown number.

I answered. "Hello, this is Special Agent Felicity Harland—"

"Harland, it's Ray. Are you in your car right now?"

"Um, yes—"

"Good. I just heard about a situation in Pinnacles National Park."

I stopped at the corner and tried to remember the way back to the freeway.

"Yes, sir, at the hotel," I said, turning the wheel. "I'm already aware."

"The hotel?"

The question in his voice made me move my foot from the accelerator to the brake. I rolled down the window and shifted into park, deciding that this conversation warranted my full attention. Because if Ray Eskill *wasn't* calling about the situation at the Pinnacles Grand Hotel, then what the hell was he calling about?

"The manager called me about a potential homicide on hotel property," I said. "You're calling about something else?"

"He called you directly?"

"Yes, why?"

"How did he get your number? The rangers are supposed to call the switchboard."

"One of the rangers down there had my number, apparently. I get the feeling the hotel manager wants to keep this one on the down-low."

Ray harrumphed. "Yeah, well, he's in luck. Usually the FBI would be all over any shenanigans at a fancy hotel, but they're busy. There's a legit terrorist threat at SFO right now."

SFO was the San Francisco International Airport, a mere ten minutes north of where I was parked. At precisely that moment, I noticed the flock of helicopters soaring toward the airport. Sirens wailed in the distance. I felt a pang of regret, not being part of that chaotic, high-stakes world anymore, but it passed quickly.

"Is it under control?" I asked.

"Not at the moment. Could be a while."

I decided to try and refocus the conversation before Ray claimed he had to hop off the phone for some reason. "So are you calling about the possible homicide at the Pinnacles Grand?" I asked. "Or something else?"

"*Homicide?* Christ." Ray took a swig of something that was almost certainly bad coffee. He preferred instant, not for the taste, but because he was a cheap bastard. "No, Harland, I don't know anything about that—which pisses me off, to be honest. That's why we have a goddamn switchboard."

"Yes, but—"

"A park ranger called about a missing person." He huffed. "They need help."

The Park Service usually handled overdue hikers on their own, but if they were concerned about foul play, they were supposed to reach out to law enforcement for assistance. Sometimes, though, it was hard to distinguish a wayward tourist from something more sinister. "They're sure this isn't just an overdue hiker situation?" I asked.

"No. Apparently they found a shoe on the trail down there—a pretty nice one. You know, the kind a lady might wear on a date. It looked brand new, not like something that'd been out there a while."

"And that feels suspicious to the rangers? A shoe?"

"Look, don't shoot the messenger. They're thinking this Cinderella might have wandered away from the hotel bar and got herself into trouble. You gotta understand, Harland, nobody likes the idea of a fancy new resort being built in an area with such poor access. The rangers, especially."

The clock on the dash ticked forward another minute. *So much for Cold Case Sunday,* I thought, which was how I approached my weekends these days.

With Ray still on the line, I entered "Pinnacles Grand Hotel" into Google Maps; it was showing a two-and-a-half-hour drive to the Chaparral Trailhead Parking lot, but it would take four if I drove back to my hotel in Millbrae to shower and change. And then, of course, there was that four-and-a-half-mile hike.

I'd been with ISB long enough to know that these time-sensitive calls were a part of the job, and that it was best to pack ahead of time and think later. In my trunk were my backpack, hiking boots, a tent, and a week's worth of food, water, and supplies.

As much as I relished the thought of a hot shower, it just wasn't going to happen.

"I'm on my way to Pinnacles now," I said. "I'm going to start at the hotel; I'd like to try and get there before the M.E.'s office comes to get the body." I put my phone on speaker and pulled onto another street where the fifteen-hundred square-foot houses went for well north of two million. "Is there a search-and-rescue outfit working the missing persons case?"

"The chief ranger is mobilizing a team as we speak," Ray said, before something else stole his attention. "Dammit—I got another call coming in. Just get to Pinnacles and we'll touch base when you get there. If the service is lousy, use your sat phone."

After he ended the call, I thought about grabbing my clothes out of the trunk and changing right there in my car, but every minute counted in Bay Area rush hour. I plucked my sunglasses off the dash and slid them over my nose. If a state trooper pulled me over in this get-up, I'd never live to hear the end of it, but that was a risk I was prepared to take.

It was onward to Pinnacles—home to rock formations, caves, and at least one dead body.

3

I HAD LEARNED FROM my research into the cold case I'd been working on that Pinnacles was one of the country's newer national parks. In the early twentieth century, a tight-knit group of homesteaders, who owned property in its unique landscape of igneous rocks, rolling hills, and volcanic formations, worked to make it accessible to the public. That tradition had continued into the next century.

I wondered, though, if those homesteaders had ever intended for a luxury hike-in lodge to make its way into the park. At some point, it would be important for me to learn more about the politics behind the hotel's development, but for now, I was focused on getting there.

And *fast*.

Google Maps informed me that Pinnacles National Park had two ways in: a west entrance and an east entrance. Both were accessible via Highway 146, a two-lane road that disappeared inside the park where it was absorbed by the 26,000 acres of hiking trails, canyons, oak forests, chaparral, and dormant volcanoes. To get from one side of Pinnacles to the other required a five-mile hike through varied and mostly exposed terrain. Driving was not an option.

Pinnacles wasn't a particularly large national park, especially compared to its California brethren, but unlike Yosemite and Sequoia, which were just a few hundred miles to the east, most of its trail network was out in the open. The lack of shade posed a danger to hikers, especially in warmer weather. I could see, then, why the rangers were concerned. If someone had ventured into the park in dress shoes, it boded poorly for their preparation and survival skills.

On the ride down the 101, I did some more quick and dirty research with my trusted friend Siri. *What is the weather forecast in Pinnacles National Park? How many people visit Pinnacles every year? How many trails are there in Pinnacles National Park?* Some of these questions, of course, she couldn't answer, but it was worth a shot. Hux could fill in the gaps; he had an encyclopedic knowledge of California's natural resources.

As for the Pinnacles Grand, the only real source of information was its website and a random news story. I played the audio:

"The Pinnacles Grand was the birthchild of a contingent of wealthy real estate tycoons who decided to build a luxury hotel near the park's western entrance. It's not easy to find, and that's kind of the point. The Pinnacles Grand isn't just for wander lusters and adventurers; it's for people who want to disappear deep into an obscure pocket of California's history."

Sounded nice, I guess, albeit not really my cup of tea. All I could think about was that hike and the mounting pressure to do it quickly. The coolest hours of the morning were already gone, which meant I'd be a sweaty mess by the time I got there.

After turning onto Highway 146, I lost cell service. Fortunately, there was no traffic, so I tried to calm my mind while enjoying the scenic ride through rolling vineyards to the park's west entrance. For the most part, though, I was unsuccessful. Something about this case was stoking my unease. Maybe it was the volcanic sprawl etched into the dry, sun-beaten landscape, hinting at hidden dangers. Or maybe it was the fact that I hadn't dealt with an "indoors crime" in so long; after so much time in remote locales, I was feeling rusty.

Just before ten o'clock, I pulled into a small parking lot for the Chaparral Trailhead. The lot was nearly full, a few hikers milling about. In peak season, I wouldn't have gotten a spot.

Past the main lot, though, was what appeared to be a newly constructed designated area for Pinnacles Grand Hotel guests. This adjacent lot had about fifty spaces, which gave some indication of the hotel's size and scope. I hoped, perhaps foolishly, that the small lot meant I wouldn't have to deal with frazzled tourists and an abundance of potential witnesses. In my experience, though, it wasn't the number of witnesses that mattered; it was how quickly they scattered. In the wilderness, there were a thousand ways to escape a conversation with an ISB agent. A hotel was more contained, but it also posed its own challenges.

After an expedient, and hopefully discreet, change into my ISB uniform, I went around to the trunk and grabbed my backpack, which always felt a little heavier than it needed to be. In addition to the standard necessities like a fully-charged sat phone, clothes, and food, I also made sure to pack some investigative tools: evidence bags, a tape measurer, and police tape. I took my cell phone along, too, to take pictures of the crime scene.

In the past, I used to wrestle my backpack onto my body in a sort of haphazard, hope-for-the-best motion that made Hux wince, but I'd learned the hard way to take things slow. I bent at the knees and hoisted the child-sized pack onto my shoulders with minimal twisting—the perfect fit for my five-foot frame. I adjusted the big straps around my hips and made sure the weight was distributed evenly. A twinge in my shoulder, a dull ache in my lower back, and I was good to go.

With a lot of unknowns ahead, I had to hoof it to get there by noon. A half-dozen people loitered near the trailhead, debating the risks of heading out in ninety-degree heat. It wasn't a great day to be out on the trail, to be honest, but I knew that the park rangers patrolled these trails pretty intensely. I slurped some cold water and trudged past them. The posted sign confirmed Dunaway's information:

"Pinnacles Grand Hotel: 4.4 miles"

My watch chimed with the ten o'clock hour. Hux liked to time himself on short hikes like these, but my goal was to haul ass as fast as possible without aggravating my back or pulling a muscle. My topographical map had already clued me into the fact that this wasn't going to be an easy trek; while the first two miles were mostly paved and flat, the last two took a rough and treacherous route through less familiar terrain.

The first half hour on the Juniper Canyon Trail was fairly crowded since it shared a route with the Balconies Caves Trail Loop, a popular tourist destination. Shortly into the hike, though, the trail diverged, heading into Juniper Canyon itself. The silhouette of the High Peaks range loomed over the canyon's flank. The dry creek bed at the base of the canyon formed a riparian zone buffeted by cottonwood trees and gray pines. The greenery offered intermittent shade that made for a pleasant hike, but it wasn't long before I emerged into a field of boulders. Looming in front of me was Resurrection Wall, a bald-faced crag that had its share of climbing enthusiasts.

I continued onto a series of switchbacks and thick brush, bypassing the sign for the Tunnel Trail. Another mile or so on Juniper Canyon, and I almost missed the sign for the Pinnacles Grand Hotel jutting out of the dirt. It looked freshly painted.

Ignoring the tiny spasms in my lower back, I turned onto the park's newest route through Pinnacles wilderness. The drape coming off my wide-brimmed hat protected me from the hot sun's scorching burn, but it did little to tamp the deluge of sweat dripping from the nape of my neck. I just hoped Dunaway didn't think me to be unprofessional for looking like a hot mess.

An hour passed in a haze of heat and sunshine, as the trail cut through more switchbacks and dense chaparral. I took a swig from my canteen and prepared myself for the final stretch. For a moment, I thought about Hux and how much I missed having him here. It wasn't that I didn't like a solo hike now and then, but embarking on a near-sprint in the midday sun was pure punishment. It was also just good practice to have a trail buddy. Accidents happened.

Don't think about that now, I told myself as a pair of hikers smiled wearily and made their way past me. There was no time to dwell on the past, even though it had a habit of creeping up on me. I ignored the scenery and focused on putting one foot in front of the other.

I passed no one else. The hotel had only just opened a week ago, and I assumed that guests were advised to hike in or out at certain times of day—and this wasn't that time, at least not during a late-October heat wave.

At last, as one flimsy cloud passed over the sun, I began a descent into a canyon that heralded my destination. A smattering of trees congregated on the creek bed, almost like they were sunning themselves in the sun, welcoming me into their reverie. As I took respite in the shade, I suddenly noticed the sprawling façade of glass and timber in front of me.

"The Pinnacles Grand."

I just stood there, admiring it for a moment. For an establishment with multiple superlatives in its name, the Pinnacles Grand offered a stunning first impression, its main building nestled into a gulch flanked by mossy cliffs and jagged rock formations. Some of these cliffs featured private villas that had been erected into the stone walls. The withering sunlight that had plagued me on the hike died in the canyon's towering trees. It reminded me, eerily, of the forest at the bottom of King's Canyon in Australia, where my late husband, Kevin, and I had been stranded for days before he finally agreed to go off and find help.

Unlike that remote canyon, humanity had clearly made its mark on this place. The shaded, secretive trail through a canyon of rock formations and clear blue pools ended at an architectural marvel. Whoever had designed the hotel complex had gone to great lengths to assimilate it into the scenery, and for the most part, they had succeeded. Still, it made me a little sad to see yet more evidence of human activity encroaching on Mother Nature's raw beauty. I would have preferred a bare-bones campsite or, at most, a travel shelter.

Dunaway had asked for my discretion on this case, but I wasn't about to go into an uncertain situation unarmed. I holstered my Glock and made sure everything was in order on that front, which it was. I took the hairband out of my ponytail, combed my fingers through my sweaty hair, and tucked it under a baseball cap. I wiped the lenses of my sunglasses and put them back on. *At least you* look *cool,* Hux would have said.

Following the signs for the reception area, I made my way to the hotel's main entrance. Guests and staff crowded the paths out front, enjoying the mild weather. If anyone was aware that a murder had taken place on the property, it wasn't obvious. The conversations I overheard were mostly about conditions out on the trail and the quality of the food.

The color scheme of the main building was mostly bronze and gold, with a hint of green to complement the moss that thrived in the damp shadows of the canyon. I expected the air to taste thick and musky, but the windows were open, and a cool breeze moved through the interior.

I took immediate note of the guests in the lobby. A fit, older couple sat by the fireplace, bickering about the route on their map, while a male hiker in his thirties munched on a banana outside the ladies' room. There were no children, not that I expected any. The Pinnacles Grand didn't strike me as that kind of place. Like Old Faithful Inn in Yellowstone, El Tovar in Grand Canyon, and the Majestic Yosemite Hotel, the Pinnacles Grand mirrored the spectacle of its surroundings in size, scope, and ambiance. In other words, it was way above my pay grade.

Not that I planned on staying the night here anyway. I had my tent with me, and there was no point in charging a luxury room to the federal tab. Hux wouldn't want to waste Uncle Sam's money on a place like this either. Aside from his cabin, he much preferred sleeping outdoors.

I walked up to the front desk and smiled at the woman standing there.

"Hello," she said. "Welcome to the Pinnacles Grand." The pin on her white blouse gave her name: "Elizabeth." "Checking in?" Her smile was practiced but genuine.

"No, ma'am," I said, doing my best to be pleasant. "I'm Special Agent Felicity Harland with ISB; I'm looking for James Dunaway." I decided to hold off on flashing my badge, which didn't feel necessary in that moment. It could come in handy later, though.

"You're with the Department of the Interior, you said?"

"I'm with the Investigative Services Branch. We're kind of like the FBI."

Her smile faded. "Oh. Um—yes. I'm sorry. Mr. Dunaway told me you were coming, but I, um, I was expecting someone more . . ."

Taller? More male? I decided not to humiliate her by finishing her thought, but my wry smile probably told her that I knew what she was thinking.

Her cheeks turned a faint pink. "I'm sorry."

"Don't be."

She did her best to resuscitate her practiced smile. "Well, um, Mr. Dunaway is waiting for you at the Peregrine suite, which is a little way down the trail."

Fumbling with a pen, she slid a map in my direction and cir-
cled a location that was about a quarter-mile away from the lobby.
"Go out the main entrance, turn right, and follow the signs for
Peregrine. I'll let him know you're on your way." She glanced over
my shoulder at the line forming behind me, undoubtedly aware of
how badly this could go for her if word got out I was investigating
a crime on the property. "Is there anything else I can assist you
with?"

"No, that'll be all, thank you." I put the map in my backpack's side pocket and made my way to the exit. I was tempted
to hang around the lobby for a little bit to see what I could glean
from the guests and their surroundings, but there was no time for
that. First, there was the morbid reality of a body decomposing
in a hotel room. Second, there could very well be a killer at large.
Third, human beings were curious creatures, even when it was in
their best interest to mind their own business. It was not going to
be easy to keep this one sealed up tight.

I went outside and, observing the signs, made my way to the
Peregrine suite, which appeared to be located within a cluster of
other animal-themed guest rooms. The path followed a serpentine
route through volcanic formations and awkward boulders, which
only reinforced my impression that access was going to be a problem. A *big* problem. It wasn't that I relished the FBI's involvement
in some of my cases, but I couldn't do all the forensic analysis on
my own.

Which made me think of Bodie Cramer, an old friend from
my FBI days in Chicago. He had since relocated to San Jose, where
he was recovering from heart surgery, but the bureau had yet to
clear him for field duty. In the meantime, he was working from
home. I knew he was anxious to get back out there, though. He
had told me as much in a text just last week, when he'd heard I
was going to be in the area working on cold cases.

I took out my phone and checked for a signal. Fortunately
for me and my investigation, the hotel had reliable Wi-Fi. I sent
Bodie a quick text. A part of me wondered what Hux was going
to think if Bodie joined our efforts here. Would he feel threatened
in some way?

No, I decided. *That's ridiculous.* They had completely different
skill sets. It wasn't going to be a problem. As for the personal stuff,

well . . . Hux didn't have to know about my history with Bodie. I knew Hux wouldn't care anyway, but I didn't even want to have the conversation.

While waiting for Bodie to respond to my text, I continued down the trail, where I passed the first collection of rooms named Bobcat, Red Frog, and Eagle. For the most part, they were cozy creek side cabins with what looked like private hot tubs in the back.

While the other guests walking the trail barely acknowledged me, the staff never missed a chance to offer a pert greeting that made me feel not just welcomed, but also valued. That was the signature feature of high-end hotels: the service. Establishments like these made it their mission to make every guest feel like a celebrity. Dunaway had trained them well.

I made a sharp turn after Eagle onto a path ending in a set of footholds that served as a makeshift set of stairs. A pair of railings offered added support. I had heard that Pinnacles had several trails like this, and every single one of them made me nervous. I didn't mind difficult trails; I just wasn't a fan of railings and footholds and other human attempts to change the landscape to make it more accessible. Half Dome in Yosemite was a prime example of this. I still hadn't been up that demonic crag and hoped to avoid it forever.

The Peregrine suite was perched high on the cliff, with a sprawling view of the canyon below. I wondered how the hell this place had gotten around ADA regulations. Then again, maybe they hadn't. I made a mental note to look for an elevator later.

The footholds turned into an agreeable set of stairs halfway up. Two flights up, I encountered a man standing on a small platform. He had positioned himself next to a door that was slightly ajar. The stairs continued upward past the door, leading to what looked like another villa, but I knew I had the right one because of the peregrine painted on the door.

The man spoke. "Agent Harland?"

"Yes," I said. "You must be Mr. Dunaway."

He was on the shorter side, with dark brown hair that he kept neatly trimmed around his ears. His perfunctory but not inexpensive suit gave him away as hotel management.

"I am," he said, with a sigh that betrayed his relief at seeing me.

We shook hands.

I pointed at the door behind him. "Is the body in there?"

He nodded. "I was just airing out the room a bit. Here, it's this way—"

"Hold up a second," I said, jostling him a bit as I moved inside. I unholstered my Glock and stepped over the threshold onto a smooth, cream-colored carpet. The lights were off, but bright sunlight streamed through the balcony window. Remembering my training, I slipped on a pair of gloves and checked the closets, the bathroom, even underneath the furniture. In the main living area, it was hard to ignore the body lying on the floor, but I wanted to make sure the room was secure first. I stepped over the victim to check under and around the bed.

"Agent Harland?" Dunaway called out from behind me.

"It's all clear," I said. "You can come in."

He tripped over the threshold, eliciting an awkward grunt. Dunaway glanced at the well-appointed bathroom to his right before coming to a stop right where the hallway opened up into the living area. He seemed reluctant to look at anything but the floor.

"That's, um—there he is," Dunaway said, pointing. I didn't need an orientation, of course, but I understood the impulse to fill the silence.

On the carpet near the foot of the bed was a man, facedown, very clearly dead. A jagged shard of glass protruded from the flesh between his shoulder blades. The blood from the wound had saturated his shirt, leeching out onto the fibers of the carpet. One arm was under his body, the other was reaching out into empty space. His positioning suggested that he had likely staggered out of bed.

I drew closer and noted a silk tie around his neck—cinched tight, knotted at the back. There was bruising around his neck, mottled to a deep plum color. He was naked except for that tie. A suit jacket was strewn across a chair next to the bed, but the rest of his clothes littered the room like they'd been thrown or tossed there. *A sexual encounter gone wrong?* I considered that possibility for a moment before realizing that there were no other clothes around. It was just his. In fact, there were no obvious signs that anyone else had been here at all—not that I could see, anyway. That's where Bodie came in.

I turned to Dunaway. "I assume you have a copy of the room reservation?" I asked.

"Yes."

"Do you know who this is, then?"

He stopped holding his breath to speak. "The name on the reservation was Chris Mason," he said. "But his wife said that's an alias. His last name is Denton."

I took down the name on my phone's Notes app. "And he's the one who paid for the room?"

Dunaway cleared his throat. "I'm not sure. The room was paid for in cash."

Another curveball. *Who paid for a seven-hundred-dollar room in cash?* Someone with means, yes, but also someone who didn't want to leave a paper trail. An affair seemed most likely, which made the spouse or a secret lover the most obvious suspects at this point.

"Don't your guests have to leave a credit card for incidentals?"

"No," he said. "We have cryptocurrency as an option, however."

I quirked an eyebrow at him. "Why?"

"Anonymity is important here. It's part of the allure of a hike-in hotel. Some people don't want to be found."

Found out, is more like it, I thought, but I kept my mouth shut. "Do you know when he made the reservation?"

Dunaway shifted his feet as he glanced down at his phone. "Yesterday. We were completely booked for the weekend, but there was a cancellation."

An impromptu trip, then. That changed things a little bit. It made premeditated murder less likely, but I wasn't prepared to rule it out yet.

"You said housekeeping found the body this morning," I said. "What time was this?"

"Around seven AM."

"Your staff cleans the rooms at seven AM?" I asked, raising my eyebrows.

"Not routinely, no. Our housekeeper assigned to that block of rooms was attending to a different room when she noticed the door to Peregrine was open."

"And what is her name?"

"Marta Bautista."

I took out my phone and added it to the file. "And the door was unlocked, or literally open?"

"It was ajar, she said. Just a crack. She went inside to make sure everything was all right—against protocol, mind you, but she was genuinely concerned for the occupant's welfare."

I tried to imagine what that poor woman must have thought when she walked into that room. Hux and I would have to talk to Marta Bautista before the day was over, of course, but I hoped that by then, she had some time to process the harrowing scene she had encountered.

"Was someone staying with Denton?" I asked. "You mentioned the wife."

Dunaway dabbed at his nose with a tissue. I noticed then that it was a little raw, but he had done his best to cover it with makeup. "She was on the property, but to our knowledge, she wasn't staying with him."

"Pardon?"

"Mr. Denton was here with another guest. They checked in together."

I looked up from my phone and met his gaze. "And who would that be?"

"I don't know. Her name wasn't on the reservation."

Of course it wasn't. Was this a love triangle gone wrong? I had seen my fair share of those before; some were pretty straightforward, others a tangled mess. "What about the wife?"

"Marta found Mrs. Denton in this room here when she went in. She was standing over the body."

I did my darndest to keep a straight face, but that was no easy feat. *The wife was standing over her husband's dead body?*

I arched my back and put my hands on my hips to add some street cred to my diminutive stature. The story was starting to come together, but I would have to talk to Denton's wife before drawing any conclusions. In my experience, most people knew if their spouses were fooling around, even if they didn't *want* to know.

"I'm trying to get this straight," I said. "Denton used an alias to book the room, but housekeeping found him here, dead, with his wife standing over his body. But you're saying she wasn't staying with him—that he was here with someone else?" I waited for him to answer, but he just shifted his feet. "Mr. Dunaway?"

He rubbed his nose again. "It appears that way, Agent Harland. Mr. Denton's name was the only one on the reservation. We don't have any record of Mrs. Denton staying at the hotel last night. To be honest with you, I don't know how she got into the room."

"What about security cameras?"

"They're installed, but not online yet."

I bit my lower lip to keep myself from making an unwelcome comment. "Who saw Mr. Denton with this other woman? Could I talk to them?"

"I've been here guarding this room the whole time," he said. "I haven't had a chance to talk with any of my staff except Elizabeth, who confirmed that they checked in together." He gave me a pointed look, like, *Isn't that your job?*

Feeling a little ruffled, I shoved my phone into my pocket. The good news was that we were going to have ample opportunity to collect information, even if it took a few days.

"Where is the wife now?"

"Upstairs."

"The officer from Hollister is with her?"

Dunaway's phone chimed with a new message. He glanced down at it and frowned, deepening the lines in his brow. He sighed loudly. Before he could even look up, it chimed again, which made him shove the thing into his pocket.

"Mr. Dunaway?"

"Yes," he said. "She's in the Condor suite."

From one bird of prey to another, I thought. *But who's the real predator here?*

The answer, perhaps, was only one floor up from where we stood, but talking to the victim's wife now meant abandoning a crime scene. I never liked to turn my back on evidence, especially with so many people hanging around the property and so many chances to disturb something important.

Mrs. Denton, though, was her own time-sensitive situation. She could call a lawyer. Have a change of heart. Demand to leave.

I decided to call Bodie to see if he, at least, could buy me a little time. The good news was that he was coming. *"Your text made my week,"* he had written.

I checked the Wi-Fi signal, which up here in the villas was password-protected. "Is there a password for the Wi-Fi?" I asked Dunaway.

"Certainly," he said. "The password for the Hotel_Employee network is *talus*."

"Pardon?"

"T-A-L-U-S. Courtesy of our IT department."

I wasn't sure what that meant, but I entered the password and got onto the network. In Hux's opinion, Wi-Fi had no place in national parks, but for now, it was working in our favor.

There—another text from Bodie. He was telling me to call him. I dialed his number and waited. He picked up on the first ring.

"Felicity," he said, a smile coming through in his voice. "I'm so damn happy you called me."

"Hey," I said. "I got your text. I'm so sorry to ask you to drop everything and come all the way out here, but I could use your help."

"Totally understandable. You heard what's going down at the airport?"

"Yes," I said, recalling Ray's curt update. "Everything okay there?"

"Major terrorism threat. I figured that's why you were calling me; the whole FBI field office is at SFO right now." It sounded like Bodie was zipping up a duffel bag or suitcase of some kind. "But don't worry, I can be at Pinnacles in a couple hours."

The fact that the FBI was still otherwise occupied left me with mixed feelings. On one hand, they wouldn't be all up in my business, telling me what to do. On the other, I wasn't going to have many resources to work this case, at least not initially. Hux was en route, too, but I was on my own for now.

"You have to hike in," I said. "It's a little over four miles from the parking lot."

"Seriously?" He forced a laugh. "Man, that's a bummer. I can do it, though."

"Are you sure?"

"Oh, yeah. I'm good. Super fit right now."

I'd never thought of Bodie as "super fit," but he talked a lot about the various sporting organizations he belonged to: the running club, the water polo team, the adult soccer league. Back in my Chicago days, he was always the first person to arrive at the bar and the last to leave. It wasn't the booze that appealed to him, though; it was the conversation with colleagues, the chance to connect with people that understood the nature of the job. I had to assume this medical leave was killing him.

"Go to the west entrance and follow the signs to the hotel parking lot," I said. "Make sure you put 'Chaparral Trailhead' into your GPS because otherwise you'll end up at the east entrance. Can you text me when you get here?"

"Sure thing. Is there good cell service there?"

"I'm on the hotel Wi-Fi right now, as it turns out."

"Oh, perfect."

I hung up without saying good-bye, acutely aware of Dunaway's ability to overhear our conversation. He had started pacing the small hallway outside the bathroom.

With Bodie on his way here, I felt a little better about shifting gears and talking to the wife. After all, with her confession, the evidence wouldn't matter quite as much.

"All right," I said to Dunaway. "Let's go."

4

FROM MY PERSPECTIVE as an investigator, Peregrine's isolated
location was an asset for multiple reasons. It had only one
obvious entry point: the footholds and narrow wooden stairs that
traversed the cliffside. If Dunaway wasn't going to let me put some
police tape across the stairwell, then I'd make sure he assigned an
employee to stand guard outside the room.

On our way back out the door, we bypassed the Nest thermostat that was currently set to sixty degrees. *Nice*. It was hard to beat
a climate-controlled crime scene. I'd heard about a case in Death
Valley where the evidence had all but evaporated in the heat before
the agent could get there.

As Dunaway stepped outside, his cell phone rang. "Excuse
me," he said, before answering in a hushed tone. "Yes," he muttered into the phone. "Yes, all right. I'll be there in a few minutes."
He hung up and turned to me.

"Something important?" I asked.

"I'm afraid so. I need to deal with a situation down in the
lobby."

"That's fine, but I'll need to put up some police tape."

"I'll be back in just a minute, Agent Harland."

While Dunaway raced down the steep flight of stairs, I took
out my phone and called Hux on his sat phone. He picked up on
the first ring, too.

"Hey," I said. "Where are you?"

"Twenty miles from the parking lot," he said. "What's the situation there?"

"I've got a body in one room and a suspect in the other," I said. "It looks like a homicide." I glanced at the hand-painted rendering of a peregrine falcon on the door, with its sleek gray head and white belly. Peregrines were efficient killers and the fastest member of the animal kingdom. I wondered if this was a harbinger of things to come, a bad omen of sorts.

Hux asked, "So who's the suspect?"

"The wife, as it turns out."

"Makes sense. Have you talked to her?"

"Not yet. A deputy from the local police department is holding her, so we have a little time, but not much." I could hear a bit of wind in the background; Hux liked to drive with the windows down. Ollie did, too. I missed my dog and was excited to see him. Hux had kindly offered to take him while I cleared out my apartment and tackled some cold cases.

"Are you thinking of calling in the big bads for this one?" Hux asked.

By "big bads," I knew that he meant the FBI. "I can't. They're all-hands-on-deck at SFO investigating a terrorist threat. Plus, access is a problem given the hike from the parking lot."

There was a pause. "What was your time?"

I could hear the smile in his voice. "It wasn't good." I sighed.

"Come on, Harland. Throw me a bone here."

I glanced at my watch. "An hour fifteen from the trailhead sign to the hotel lobby."

Ollie barked in the background, which I took as a show of support for my best effort out on the trail. As a newly minted NPS Bark Ranger, Ollie had assumed a more official role in our investigations, and I was grateful for it. Every park had its own rules and regulations about domestic animals, which made sense. Ollie wasn't just a happy-go-lucky trail buddy, though. He had a natural instinct for tracking.

"Good to know," Hux said. "I should be at the hotel by thirteen thirty."

"Don't kill yourself. I'll hold down the fort until you get here."

"All right," he said. "See you soon."

Since no one was here to guard the Peregrine suite, I decided it made the most sense to wait out Dunaway's return by taking one more look at the crime scene. After all, in witness interviews, first impressions were critical. Hux was less than an hour away, and I wanted him with me for this conversation; he often fared better with middle-aged women than I did.

I used the keycard Dunaway had left for me to regain access to the Peregrine suite. As before, I put on gloves and booties to make sure I didn't disturb any evidence.

The chilled room felt more like a refrigerator than a luxury accommodation. The rush of cold, artificial air made my hair stand on end as I stepped back inside.

Denton's body was about fifteen paces from the entry door, but my legs were of the petite variety, so for Hux, it was probably closer to ten. I walked over to where the victim lay and bent down, careful to avoid the congealing blood on the carpet. There was no way for me to say when the victim had died, except to say that the room's occupant had checked in yesterday afternoon, so he had to have died sometime in the last twenty-four hours.

I took a closer look at the wounds Denton had suffered either prior to or at the time of death. The bruising around his neck indicated this was most likely a premortem injury, but judging by the massive blood stain on the carpet, he had bled out quickly. The shard of glass had gone in deep—at least a few inches—which meant it had almost certainly punctured a vital vessel, maybe even his heart. *Bad luck . . . or a perfect hit?*

I went out onto the balcony and looked down. It was about forty feet to the bottom, with rocky outcroppings on the way down that would have made for a nasty fall. The path itself wasn't exactly cushy. Had the victim made it all the way out to the balcony and somehow managed to get over the railing, it wouldn't have ended well.

Then again, it wasn't like he'd had time to think it through. The state of the bed pointed to a frenzied encounter. The top sheet was mostly on the floor, except for one corner that was still tucked into the mattress. The bedspread was also pulled to the side, most of it puddled on the floor, along with two of the pillows.

As if that wasn't enough chaos, there were blood spatters everywhere: the wall behind the bed, the sheets, the plush white comforter. Even the lampshade on the bedside table was covered in little red specks on the side facing the bed.

I went over and had a look at the other side of the lampshade. *No blood stains there.* This suggested that Denton had almost certainly been stabbed while he was still in bed, perhaps even while sleeping. I made a mental note to ask Mrs. Denton if her husband slept on his stomach, not that I expected her to tell me very much. If she was smart, she wouldn't tell me anything at all.

As for other bodily fluids that might be a part of the picture . . . well, I'd leave that to Bodie. I didn't *see* any semen on the sheets, but there was so much blood it was hard to discern much of anything besides that. In any case, a scene like this was Bodie's bread and butter.

One advantage we had was the newness of this hotel; the sheets, as it were, had never been slept in, except presumedly by Chris Denton and his bedfellow, if he had one. That crucial question had yet to be answered, but it was near the top of my list.

I made my way over to the framed painting on the wall that had, like Mr. Denton, taken a beating. Several glass shards were still stuck inside the frame, but the painting—a print, from the looks of it—was intact. There was no blood on any part of it, which suggested that the killer had smashed the glass with a hard object while wearing a glove. *But why?*

There were easier ways to stab a person—with a knife, for example. Then again, hotel rooms didn't stock knives. Maybe the killer had improvised or brought their own. Even so, glass was risky. Unwieldy and unpredictable, it made no sense as a murder weapon. There was a grandiosity to the bloody struggle in this room that struck me as a bit unusual.

I went back over to the victim and looked at the jagged, eggplant-sized shard protruding from his flesh. From my limited perspective, the handle portion looked clean: no blood, no smears, no obvious fingerprints. Bodie would analyze the hell out of it, of course, but it seemed to me that this shard of glass had either floated from the broken frame into Denton's body (unlikely), or someone had wiped it down after the deed was done. Either way, it was hard to imagine the killer had escaped unscathed. I was eager to take a look at Mrs. Denton's dominant hand.

As I was considering how and why someone would go through such care to stab their victim with a piece of glass only to strangle them with a necktie after the fact, I felt my cell phone vibrate in my pocket with a new message.

It was Hux.

I'm here, he'd texted. *Just got myself a map.*

I texted back: *Come on up to Peregrine.*

I was putting my phone away when a knock came at the door. *Huh*, I thought. Hux was fast, but not that fast. I maneuvered around the body and cautiously approached the door with one hand on my Glock, just in case. Sure, we had a suspect detained in another room, but I was a long way from declaring that she was the killer. I hadn't even met her yet.

"Who's there?" I called out.

"Uh, this is Nate," came the answer. "Nate Horvath. I'm with the Park Service."

I peered through the aperture in the door to see a young Black man, maybe twenty-five or so, standing on the platform in his Park Service duds. He was tall and lean, with dark brown eyes that glanced nervously over his shoulder. Nate Horvath looked like your typical ranger, except for his race, which put him in an underrepresented group as a Park Service employee.

I opened the door. "Sorry for making you wait," I said. "I'm doing my best to keep the scene secure, at least until we can process it."

"I understand." He stole a glance at my holster. I noticed he wasn't armed. "Are you, um—are you the ISB agent?"

"I am." I extended a hand for him to shake. "My name is Felicity Harland." Picking up on the fact that Horvath didn't seem too anxious to come inside, I stepped onto the small platform outside the door. "How long have you been with the Park Service, Nate?"

"About a year." He scratched a spot above his left ear.

"How are you liking it?"

"Pretty good. It wasn't Plan A, but I'm happy with it."

"What was Plan A?"

His smile eased up a bit. "Baseball—got drafted right out of college. Just didn't work out." He moved his left arm around. "Shoulder problems."

"I'm sorry to hear it," I said. "I'm sure the Park Service is happy to have you on board."

He nodded. "I just—damn, I wasn't expecting this. This hotel's brand new, never thought I'd be called up here for a murder."

"Were you on patrol here?"

"Yep. My chief wanted somebody on-site for the first week or two. He put me on it because I'm still kinda the new guy, and he figured it'd be an easy assignment."

He sure had the *look* of the new guy, especially with the way he was shifting his feet, fidgeting with his hands. I knew that the police officer from Hollister had seen Denton's body, but Dunaway hadn't said much about the park ranger on the premises.

Then again, this wasn't unusual. For the most part, I got my information piecemeal, especially out here in the wilderness. The hotel was more of a controlled environment, which was good in some respects, but it also posed some unique challenges.

From somewhere down below, a voice echoed in the canyon. "Harland? That you?"

I looked over the railing to see Hux standing at the bottom of the stairs, one hand shielding his eyes from the sun as he peered up at us. Ollie was there, too, sitting on his haunches. Neither one looked the least bit winded. *How does he do that?* I wondered. Keeping up with Hux was the hardest part of this job.

"Come on up," I called out.

Hux took the stairs two at a time with my shepherd dog close at his heels, almost like they were gliding on air. Nate seemed impressed by their agility, too, not that the young ranger was any slouch. You had to be fit to cut it in the Park Service.

When Hux joined us on the platform, he smiled broadly at me, that same boyish smile I'd come to relish during our time together. Despite the nature of our work, he tackled every new case with fresh-faced enthusiasm, which kept me going through the constant ups and downs of this job: the hard treks through the wilderness, the frustrating interviews with uncooperative witnesses, the physical altercations with bad actors. Hux kept me on task, but he also helped me find joy in my work. We both had our troubled pasts, but we didn't dwell on them.

Not that I planned on telling him any of that, and certainly not right then. I had decided long ago that it was important to project the utmost professionalism at the start of any new investigation, especially in front of other personnel. Male personnel to boot.

"You're a little late," I said to Hux, which elicited a tiny smirk from him that made me smile. I ruffled Ollie's fur and let him know that I was glad to see him. Content, he sat at my feet and made himself comfortable. He was probably going to be there a while, but Ollie had the patience of an ox.

I turned to Horvath and made the introduction. "Hux, this is Nate Horvath, the park ranger on patrol here. He's the one who told Dunaway to call us."

"Hey, man," Hux said. They shook hands, Nate giving in to a more relaxed vibe as he responded to Hux's easygoing nature. "You must have your hands full."

"Yeah, you could say that. The hotel manager called me just after seven AM and said he had a dead body."

With a glance at Hux, I asked Nate, "What did he say, exactly?" I knew that Hux was chomping at the bit to get inside the room and have a look around, but I wasn't ready to let Nate Horvath go just yet. Park rangers could be difficult to track down after the fact.

"He said one of his housekeepers found a dead body in one of the rooms. I asked if it was a medical situation; he said no, it was a murder situation."

I caught myself doing a double-take. "He said 'murder'?"

"Well, uh—I can't remember. But I could tell he was freaked out."

"So what did you do?"

"I told him to call the police."

Hux already had his notepad out and was making some short-hand notes on the pages. Over the course of our investigative partnership, he had learned to parse out the critical information from the excess. I trusted him to take good notes, which he usually did on his phone. For now, he was keeping it old-school.

"And did he?"

"He already had. The officer was there, dealing with the witness. She said her department didn't investigate crimes in the park, so I told him to call you."

I cleared my throat. "ISB has a switchboard, you know."

"Yes, ma'am, but I heard that the agent who's supposed to be covering Pinnacles is, well . . ." He scratched that same spot on his scalp. "Anyway, word on the street is that when it comes to ISB, you want the duo."

"Sorry?"

Nate's cheeks turned pink. "You're partners, right? I was told most ISB agents work alone, so . . . um . . . anyway, everybody likes Harland and Hux." The pink in his cheeks turned red. "That's what they call you."

"I see." I dodged Hux's gaze even though a part of me was dying to know what he thought about our moniker.

I didn't have to wonder long. "Hmm. I like it better than Watson and Holmes, don't you?" Hux looked at me with humor shining in his eyes.

I turned back to Nate. "All the rangers should use the switchboard. We've got our protocols."

"Yes, ma'am," he said, chastened.

"Look, I'm glad you called us," I said. "For the record, I don't care how you get in touch with ISB, so long as it happens. I just have to let you know that there *is* a protocol."

He nodded, but the whole situation seemed to be wearing on him. I decided it was time to wrap up the crime scene investigation for now and deal with Mrs. Denton before she bolted.

"Have you met the victim's wife?" I asked Nate.

He grasped the brim of his hat and twisted it in his hands. "No, ma'am. I was told housekeeping found her standing over the body when they went in to clean the room, but that's pretty much all I know. The deputy put her in that room upstairs, and she's been there ever since."

Nate's satellite phone chirped with an incoming call. "Sorry," he said. "That's my chief." He answered the call while Hux and I waited for Nate to finish up. It was a brief conversation, but the young ranger was frowning when he hung up.

"I gotta go," he said. "We've got a situation out on the High Peaks Trail."

I saw Hux look up from his notepad. We exchanged a glance that Nate must have noticed because he furrowed his brow. "Wait," Nate said. "Does that situation have something to do with *this* situation?"

"We heard about a missing person out in the park," I said. "But we don't know much more than that."

Hux twirled his pen in his hand, waiting for the young ranger to say something. At last, Nate said, "My chief hasn't said much, but I heard they found a shoe out on the High Peaks Trail."

"What kind of shoe?"

"A woman's dress shoe. Sorry—that's all I know."

"And that trail is where, exactly?"

"It's a loop, but right now they're down on the south end, close to Monolith, where it links up with the Chalone Peak Trail. On a hot day, it can be brutal—not much shade at all. Chalone Peak is kind of like a fire road; some parts aren't well-maintained."

"Is it easy to go off-trail?"

"Not really," he said. "But, well, it can happen."

Yes, I thought. *It certainly can.*

Nate looked at me and Hux before dropping his gaze to the ground. "I just wonder . . ." Nate said, his voice tapering off as the wind picked up and drowned him out.

I said, maybe a little too loudly, "You wonder what?"

"I just wonder who it could be."

"What do you mean?" Hux asked.

"Well, the wife's upstairs," he said. "But this guy wasn't here with his wife."

"You know that for sure?"

He released a long exhale. "Oh, yeah," he said. "I only just got here, but the rumor mill's firing on all cylinders."

"From who?"

"Well, when I got here, the first person I talked to was the lady at the front desk—and *she* said Denton was here with a much younger woman."

"What else did she say?"

Hux adjusted his grip on his pen as he prepared to take notes.

"She seemed to be under the impression that the girlfriend was dead, too, since she hadn't seen her since the night before."

"What time the night before?"

"Around midnight. She came down requesting another room."

Another room? Why? Had an argument gone bad? Was there some other reason?

I didn't like that we had a potential witness completely unaccounted for, but I decided that she wasn't our top priority right now.

We had to talk to the wife.

5

T HE THREE OF US stood outside the door, congregating under the creepy eye of the hand-painted peregrine, while Ollie gnawed at a bone. I was anxious to get upstairs, but I also knew that we might only get one shot at Mrs. Denton. These kinds of interviews required some strategizing beforehand, especially if the suspect knew their way around the legal system. Hell, anyone who'd ever listened to a true crime podcast understood that the smart thing to do in these situations was to call a lawyer.

Hux was trying to get onto the hotel Wi-Fi. "The password is 'talus'," I told him.

"Thanks." While Hux saved his notes to a newly created master file on the cloud called "Denton/Pinnacles," Nate went off to take another call on his satellite phone. I suspected it was his chief again, telling him to get his butt on the trail.

"I'm gonna see what I can find on Christopher Denton," Hux said, as he pulled up his internet browser. He typed Chris Denton's name into Google, which brought up his LinkedIn page, among various other social media links. Hux clicked on the networking site.

Denton's profile photo featured a good-looking guy who appeared to be in his mid-forties. His blond hair, tanned face, and white teeth reminded me of a Florida real estate agent, but his penetrating gaze had a slightly unsettling quality. In his headshot, he was wearing a dress shirt but no tie, which fit the bill for a Silicon Valley type, where the intent was to look California cool while working yourself into the ground.

His actual profile, though, hinted at something other than a hard-driving entrepreneur. Despite his position as "Founder & CEO of Chips & Trips, Inc.," which looked to me like some kind of poker company, I was having a hard time understanding the scope of his job and the nature of his business. From what I could tell from Hux's brief online search, Chips & Trips didn't seem to have any other employees. Denton himself had jumped around a lot the last few years, never seeming to find his niche anywhere.

How, then, could he afford this place? I wondered. Dunaway had shown me the receipt for the room; the base rate was $695 a night to stay in the Peregrine suite. That was some serious money, well above the standard fare for something like a Holiday Inn.

I pulled the internet up on my cell phone and ran a search on Colleen Denton. Her online footprint, as it turned out, was sizable. Google had plenty of evidence to suggest that *she* was the real tech wunderkind, with a long stint as chief operating officer at a media conglomerate with offices in L.A., San Francisco, and New York. I searched her social media profiles, too, but she only used Twitter to promote her company, while her Instagram was set to private. Interestingly, I couldn't find any photos online of her and her late husband together. *Trouble in paradise?*

I had worked all sorts of cases involving spouses who kept secrets from each other, but I had also dealt with couples who *knew* each other's secrets and chose to look the other way. In my own life, I liked to think I knew everything about my late husband, Kevin, but that just wasn't true. No one could know another person inside and out; human beings were complicated creatures with lies they told themselves on a daily basis. *"I don't need to know all your secrets,"* Kevin had told me once, early in our marriage. *You're entitled to them.* And then, in a cruel twist of irony, he had left me with the one secret that mattered most: what happened to him in the last days of his life.

"Harland?" Hux asked, nudging my elbow. "You still with us?"

"Yeah, sorry," I mumbled. Hux and I had only talked about Kevin a handful of times in all the hours we'd spent on a trail together, mostly because I avoided the subject. Hux was aware of the fact that eight years ago, I had gone to Australia on a backpacking trip with my husband, but only one of us had come home. He also knew that I blamed myself for what happened.

The truth was, talking to Hux about it probably would have been therapeutic. For me, though, the difficulty wasn't so much about my *feelings*, but coming to terms with the facts. Maybe someday, somehow, Hux could help me put the pieces of that puzzle together, but I wasn't about to invite him to Australia for a tracking expedition focused on the ghost of my dead husband.

Hux put his hands on the railing and leaned up against it. "So, what's our play here?" he asked, a welcome congeniality in his voice.

I turned to face him. "I know you want to see the crime scene, but we'll have to make it quick. Colleen Denton's probably waiting on her lawyer, and once he gets here, we're done. She must know this doesn't look good for her."

"I can just look at the photos you took, if that's easier . . ."

"No. It's always better to see it in person." As I went to place my card on top of the key reader, Nate walked back over to where we were standing on the platform. He slipped his sat phone into his back pocket.

"Sorry," he said. "There's some trouble at the west entrance, and all the other rangers are tied up. I gotta head out there."

"No problem," I said. "We'll meet up with you later."

While Nate took off down the stairs, Hux and I braced ourselves for a critical foray into the doomed Peregrine suite. Hux took a breath and held it for a moment. I could tell he was nervous, but only because he knew, like I did, that we couldn't afford to make any mistakes when it came to gathering evidence and processing a scene.

The lock disengaged with a soft click. Hux stepped to the side, giving me a wide berth. With him, it was ladies first, always.

"Ten minutes, tops," I said as he followed in step behind me. Another cold blast from the air conditioner sent a chill down my spine. The afternoon light cast an eerie glow on the walls.

Hux took out his phone and affixed the little doo-dad he used to take crime scene photos. More than once, Hux's photos had passed muster with a hard-boiled prosecutor, and for the most part, the DAs we worked with had stopped giving us a hard time about not having a high-quality camera. For the crimes we tended to investigate, which occurred in remote landscapes where packing light was critical to survival, heavy cameras weren't feasible, either. And so, we relied on our phones, among other tenets of modern technology.

I noticed another text from Bodie flash up on my screen: *On my way!* Hux seemed to catch it, too. I could tell by the subtle frown that he might have seen the sender's name.

"What?" I asked him.

"Nothing."

"It's something."

"He's just—well, it's Bodie, right? Are you bringing him in on this one?"

"We need him, Hux. We've got a lot of evidence to process, and the Feds are tied up."

He grunted. "Yeah, but he's always so enthusiastic. It bugs me."

I couldn't help but laugh. "*Always?* You've only met him once."

"Yeah, but his text messages and emails . . . all those exclamation points . . ."

I could tell he was joking—sort of. Hux wasn't the type to harp on other people's flaws, but he had never warmed to Bodie. They'd met once last summer during a training event in Sequoia, where Bodie had been invited to speak about criminal forensics to the park rangers. I wasn't there, but the two of them had somehow discovered their mutual connection: me. Hux had come away from that conversation thinking that Bodie and I had dated years ago in Chicago.

Which wasn't true, although I had long suspected that Bodie might have made a move if Kevin hadn't been in the picture. To be fair, Bodie had never done anything inappropriate, but we were friends. Confidantes, even. Maybe Hux felt insecure about that, for some reason. *You could just ask him*, I chided myself, but of course I wasn't going to do that. With Hux, I always preferred to just let things blow over.

Another text message lit up my phone. A team from the medical examiner's office in Salinas was on their way to pick up the body via helicopter. "ETA 15 minutes."

With all these different parts in motion, I saw this as our last chance to view the crime scene in its primitive state. Later, Hux and I would go over the photos we'd taken, but there was no substitute for the real thing. Something about the smell of the carpet, the taste of the dry air, the aura of death and violence confronting you at every turn.

Standing in the shadows of the Peregrine suite, I got back into my gloves and booties and tried to picture the room as it must have looked in the moments before Chris Denton died, through the eyes of his killer. Was he asleep? And if he *was* asleep, in bed with his wife, it seemed like a stretch to imagine her putting on some heavy-duty gloves, smashing a framed photograph that wasn't even that close to the bed, and chasing her husband around the room. It would have been quite the production.

Even if the wife had killed him, however, there were easier, cleaner ways to dispose of someone. An "accidental" overdose. Poison. A gunshot wound to the head. She could have smothered him with a pillow or hit him over the head with a baseball bat. There was no reason for her to get out of bed and make such a horrid mess of things. For one thing, she risked Denton getting away from her. For another, all that blood left a trail of DNA evidence.

Which brought me to the so-called third-party theory, in which Chris Denton had been in bed with someone other than his wife when the killer entered the room. After all, Denton was a good-looking man who clearly had a thirst for adventure and scandal, or at least some degree of risk. And Nate had all but confirmed that Denton had checked in with someone else, at least according to the woman working the front desk at the time.

As for risk, if Denton *had* been cheating on his wife, then the Pinnacles Grand Hotel made sense for several reasons. It was posh, impressive, new—and way off the grid. That well-timed cancellation must have made it a no-brainer.

In this third-party scenario, the killer would have entered the room to see the two lovers asleep in bed, with the balcony door cracked open to encourage a breeze. Whoever it was had presumably gained entry with a key card, but that was another loose thread that would need tidying up later. At a place as new as this, it was reasonable to expect that the hotel tracked every entry and exit where an electronic key reader was involved. I might need a warrant to get it, but the information was there. *Add it to the to-do list.*

While Hux had a look around the bathroom, I decided to inspect the paintings on the walls. All were landscapes, clearly prints or duplicates rather than originals, but tastefully framed and arranged, and protected by what appeared to be thick, smear-free glass. The largest and grandest one was a majestic rendering of Pinnacles' signature rock formations at dusk; it stretched the full length of the mantle. The others were smaller in size, but the style was the same. Indeed, they all shared the same signature in the lower left corner: *Marchand.*

As I'd noted on my first walk through the scene, the broken glass had come from the painting next to the bed. The painting itself was about eighteen-by-eighteen inches, embedded in a heavy wooden frame. The subject of this one was a nondescript cave, its dark aperture beckoning to the artist who had rendered it. There was no text or placard to indicate the cave's location. As for the glass, it was nearly three millimeters thick.

I stood back a bit and tried to reimagine myself as the killer, standing before this piece of art moments before using it as a murder weapon. Had it happened in a fit of rage? Or was it complete indifference that had compelled the killer to shatter the glass?

Either way, the broken glass would have woken the room's occupants. Chris Denton, startled at first and terrified soon after, surely would have tried to run away from his intruder.

Denton hadn't gotten far. Then the necktie had come into play.

There was also the issue of Denton's bedfellow—assuming there was one. If it wasn't the wife, then who was it? And where was she?

Also, where were her clothes?

There was a lot to work out here, but despite the loose ends and strange discrepancies, I was feeling cautiously optimistic. Denton had had several points of contact with the staff since check-in, any one of whom could provide useful information.

I walked over to Denton's body and lifted his left foot. There was a small laceration on the top of his big toe that looked recent: an injury he'd sustained falling out of bed, perhaps.

The tie struck me as a haphazard weapon, something the killer had grabbed out of desperation in the midst of their carefully laid plan that had, for whatever reason, gone awry. I checked the dresser drawers for other clothes but found none.

"If there's a third party or a girlfriend or whatever, where are her clothes?" Hux asked from the hallway. He was also wearing gloves and booties, which was a deviation from the norm for us. We weren't used to dealing with an abundance of evidence. "Nothing in the drawers, there?"

"No," I said. "Did you find anything in the closet?"

Hux extricated himself from the hallway closet with a suitcase in his hands. "Just this." He held up a travel-sized piece of luggage. "Can I open it?"

"Just be careful with it. Make sure you photograph and log everything that's inside."

Hux carried the suitcase into the main living area. Careful to keep the contents as undisturbed as possible, he placed it on the luggage rack and unzipped the main compartment. I caught myself holding my breath.

My excitement was short-lived. Inside were several pairs of boxer shorts, T-shirts, some dress clothes, men's running shoes, and sweatpants, all thrown inside without much thought or care. Some of Denton's clothes were literally bunched up into little balls and squeezed into the corners. Hux took photos of everything.

No women's clothes whatsoever.

"Is Denton's packing style giving you a seizure?" I teased Hux, who always folded his clothes into works of art. He claimed it was a habit he'd developed in the military.

"A little," he said with a smirk.

He leaned back on his heels while holding a crouch, like a catcher loosening up a bit at home plate. Hux could stay in this position for hours; the guy had knees of steel.

I remarked, "Either he packed in a hurry, or Denton was a slob."

"I'm going with slob," Hux said. "Even when I'm tight on time, I don't just throw my toothpaste in with my underwear."

I waited for him to say more, but he didn't. "I'm getting the sense you don't like the guy."

He shrugged. "It looks like he cheated on his wife. I'll leave it at that."

I wasn't ready to leave it at that, though. I wanted Hux to see the other side of it; as an investigator, he had to be able to do that. "Maybe they were separated," I said. "Maybe she abused him. Maybe they had an open marriage."

Hux put his hands on his knees and pushed himself up. "Nah." He looked me in the eye. "You're making excuses for him."

"No, I'm not. I'm looking at this situation from multiple angles, not just the most obvious one. You've got to keep an open mind, Hux. Bias is a dangerous thing."

"I know," he said, his tone softening. "I remember the module."

The toiletry kit was just as disorganized as the suitcase. Inside were the standard personal items: a toothbrush, a razor, shaving cream, contact lenses, and Chapstick. But the toothpaste, as Hux had pointed out, was in with the underwear. Either way, there was absolutely no evidence that more than one person had packed any of this stuff—and certainly not a woman.

Hux reviewed his photos of everything while I made a meticulous inventory of all the items.

"Was there anything else in the closet?" I asked.

"No," he said. "I searched every inch."

"Did you check the minibar?"

"Yeah. Fully stocked."

"See any wine glasses anywhere?"

He shook his head. "There was a half-full glass of water in the bathroom, but that was it."

"Bodie will see what he can get from that." I glanced at my watch. "Let's have one last look around before we head upstairs."

Starting at the front door, we covered every inch of the room in a rapid, coordinated effort. We searched between the sheets, under the mattress, behind the TV . . . but found no evidence that another person had been here. And yet, it felt like someone other than Chris Denton's wife *had* to have been here. I could feel it, or maybe smell it—something floral and feminine, clinging to the bedsheets.

Hux peered over the balcony. "Maybe there *was* no girlfriend."

I went out and stood next to him. The afternoon hour had brought out the crowds. "According to multiple people, we have at least one eyewitness placing her on the property."

"Could she have checked out before seven AM?"

"Maybe. But to leave nothing behind? It's odd—and suspicious."

He considered this. "How long after the housekeeper found the body did the police get here?"

"Within the hour."

Hux rubbed the back of his neck while I made my way over to the bedside table. An old-fashioned clock ticked ominously. "Well, it's been ten minutes."

I nodded. "We should head upstairs."

Hux, though, lingered on the balcony, leaning over the railing as he scanned the cliff face on either side of the doorway.

"Hey, careful there," I said. "I don't need another fall-from-height case on my docket."

"Look over there." He was pointing to a sprawling wall of moss to his right, just below a window belonging to another room. "Do you see that?"

I *did* see it: a white plastic card, serendipitously jammed between two small branches. Hux stretched his long arm as far as he couch reach, which made my stomach churn. With the tips of his gloved fingers, he grasped the card.

It was a driver's license.

Hux flipped it over, revealing the pretty face of a young Middle Eastern woman smiling tightly at the camera. Her name was Aria Privar, and according to the Washington State license she was twenty-eight years old, five feet eight inches tall, and one hundred and ten pounds. She had brown eyes and brown hair.

"Wow," I said. "Nice work, Hux."

"Thanks," he beamed.

I reached into my back pocket for my stack of evidence bags and handed one to Hux. He dropped the license inside.

"Now let's go and talk to Colleen Denton."

CHAPTER

6

As the midday sun passed behind the clouds, casting a long shadow on the floor of the canyon, Hux and I caught a glimpse of James Dunaway making his way down the trail. His suit looked a little worse for wear, but he had changed into a sturdier pair of shoes.

I understood why. He was limping a bit, probably thanks to all the climbing and hiking he'd been forced to do this morning in his polished brown loafers. There was no way he could have anticipated having to log these many miles in his first week on the job, but still, it must have been a rude awakening for him and his feet.

"I apologize for that interruption," he said once he made his way to the top, joining me and Hux on the platform. "Have you been upstairs to Condor?"

"We were just about to head up."

"Good," Dunaway said. "I'll join you."

Together, the three of us made our way up the narrow, head-spinning staircase to the Condor suite. A gentle breeze rustled the leaves on the sycamore and cottonwood trees that populated the canyon. Bright sunlight penetrated a smattering of white wispy clouds.

At the top of the stairs, the door to the Condor suite featured another hand-painted rendering of its namesake, the California condor. While peregrines were handsome creatures with their well-proportioned, muscular bodies and gold-rimmed eyes, condors looked like the oversized goblins of the avian world. They had massive, bulky torsos and shriveled pink heads. Like other vultures, they feasted on the dead. *Not a good sign.*

Dunaway made a motion to unlock the door with his keycard, but I stopped him. "I think it's best if you wait out here," I said. "Would that be all right?"

"Oh, um." He cleared his throat. "Why?"

"We're treating this as a formal interview that could be used in court later. No offense to you, but we can't have you in there."

He nodded. "I understand. I have business to attend to in the lobby anyway."

While Dunaway made his way back down the stairs, Hux and I confronted the bloated condor staring out at us from the door. I supposed *someone* must have thought it made for a nice, homey touch, but the creepy birds of prey weren't really my speed.

Ignoring the small "Do Not Disturb" sign hanging from the doorknob, Hux rapped on the door with his knuckles. *It's go time.*

After a few seconds, we heard footsteps, then a muffled voice inside the room. The door swung open, revealing a police deputy named Vee. Her last name was right there on her badge. She looked even younger than Nate, probably fresh out of the academy. This made me uneasy. I worried about amateurs making amateur mistakes, especially in the early stages of an investigation when every decision had a potential fallout. On the other hand, the newbies hadn't yet had an opportunity to develop an ego. It was a mixed bag.

Deputy Vee put her hands on her hips and said, "Glad you're here. I'm Eunice Vee, by the way." She gave our hands a firm shake before jutting her thumb over her shoulder. "You're here to talk to the wife, I bet. Well, I've got bad news: she lawyered up."

I glanced at Hux. "Pardon?"

"She called him hours ago. He's on his way here."

The good news was that Vee seemed to know her way around a criminal investigation. The bad news was that it was possible we'd missed a crucial window of opportunity while processing the crime scene. "What time did you get here?" I asked.

She glanced at the thick band on her left wrist. "Before eight. I drove up from Hollister as soon as I got the call."

"Where was Mrs. Denton at that point?"

"Still in the Peregrine suite."

"Did she ever try to leave the property?"

"Not to my knowledge. She was sitting out on the balcony by the time I got there—away from, er, the body. But she wouldn't come in."

"What was her demeanor like at that time?"

Vee flipped her long black ponytail off her shoulder. "She seemed pretty stable. Cold, even. Hardly any emotion at all. I thought it was weird."

I liked Vee's honest assessment, her casual tone. It took emotion out of the equation, which helped me take her information at face value. "And then what did you do?" I asked.

"I moved her upstairs. She wasn't happy about it."

"About being detained, you mean?"

"She liked to be in control. You could just tell. She didn't like that I wanted to move her to another room before her lawyer got here."

"The sight of her husband's dead body didn't bother her?" Hux's tone was somewhere between wry and skeptical.

"Not too much," Vee said. "Probably 'cause she killed him."

"What are you basing that on?" I asked her.

"Just the whole vibe." Her response came without any hesitation.

I wasn't ready to dig into Vee's conviction of Mrs. Denton's guilt just yet, so I let it slide. "What else did she say to you?"

Vee stiffened her posture as she folded her arms over her chest. I had to admit I was impressed by the way she carried herself. She wasn't going to be bullied. "Just that she had already called her lawyer, like I said."

"Before that, I mean."

Vee closed the door behind her, leaving it a few inches ajar so she could listen for any activity inside. She pushed that ponytail behind her ear again. "Look, this lady is no idiot. She wanted her lawyer ASAP. I told her only guilty people want lawyers, but she didn't care."

Despite what had seemed like a promising start, I was starting to get a sinking feeling about what awaited us in the Condor suite. I knew the chances of getting a confession out of Mrs. Denton at this point were practically nil, especially with her attorney en route.

"I assume you still want to go in there?" Vee asked.

"Absolutely," I said, with a glance at Hux. "Let's go introduce ourselves—no law against that. She doesn't have to talk to us."

Hux put his notepad inside his pocket. I heard him take a deep breath, a rare indication of nerves. He had a talent for keeping his emotions contained, but the stakes were high. If Mrs. Denton shut us down, we were really going to have our work cut out for ourselves.

Hux and I followed the petite but sturdy Deputy Vee into the Condor suite. The first thing I noticed was the more comfortable climate, the thermostat set to a pleasant seventy-two degrees. A cool breeze flowed in from the open balcony door.

The layout of the room was similar to Peregrine, but there were some notable differences. The hallway was a little shorter, the bathroom smaller, with a walk-in shower instead of a tub. The bed was queen-sized rather than a king.

Like Peregrine, there was a desk, a television, and a balcony that looked out at the canyon. A hearth made for a pleasingly romantic sitting area, framed by a lovely arrangement of landscape paintings. In fact, they were similar in style to the ones in the Peregrine suite.

The woman who I presumed was Colleen Denton occupied the chair at the desk. She turned her head in our direction when we walked in.

Her short, stylish blonde hair framed a pair of bright green eyes that betrayed no alarm at the sight of us. At first glance, she looked about fifty, but she could have been ten years older than that. I could see she had gone to some lengths to hide the relentless march of time: Botox, laser. Her brow didn't furrow when she narrowed her eyes at me and Hux.

"Mrs. Denton?" I said, by way of greeting.

She gave a curt nod.

"I'm Special Agent Felicity Harland, and this is my partner—"

"I've already invoked my right to an attorney," she said. "I don't have anything to say to you."

Well, that was fast. Her expression was smug, making it clear she wasn't going to budge. Her lawyer was on his way, but he would have to endure that brutal hike like the rest of us. He could be hours away, or even a day away. We couldn't hold her here if it took him that long—and she probably knew that, too, but I decided to play dumb.

"All right, then," I said. "We'll come back when he gets here."

"Am I free to leave?"

Hux and I exchanged a glance.

Vee snorted. "No, ma'am," she said. "I already told you that."

"It feels like I'm being unlawfully detained, then."

"You can ask your lawyer to sort that out," Vee snapped at her.

I decided to let the silence play itself out. A part of me sensed that Mrs. Denton *wanted* to talk; she just wanted to do it on her own terms, with her lawyer present. In this way, she wasn't unique. Human beings liked to talk. The blameless wanted to profess their innocence; the guilty felt like they could talk their way out of a murder charge.

"We'll come back when your lawyer gets here, Mrs. Denton," I said.

Vee looked disappointed, but she bit her lip.

Mrs. Denton watched us leave, tracking us all the way to the door like she didn't trust our intentions. Vee left the door slightly ajar after the three of us had filed out.

Vee said, "She's a real piece of work."

"She knows her rights," I said. "Nothing we can do about that."

"Yeah, well, she was *standing over the body*. Far as I'm concerned, she doesn't have any rights. She lost 'em when she murdered her husband."

Vee's emphatic conviction continued to take me by surprise. *Does she know something we don't?* I was under the impression that Mrs. Denton hadn't said much of anything to anyone, except maybe the housekeeper, who had gone home for the day.

"Are you sure she didn't confess?" I asked Vee.

"She didn't have to confess. I heard about the mistress or whatever. I mean, clearly this lady had motive. Why else would she even be here?"

Hux, at least, seemed skeptical of Vee's assessment, but he didn't push her on it. Instead, he peered over the railing at the trail down below, perhaps as a way to diffuse the tension that Vee was bringing to the table. The passersby never even looked up, which meant word hadn't gotten out about our investigation. This was a good thing.

I checked my phone to see a message from Bodie—*ETA 5 PM, hitting the trail now*—and several from Ray. The situation at the airport hadn't changed, apparently.

Then, as I was putting my phone away, a new message from Ray popped up: *Call me.*

"Uh-oh," Hux said, while I fumbled to type out a response on my phone.

"Ray's in a bad mood about something," I said, deciding this was probably as good a time as any to call him back. I pressed the button and waited for the call to go through.

Ray answered in a huff. "Harland?" He was clearly walking somewhere, his heavy footfalls echoing in the background. I put the phone on speaker. "What's your status?"

"Hux and I are on-site at the hotel. We processed the crime scene as best we could in a short time frame. I called in a friend to help us with some forensics."

"Good idea. You're on your own for now."

"We can handle it."

"I sure hope so," he said with a grunt. "Is this a homicide, then?"

I flashed back in my mind to Christopher Denton's mangled body, lying facedown on a blood-stained carpet with a silk tie around his neck. "Yes, sir."

"You got a suspect?"

"We've got the wife, who was found standing over the body not long after he was killed, but she won't talk. Her lawyer's on his way here."

Ray snorted. "Lean on her until he gets there."

Hux looked somewhat displeased by this comment, but then again, he was former military. He respected protocol. "She lawyered up, sir," I said firmly.

Another snort as Ray slowed his walk, slurped on a drink of some sort, and started up again. "Well, look, the Park Service is lighting up the switchboard about this missing person they've got in the park down there. I think they got wind of the situation at the hotel and don't feel comfortable handling this on their own. You've got to get out there and meet up with them."

"Out where?"

"They'll text you the coordinates."

"I'll call them now," I said. "Who's the point person?"

"I just texted you the number."

He hung up.

I pulled up the message he had sent and dialed the number. Less than a minute later, a man answered.

"Niles Griffiths here."

"Is this the chief ranger?"

"Yes," he said. "Who's this?"

"Felicity Harland with ISB. I received a copy of your incident report about a missing person."

"Yes, ma'am. Thanks for calling." Niles sounded like he was in his forties, with an unhurried manner of speaking that reminded me of a courteous and patient teacher. The gusting wind in the background made it hard to hear him.

"Can you repeat that, please?" I asked him, putting the phone on speaker so Hux could hear every word.

"We're on the High Peaks Trail. I'll send you the coordinates."

"We're dealing with a serious situation at the hotel right now," I said. "Is this time-sensitive?"

"Very much so," he said. "We don't have much of a search-and-rescue squad out here, and my team is inexperienced. I just want to do everything we can to find this lady."

I sighed, wondering if maybe Griffiths was worried about his reputation, too. Pinnacles wasn't Yosemite or Sequoia, after all, but it had gotten plenty of press after the hotel's grand opening. The spotlight was on him and his crew.

"Okay," I said. "One other thing—we just found a driver's license belonging to a woman named Aria Privar. Twenty-eight years old, Middle Eastern descent. She's five eight, a hundred and ten pounds. We think she stayed at the hotel last night, but we can't locate her."

The chief ranger let out a breath. "Sounds like this could be our gal, then."

"Could be. I'll have to look at the map, but can you give us a sense of how long it might take for us to reach you at your location?"

"From the hotel?" Griffiths thought for a moment. "An average hiker could probably do it in four hours."

I glanced at my watch. It was a little after two o'clock, which didn't give us much time to get there in the daylight. I also wanted to be on the premises this evening to interview potential witnesses at the bar and restaurant.

"I think the best we can do is tomorrow morning," I said. "We can head out at first light."

"I understand," Griffiths said, but he sounded disappointed. "We'll mobilize our resources on our end and touch base with you in the AM."

The connection deteriorated, and the call disconnected before we had a chance to say good-bye. It didn't matter. We had a plan—sort of.

Hux said, "He sounds a little overwhelmed."

"He is, but so are we."

"I bet we could do it in two."

"*You* could do it in two. I'd need a helicopter to get me out there right now." I wasn't resentful of Hux's abilities; these were just the facts. "We have a lot of people to track down and talk to— pretty much anyone who might have seen the Dentons or Aria Privar last night. I suspect a good number of them will be back for their evening shift, and we need to be here when that happens."

"What about the wife?"

"We wait for her lawyer to get here and hope for the best."

Hux nodded. He made no secret of the fact that he much preferred the expansive nature of the great outdoors to fancy hotels, which was what had attracted him to the Park Service in the first place. He relished the law enforcement aspect of our job, too, but Hux's boundless enthusiasm for the work withered a bit in enclosed spaces.

"Don't worry," I said. "We'll be out there at first light."

I rarely asked Hux personal questions, but the chaos of the morning had made it hard to check in with him. I felt bad about that. For as long as I'd known him, Hux had had my back—hell, he'd saved my life in Sequoia—and I always felt in some small way that I owed him for that. It was a joy, really, having a partner as smart, and as capable, as Hux Huxley. Most days, he was an open book, which meant neither one of us was afraid to rib the other a little bit. In that moment, though, I knew he felt like we were letting down his fellow rangers.

"I know," he said, managing a smile. He pulled a trail map out of his back pocket and showed it to me. "Here, look. I came prepared."

"Where did you get this?"

"The little brochure rack in the lobby. I popped in real quick and grabbed one."

"Where's your topo map?" By *topo*, I meant "topographical"— which gave a detailed sketch of the landscape, including altitude. Hux had about a thousand of them back at his cabin in Sequoia, at least a few of which were collector's items.

"Don't worry, I packed one of those, too," he said. "But the High Peaks Trail is no joke. We're in for an adventure if someone's gone missing down there, especially if they went off the grid at all, into those mountains."

Before I could comment on Hux's idea of an "adventure," I glimpsed a tall, dark-haired man in a crisp charcoal suit making his way down the trail below. He tugged at his tie as he grasped the railing and powered up the stairs.

"Well, hold that thought for now," I said. "Because here comes Mrs. Denton's lawyer."

CHAPTER

7

Mrs. Denton's attorney introduced himself as Jim Steinberger, followed by the name of some legendary law firm
that he clearly expected me to recognize and admire. I could tell
from the smirk on his face and the crispness of his suit that he
knew his way around high-profile cases. Despite the hike to get
here, he looked refreshed: nice hair, clean suit, tanned skin. Not
a bead of sweat on him. Unlike me, he must have found a shower
and a place to change.

"I'd like a word with my client," he said after we'd gotten
through our introductions. "Then we can chat."

"Can you make it a quick word?" I asked. "It's just the two of
us working this case right now, and we've got a lot to get through."

"I'll do my best," he said, without an ounce of authenticity.

Hux and I stood out on the landing while Steinberger went
inside to convene with Mrs. Denton. As he closed the door behind
him, I heard the deadbolt click into place. *Seriously?* I resisted the
urge to roll my eyes.

"Don't take it personally," Hux said, reading my mood.

"He thinks we're a bunch of amateurs."

"Most folks do," Hux said good-naturedly.

I felt a smile spread across my face in spite of myself; Hux had
that effect on me. "So, how do you want to do this?"

"You should take the lead on this one," he said. "She sounds
pretty savvy."

"Yeah, well, you're savvy, too. And the cougars tend to like you."

He laughed. "I appreciate the vote of confidence."

"You take this one," I said. "I'll back you up."

At last, the door with the giant Condor on it swung open, startling us both. "We're ready, unfortunately," Steinberger said. He reached up and tightened his tie. "But don't expect much. I advised her not to say anything to you."

With a nod that pretty much said, *We'll see about that*, we proceeded into the room. Steinberger seemed a little agitated, which boded well for us. *Had Mrs. Denton changed her mind about talking to us?* We were about to find out.

The balcony door was open, bathing the room in a soft yellow glow from the waning daylight. A light breeze rustled the translucent white drapes. The room smelled of lavender.

Mrs. Denton was looking a little bit worse for wear, but her grim facial expression gave nothing away. The dark circles under her eyes betrayed the fact that she'd been up all night, but she looked at us with disarming focus. Despite her weary façade, she sat ramrod straight, like she was bracing herself for a battle. *This could be tricky*, I thought, but there was no going back now. Presenting a united and confident front was an important part of the strategy here. Mrs. Denton seemed the type to exploit any weaknesses.

Hux grabbed a pair of chairs from the balcony and brought them inside. Steinberger stood in the corner. No one sat on the bed, even though it was available and convenient.

"Hello again, ma'am," Hux said, directing his attention to Mrs. Denton, almost like she was the only person in the room. His smile was the kind that invited you in. "Would you be open to a few questions?"

Steinberger shot a look at his client. "Don't answer that," he said.

Mrs. Denton leaned back a bit in her chair. She twisted her torso a few degrees so that she was facing away from us. While we waited with bated breath, she gazed out the window at the ancient rock formations rising out of the earth, the electric blue sky that almost seemed to sizzle in the sunlight.

"Colleen?" Steinberger said.

She turned back around to face him. "I'd like to say something."

"What?" He shifted his feet. "What—no. No, don't do that."

"The maid found me standing over his body, Jim. I want to explain myself."

"There's no *need* to explain yourself, Colleen. Come on."

She arched her back a bit, sternum to the sky, no slouch in her shoulders at all. Her voice oozed the kind of confidence that eluded most women. Steinberger had an imposing presence, but his client wasn't the least bit intimidated by him. I knew she wasn't going to let him talk her out of making this mistake.

Because it *was* a mistake, and we all knew it. Even *she* knew it. Just moments ago, she'd made it clear that she had no intention of talking to us. *What changed?*

Mrs. Denton looked at Hux. "I'd like to make a statement, but I'm only going to do this once. I'm not meeting you at a police station, in other words."

Hux took his cell phone out of his pocket. "Go right ahead, ma'am. We're ready."

The tiniest of smiles curled on her lips. She looked almost amused by Hux's earnestness. "Are you sure you're a real detective?"

"I'm as real as you'll find out here." He met her gaze with a thin but genuine smile. She didn't smile back, but I could tell that Hux had gotten her onto his side.

Steinberger shifted his feet. Of course his client's willingness to talk was excellent news for us. The most valuable piece of evidence in a homicide case was always a confession. If we could get that, the rest was downhill—dotting *I*'s, crossing *T*'s. Ray would be pleased, and I could get back to Cold Case Sundays, which made for a good winter project.

Don't get ahead of yourself, I thought, a common refrain for me in moments like these. As promising as things seemed, I knew that Mrs. Denton or her lawyer could shut things down in an instant. It was about riding the mood, seeing how far we could take it before Steinberger had an aneurysm. Hux had done well so far. I was prepared to let him act on his own instincts.

Mrs. Denton crossed her ankles and looked at Hux before shifting her gaze over to me. Steinberger, at this point, looked like he was about to jump out of his skin. He kept glaring at his recalcitrant client, who acted like he didn't exist. *Interesting.*

"First," Mrs. Denton said, "I'd like to say that I did not kill my husband. I'm sure you'll come to the same conclusion during the course of your investigation, but I wanted to make this clear from the outset."

I had gotten pretty good at hiding my emotions, but still, her calculated pronouncement was a blow. *So much for a confession*, I thought.

Steinberger interjected again. "Colleen, this is *not* advisable. As you know, they can use anything you say against you—"

"I'm well aware, Jim. I passed the bar, remember?"

Another blow. If Mrs. Denton had a law degree, then she understood the risks of talking to us, even with her lawyer present. If she was guilty, it certainly behooved her to stay quiet. But if she was *innocent* . . .

Her insistence on talking to us could have been a strategy of some sort, a way to deflect suspicion on our part, especially after everything we already knew. The fact that a housekeeper had found her standing over her husband's dead body was damning evidence, the kind of thing you couldn't deflect or deny in a courtroom. Maybe she was trying to get out in front of it.

"Now, I'd like to start from the beginning," she said. "Chris and I have been married for eleven years, and he's been unfaithful for ten of them." She studied her cuticles before shoving her hands in her lap. "He's a gambler, a liar, and a cheat."

Jim Steinberger paced the room, his chin tilted upward like a petulant child as he grasped his cuff links. He let out a groan.

"I suspected this early on, which is embarrassing to admit," she went on. "You've seen him—although, I suppose it's not the same, since you saw the posthumous version of him." She folded her hands in her lap. "He was very attractive, even more so when we met. He was charming and sexy and fun. I liked that he was younger than me; it made *me* feel young. I was forty when we married—a vulnerable time for a woman. You start to feel invisible."

She shifted her gaze in my direction, but this time there was a hint of condescension behind it, or maybe even envy. I knew women that resented the aging process—the wrinkles, the hormones, the attitude changes—but I wasn't raised that way, and

I couldn't relate to her contempt for it. I supposed maybe things were different in her industry, where appearances mattered. In my line of work, it didn't make sense to do yourself up every day on the job. Most days, I ended up sunburnt, battered, and riddled with bug bites.

"Are either of you married?" she asked Hux and me.

Hux shook his head. "No, ma'am."

I was slower to answer, in part because her question took me by surprise. Police interviews tended to be a one-way flow of information. It was rare for someone being interrogated to show much interest in my personal life, or to even have the gall to ask me about it. I wasn't just going to ignore the question, though, and I had a feeling she'd pick up on a lie. How could I expect her to tell the truth if I wasn't willing to do the same?

"I was married once," I said, omitting the part that I was widowed, not divorced.

"Then you know," she said dismissively.

But I *didn't* know. I had married at a time when most of my friends were still navigating the dating world. Even my parents were surprised when I told them, at twenty-three, that I was engaged. *"Aren't you too young?"* my father had asked, clearly disappointed. *"Don't have kids right away,"* my mother scolded me. *"You'll never have the career you worked so hard for."* It often felt like they were trying to talk me out of it right up until Kevin and I exchanged vows. It took years in law enforcement for me to understand why my parents were so cold on marrying young. For years during my tenure at the FBI, I witnessed the implosion of marriages and long-term relationships—to affairs, job obsessions, addiction, even murder.

The Dentons' marriage had collapsed, too, clearly, but I wasn't convinced I had the whole picture as to why. Mrs. Denton, perhaps, had made a lousy choice when it came to a mate. Kevin wasn't a lousy choice. For me, he had been a safe choice.

"What was your marriage like?" I asked her.

"Terrible, practically from the start. He didn't want children, and neither did I, but soon, it became apparent that he didn't want *me*, either." She tapped on the desk with fingernails that looked recently painted. "I put up with the affairs, at first. He was always sorry. He said they were just flings that didn't mean anything to him." She heaved a sigh as she curled a strand of hair behind her ear. "I believed him."

"What changed?" Hux asked.

"Aria." She snorted. "When she came into the picture, I knew it was different."

I tried to keep my expression neutral, but hearing the confirmation that Aria Privar was Colleen's late husband's lover changed the game. It gave us motive, for one.

"Different how?"

"He was in love with her." Her voice soured.

Steinberger muttered, "*Christ,*" but Colleen shot him a look that sent him cowering. He looked out the window at the picturesque scene off the balcony. I wasn't sure if it calmed him. *Probably not*, I thought. He was wound up tight, and for good reason. His client was giving us a lot of ammunition for a trial, if it ever came to that.

"The thing about Aria is that she was clueless," Colleen said. "She knew Chris was married, but he told her we were separated, and she believed him."

"How did you know?" Hux asked. "He told you?"

Steinberger cut in, "Colleen, don't even *think—*"

"I hired a private investigator," she said, which made Steinberger wither even more. His cuff links weren't going to survive this ordeal, that was for sure. "I wanted to get my information first-hand, not through my lying cheat of a husband."

"Makes sense," Hux said. "So he passed you information about the affair?"

"Oh, yes. Photos, emails. At first, I was embarrassed that I had fallen for Chris's lies, but you have to understand, he was a master manipulator. He grew up in foster care in Modesto and has been hustling ever since. He lies, he cheats, he gambles—whatever it takes to make his way in the world." She reached for a glass of water on the table and sipped it slowly. If she had any compassion left for her husband's difficult childhood, it didn't come through in her voice.

"That must have been difficult to deal with," I said.

"Oh, it was. I suspect he was into hard drugs as a youth, but he never talked about it. He's been sober for as long as I've known him, but I don't think addiction was ever his real problem." She lowered her voice. "He's rotten to his core."

Yikes. Even Hux looked a little taken aback.

"So he didn't use alcohol or drugs, to your knowledge?"

"No," she said. "Not that it matters. He has other flaws."

"Such as?"

She tightened her grip on the glass but made no move to drink it. "Last year, he got Aria pregnant. That, for me, was the turning point." Her expression was molded into place, like a mask, but I could feel the rage simmering behind it. Steinberger put his hands on his knees and bent over to suck in a breath.

"I decided I wanted him dead," she said, which made Hux flinch. He glanced at his phone, probably to make sure it was still recording.

It was.

Steinberger walked over to the desk and stood next to his client. I wondered if he thought his physical presence might change her mind.

No such luck. She stiffened when he bent down and spoke into her ear, as if his proximity offended her. Again, this was good for us—very good. Here I was, thinking this law school educated woman was going to put up walls a mile high and take us for a ride on this "interview." Instead, she was giving us keys to the kingdom.

For now. I couldn't help but feel that this story, as elaborate as it was, had a punch line. It just hadn't come yet. When it did, it was going to hurt.

"What did you do then?" Hux asked.

"I seriously considered hiring a hit man in April, but when I heard about the pregnancy—"

"Wait, what?" I interrupted her. "I'd like to go back to the hit man."

"Don't answer that," Steinberger grunted.

"I didn't hire anyone," she said, reducing her voice to a low growl. "It's a moot point."

I looked at Hux, who seemed to be momentarily stunned into silence by this development. I had to admit it was new territory for me, too.

"All right, then," Hux said. "You canceled the hit man. Go on."

"Chris claimed the relationship was over, that Aria had had an abortion and he had nothing to do with her anymore. You have to understand, I *wanted* to believe him. That's the most pathetic part of all this: I was still in love with him. I hated him, but I loved him." Colleen put the drinking glass down, the ice clinking the sides at a deafening pitch. I noticed her hands were shaking. "For the summer, things were good. We traveled together—Vegas, Europe, Bali. I was busy with work, but I took a few weeks of personal leave to work on my marriage." Her voice curdled. "And then I saw him with *her*. Again."

"When was this?" Hux asked.

"A couple months ago."

"Where?"

"At a restaurant in Palo Alto." She threaded her fingers through the tapered ends of her hair, which were completely and utterly blond, not a twinge of gray. "At that point, I asked my guy to follow them, not that I needed any more confirmation that they were back together. Chris was only marginally employed, so he was using *my* money to wine and dine her."

"Marginally employed?" Hux asked. "You mean Chips & Trips?"

Colleen rolled her eyes. "He was trying to get into the artificial intelligence space. It's all the rage now in poker. The trouble is, he never really understood the concept. I burned quite a few investor relationships trying to get him started."

I could now see why this woman had ultimately turned against her husband, but how far she'd gone in that regard was still unclear. The hit man piece was an important lead, and I was shocked she'd even admitted it. Getting access to emails and cell phone records wasn't always a guarantee, but we weren't going to have any trouble getting a warrant based on what she'd given us so far. Much to the chagrin of her lawyer, she was doing a lot of work building a circumstantial case against herself.

"Did you ever reconsider hiring the hit man?" Hux asked.

She shook her head. "No," she said curtly. "I realized it was stupid to put so much trust in a stranger for a task like that. But when my guy told me yesterday that Chris and Aria were packing up for what looked like a camping trip, it changed things for me."

"Changed things how?" Hux asked.

She was quiet for a moment. "Chris and I had always talked about going off the grid for a real wilderness adventure. You know, back when things were good."

"That must have hurt," he said. "To hear he was going on your wilderness adventure with someone else."

She shrugged, but I could see the tension in her shoulders, the anguish in her expression. Colleen had allowed her toxic obsession with her own husband to get the best of her. It was sad, but not uncommon.

"So what happened next?" Hux asked.

"Well, as I mentioned, Chris was a careless person in pretty much all aspects of his life, so it didn't take much for my PI to figure out where he was going."

"Pinnacles, you mean?"

She nodded.

"Got it," Hux said. "So your guy told you what he found out. Then what happened?"

Colleen went back to curling the ends of her hair. I could tell she was losing steam, but Hux was just getting started. "It was all very rushed," she said. "My investigator posed as a neighbor while they were packing up for their trip and asked where they were going. I was in a meeting at the time, so when he called, I had to drop everything rather quickly."

"On a Saturday?" I cut in.

"Yes," she said. "I work every day of the week."

Good for you, I thought. Her self-righteousness grated on me even though it wasn't supposed to. Hell, *she* grated on me. There was just something about her.

"So you got in your car and drove here yesterday?" Hux asked. "What time did you leave?"

"I left around eleven. I didn't know there was going to be a marathon hike at the end."

"What were you expecting to happen when you arrived?" Hux asked. "Did you have a plan?"

She didn't answer.

"It's a three-hour drive from the Bay Area," I said, interjecting before she could use the pause as an excuse to end our conversation. "You would have had some time to think about it."

Steinberger slapped his hand down on the table. "Colleen, you've said enough. You made your statement; now they're just trying to goad you into a confession."

Something in Steinberger's tone seemed to give her pause. She looked out the window, which at this time of day offered a seductive, sun-drenched view of the canyon. After a brief hesitation, she got up off the chair and walked out onto the balcony. Hux tensed a bit, and for a moment there, I thought we were going to witness a suicide. Colleen Denton didn't strike me as mentally unstable, but I wasn't about to take any chances.

Hux and I followed her over to the balcony door while Steinberger downed his bottled water in three swift gulps. When Colleen noticed how close we were, she backed away from the terrace. "I'm not going to jump," she said, barking a laugh.

"Good," Hux said. "Nobody wants that."

She inhaled deeply, savoring the delicate scent of chaparral, the savory taste of freedom. "I thought about what would happen on the drive down here," she said. "I thought about confronting him once and for all. I wanted to humiliate him in the worst way—her, too. She moved in on my marriage like it was hers for the taking." Her voice cracked, but only for a moment; she recovered quickly and decisively, banishing this ripple of weakness like it was a regrettable mistake. "I didn't get to the park until two o'clock, but I caught up to them on the trail. Chris was always a flake when it came to logistics. Sure enough, he was in sandals, carrying his suitcase over all those rock formations like a bumbling idiot." Another snort. "He always depended on me to be the sensible one."

"What about her?" Hux asked.

"I don't know. I don't remember."

This sounded like a lie, but I didn't understand why she would feel compelled to dodge the question. I wondered if at some point she was going to try to convince us that she hadn't seen Aria Privar at all. *Does Colleen know something we don't?* I wondered.

"You said he had a suitcase," I said. "Did she have any luggage?"

"I don't remember."

Steinberger's phone rang—loudly, almost obnoxiously. He glared at his client before taking the call down the hallway, still within earshot of our conversation. It didn't take long for him to start shouting at whoever was on the other end. *His assistant, maybe?*

A paralegal? My grandmother always said you could tell a lot about a person by the way they treated the "little people"—not the term you'd use these days, but the spirit of her words still held true.

Hux moved in quickly with another question. "Is it possible they saw you?" he asked.

"No."

"How can you be sure?"

"Oh, I'm quite sure. Chris has a one-track mind when it comes to women—especially *that* woman. He wouldn't have noticed a mountain lion if it was about to eat him."

And yet you were desperate to go on an outdoor adventure with this man, I thought. Everything Colleen had said so far was building to a deep-seated love-hate relationship with a man that had gone bad. But *how* bad was the question. Her marriage was not what she had hoped and dreamed it would be. What was worse, though, was that she had clearly held on to that hope, despite all signs telling her that it wasn't going to happen. A woman like Colleen Denton didn't strike me as the type to take no for an answer, even in her love life. Had the dismantling of her dream marriage ended in murder by her own hand? Or was she telling us the truth?

"What time did you get to the hotel?" Hux asked.

She thought for a moment, even though I suspected she knew every detail of her pursuit of Chris and Aria, including the timeline. Colleen just didn't want us to know that she did.

"It was late afternoon, but I couldn't tell you the exact time," she finally said. "I was sitting in the lobby, just close enough to the reception area to hear their conversation but far away enough that they wouldn't notice me. It was busy at that hour—easy to blend in."

"Okay, so what did you glean from that conversation?" Hux asked.

"Pretty much what you'd expect. Where the pool was, what time the restaurant was open . . ." She squeezed and twisted her fingers, one of which was adorned with her engagement ring. *Had she paid for that, too?* I wondered.

"Then what happened?" Hux prompted her.

She covered her ringed finger with her other hand, blocking it from view. "After they checked in, they went to their room. Chris was drenched from the hike, so I imagine he wanted to shower." Her tone was withering. "After about an hour, they came back for dinner out on the terrace. I went out and sat by the pool. It was dark by then, which meant I could see them, but they couldn't see me."

"What time was this?" Hux asked.

"I don't know," she said, betraying a slight irritation. "I'd say they sat down for dinner at around seven and finished up at the bar at ten or so. They weren't in any hurry."

Hux glanced at his phone to make sure it was still recording. "Then what happened?"

Steinberger barked at his client, "*Colleen*. Haven't you said enough?"

"Not quite." She looked back at Hux. "I followed them down the trail to their room."

"Did they seem drunk to you?" Hux asked.

"Chris wasn't. I saw him drinking cranberry juice."

I cut in. "What about Aria? You said they sat at the bar for a while; it would help us to know if she seemed intoxicated."

"I can't recall."

It intrigued me, her tendency to be evasive when it came to Aria. This was an important detail, too. For Chris Denton, the toxicology report would tell us a lot, but we had nothing concrete on Aria. At the moment, we didn't even know if she was alive.

"Okay," Hux said, changing course. "What happened when you got to the room?"

"I saw the stairs and decided to hold back a little bit. I wasn't worried about Chris seeing me, but I didn't want to do anything needlessly stupid."

"Are you sure *she* didn't notice you?" I asked.

Colleen shrugged. "I don't know. If she did, I doubt she knew who I was."

"But you said she knew Chris was married."

"Well, yes, but I highly doubt she took it any further than that."

I wasn't usually one to harp on generational differences, but in my opinion, a twenty-eight-year-old woman dating a married man absolutely would have taken it further than that. She would have scoured the internet for whatever she could find about her boyfriend's wife, and she would have uncovered a lot—including

Colleen's photo. I actually thought there was a pretty good chance that Aria Privar had seen Colleen over the course of that afternoon and evening, especially since Colleen herself had been a little careless.

"Did you have a plan once you got up there?" Hux asked.

"Don't answer that," Steinberger ordered his client.

Colleen met his gaze, acknowledging that she'd heard his admonition, but then she said to Hux, "I knew that if I knocked on the door, Chris would answer—and he wouldn't be able to talk himself out of what was going on. He'd have to tell me the truth about Aria and how he felt about her."

"And why was that so important to you?" Hux asked.

"I knew it was over," she said brusquely. "I just needed to hear it from him."

Even though a direct confrontation like this wasn't the smartest move, I understood the impulse. Colleen was the jealous wife who still held a torch for her philandering husband. She wanted to know about the other woman—not just her name, or what she looked like, but what her husband saw in her. While Colleen struck me as a detail-oriented woman, she probably wasn't satisfied with her private investigator's dry reporting of Chris and Aria's affair.

"So, did you knock?" Hux asked.

"Not right away," she said. "I heard them talking for a while, then . . ." She cleared her throat, barely holding back her disgust. "The balcony door was open. I could hear everything."

"What time was this?"

"I don't know . . . probably around ten o'clock."

I asked, "How long did you stay out there?"

"An hour. Longer." She spoke in a strangled voice. "I don't know. Hearing them have sex, it made me nauseous. I could picture it in my mind . . ."

Hux and I exchanged a glance. He was still recording, thankfully. I could see the time stamp ticking away.

Steinberger cut in again. "Colleen, I *must* counsel you—"

She held up a hand. "For the last ten years, I've lived with a man who habitually lied to me." Her lips curled up in a grimace. "The truth will set you free, right?"

Not if you go to prison for murder, I thought, but I kept my mouth shut. She was about to get to the punchline . . . if there was one. Maybe she had changed her mind about confessing. These things happened sometimes. People were funny that way. The smart thing to do in these situations was to shut up, but human beings liked to talk and unburden themselves.

"After a while, their sexual escapades ended," she went on. "It felt late, but I don't know what time it was. I was in a fog. At one point, I tried to open the door, but it was locked."

"The door was locked?" I asked, eager to nail down the details on this point. "Are you sure?"

"Yes," she said. "I didn't have a key to the room, obviously."

"But you got in eventually because the housekeeper found you that morning," I pressed her. She was going to have to explain her presence there one way or another. "Isn't that correct?"

She made a little snort. "That was much later. At some point, I went back down to the lobby. I wasn't going to hike back to the trailhead in the dark, so I lay down on one of the cabanas by the pool. When I woke up, the sun was up. I felt more like myself. I was in the mood for a more level-headed confrontation—you know, go in there, tell Chris and his whore to go to hell, and end our marriage."

"What time was this?" I asked.

"Six fifteen AM. I have a daily alarm that goes off then."

"For what purpose?"

"Yoga."

Hux nodded agreeably so she wouldn't think he was being judgmental. It was a good thing Colleen had consented to be recorded. There would be time later to analyze every word she said.

While Steinberger paced the room, Colleen drank the remains of her ice water. I knew he wasn't going to interrupt her again. At this point, she had won the war against him; she was determined to tell her side of the story.

In a softer voice, she said, "I should have hiked back to my car. I mean, that would have been the smart decision. But at that point, I felt prepared to tell Chris that our marriage was over and that he should look forward to dealing with my lawyer." She glanced at Steinberger, who was still bristling in a corner. "My *divorce* lawyer."

"Of course," Hux said, like he knew all about lawyers. It almost made me smile.

"So you went back to their room," I interjected.

"Yes, she said. "I went back."

"Did you stop at the reception desk first for a key?"

She looked at me with withering disapproval. "No, Ms. Harland, I'm not into spy craft. I went back up to the room with the intention of knocking on the door."

I raised an eyebrow at her, as if to say, *Go on.*

"But the door was open—ajar, I mean. Like someone had just stepped out. It was odd."

"What time was this?" Hux asked.

"I don't know. I imagine it was sometime between six thirty and six forty five."

"The door was wide open?" he asked.

"About three or four inches. It gave me a bad feeling."

"A bad feeling, how?" I asked.

"Like the room had been broken into—which didn't make sense. You've seen this hotel, the people staying here. Security is very good." She placed her hands on her lap. "In any case, I became worried. I called out, but no one answered."

"You called out for your husband?"

She nodded.

"Did you hear anything at that point? Any response at all?"

"No. So I went inside, and that's when I saw Chris—dead, on the floor." Her tone lacked emotion, not so much as a quiver in her voice. She wasn't wringing her hands anymore, either.

Hux looked over at me, understanding as I did that this was a crucial point. "So he was dead when you got there," Hux said. "Is that what you're saying?"

"Yes." She looked him in the eye as she said it.

"How did you know he was dead? Did you try to help him?"

"You saw him," she said, snorting. She grasped the edge of the desk with her fingers. "It was pretty obvious to me that he was dead."

Hux put his notepad back in his pocket and struck an almost casual pose, even though I knew he was feeling anything but. "And where was Aria Privar at that point?" he asked. "Was she in the room with him?"

Colleen glanced at the framed painting mounted on the wall above the fireplace. Like the artwork in Peregrine, the painting was a lovely landscape that captured Pinnacles' splendor with its sultry green and golden hues. It had all the classic features of Marchand's work.

As Colleen sat there, studying the expansive vista captured in a frame—*trapped* in a frame, as it were. The same way she was trapped in this room.

I could tell that she had lost her momentum. It was Hux's mention of Aria, oddly, that had seemingly shut her down. But then, Colleen had been evasive about her from the start.

"Colleen?" Hux pressed, sensing this shift in tone. "Do you know where Aria is?"

Steinberger took advantage of his client's momentary lapse in concentration before I could. "That's the end of this interview," he said and grasped her arm. "Colleen, we're done here. If you want to sleep in your own bed tonight, we better leave now. I'm not hiking in the dark with a killer on the loose." He made no effort to hide the edge in his voice.

"They think I did it," she said, barely a whisper. All that vitriol and conviction and confidence had suddenly left her, but was it an act? A last-ditch attempt to get us back on her side? Even Hux looked skeptical. A little frustrated, even.

Steinberger blustered, "Do you really want to stay the night at this hotel, Colleen? Think carefully about this. The Feds could be on your doorstep tomorrow, and then you're really screwed. These two park rangers here, this is small-time. But as soon as the FBI gets involved, there's no going back."

She finally looked away from the painting as Steinberger's words seemed to register in her mind. His disparagement of Hux and me should have offended me, and maybe at one time it would have, but I didn't flinch. It was all part of the game, a way for her disgruntled attorney to get into my head. Hux, who had heard me talk about the things lawyers said to psyche me out, projected the same steady calm.

Not that it mattered; Colleen's silence meant that Steinberger had clearly gotten the result he wanted.

Her expression hardened as she looked back at Hux and me.

"I didn't kill anyone," she said. "But I'm glad Chris is dead— and I hope she is, too."

8

STEINBERGER USHERED US out of the room in a hurry before Colleen could give us any more ammunition when it came to motive. Hux and I grabbed our backpacks off the platform outside the Condor suite and descended the stairs back to Peregrine along with Ollie, who trotted behind us. I figured it was a good time to catch up with Bodie anyway.

Hux looked tired, a rarity for him. I could tell the interview had taken something out of him.

"Sorry, Harland," Hux said. "I know that's not what you were hoping for."

"You mean a confession?" I said, holding back a snort, which I hoped made him feel better. "I knew as soon as we walked into that room we weren't going to get that. Her lawyer was there, she's well-versed in the law, and she *still* wanted to talk to us? That to me means she's either exceptionally self-assured or just plain innocent."

Hux slid his phone into his back pocket, snug against his palm-sized notepad. He grabbed his water bottle and took a swig. I did the same, even though I was more in the mood for a cheese-burger than some tepid water. It was coming on to dinner time, and I'd missed lunch.

"So which one is it?" he asked me after he'd quenched his thirst with a few generous gulps.

I shrugged. "Hard to say just yet. It's interesting to me, though, that she wanted to talk to us. Most guilty people shut up quick when their lawyer tells them to."

"She's got motive, though."

"Plenty of it," I said. "And opportunity."

"Physically, though, could she have done it?" He stretched out his arms and breathed in the fresh air. "I mean, for someone like her to get the jump on a guy like Denton—I just don't see it. He was pretty fit from what I could tell. Even if she did manage to stab him while he was still in bed, I don't really see how she could have strangled him while he was trying to fight her off."

"He could have been intoxicated. She said he was at the bar until ten."

Hux nodded. "Yeah. Maybe."

Truthfully, though, Hux had a point. Colleen Denton was a slender woman with toned arms that might have served her well as a yoga enthusiast, but taking on a grown man was a different story. Even if she had managed to stab him while he was still asleep, he wouldn't have succumbed right away—and he *hadn't* succumbed right away. He had managed to get out of bed, only to lose the battle on the floor. That kind of encounter would have left her bruised and battered at the very least. I thought back to the engagement ring on Colleen's finger. There was nothing notable about her hands—no bruises or cuts, nothing to suggest a recent fight.

"I hear what you're saying," I said. "But then there's the hit man theory."

"She did admit to reaching out to one," he said wryly.

"Yep, that was a first for me. The problem is, that individual won't be easy to find."

"What about emails? Cell phone records?"

I took another drink from my water bottle, but it did nothing to soothe my growling stomach. "I don't expect to find a paper trail on her end, but we can try. We're better off talking to anyone who might have seen someone looking suspicious at the hotel last night."

"Someone traveling solo," Hux surmised.

"That would be my guess."

Hux's phone chimed in his back pocket. He didn't often leave the volume on, but I figured he'd forgotten to turn it off after the interview. "Sorry," he said. "It's my brother."

"Is everything okay?"

He nodded. "He's going through a rough time in his marriage right now." Hux smiled sadly. "On topic, I know."

"Why don't you call him back? I'll see if I can score us a table at the restaurant." Seeing the look on his face, I quickly added, "For you, me, and Deputy Vee."

"Got it."

I could tell that Hux was reluctant to take a personal call on the job, but everyone had families and lives and obligations, and sometimes those things unraveled at the worst times. Law enforcement was a big part of my life, but it wasn't my *entire* life. Ray had a different opinion on the matter, of course. I had heard other women in our division complain about the demands on their schedules—the nights, the weekends, the endless hours on the trail—which became all but impossible when they had children. Ray leaned on me for the less desirable cases precisely because I didn't have children. It was a double standard, sure, but I was okay with it. The frequent travel kept me on my toes.

It was a surprise, then, in some ways, to see my twenty-something male partner struggling with a family conflict while I roamed freely, unattached and unencumbered. My sister, a working mom of three, liked to tell me I was "living the dream." I liked to tell her she didn't understand my lifestyle any better than I understood hers.

"Okay, I'll meet you at the restaurant, then."

"Why don't you try the bar first?"

He raised an eyebrow. "What do you mean?"

"I'm thinking it's best if we divide and conquer—and you're taller than me. It takes me hours to get a bartender's attention."

He laughed. "You sure you don't want to hit the bar together and I'll just *buy* you a drink?"

I felt my smile falter, my stomach flutter. *Hell yes*, I wanted to say, but something stopped me. It was just the two of us. We couldn't sit at the bar and drink Manhattans. While Hux had let it slip recently that he had ended his relationship with the anthropologist in Alaska, that didn't mean he was fair game. Not for me, anyway.

"I should text Ray," I mumbled, which came off as a callous response to a perfectly benign suggestion. Hux's expression was even worse. He seemed hurt—embarrassed, even.

"Yup," he said. "I'll see you in a few."

Unable to come up with something to say, I watched him go down the stairs to the trail below. He didn't look up, not that I expected him to.

Dammit.

I checked my phone for more messages from Ray, but there were none. The medical examiner, however, had gotten my number; he'd left a message indicating that he hoped to have a preliminary report done by morning, assuming he received the body within the next few hours. The toxicology reports always took longer, but I was prepared for that.

Ollie looked up at me and barked. He was hungry, too. It was time to get a move on.

As I was navigating the footholds below the stairs, Vee called out to me from the trail. "Mrs. Denton's headed out," she said. "I assume you're good with that?"

I nodded. "The law says she's free to go."

"Not for long, I hope," she muttered.

As Vee and I hiked over to the restaurant with Ollie in tow, I heard someone coming up fast behind us.

I turned to see Mrs. Denton and her lawyer, hoofing it down the trail. Steinberger glared at me with real menace in his eyes, but Colleen didn't so much as glance in our direction. I had no intention of badgering her anymore, anyway. She had said a lot; now all we had to do was parse out the facts from the fiction. She and her lawyer could talk strategy until they were red in the face.

When they were gone, Vee remarked, "Maybe they'll get lost on their way to the parking lot."

"Let's hope not," I said. "She's a critical witness in this case, not to mention the last person to see Chris Denton alive." Before I could get into an argument with Vee about Mrs. Denton's guilt or innocence, I decided to broach the topic of dinner. "Are you able to stick around for a few more hours? I'd like to debrief with you and Hux."

Vee brightened. "Oh, yeah, absolutely."

"I was going to get us a table at the restaurant," I said. "We have to talk to the staff anyway."

"I hear the food is *awesome.*"

"Even better." I smiled at her, which was all the encouragement she needed.

"Thanks so much," she said.

Ollie ran up ahead. When he was hungry, he always let me know it. I had no interest in a fancy five-course meal, but I also wasn't going to say no to a burger. It would be a good opportunity for us to put our resources together.

As we walked, I tried to forget about the California condor's beady little eyes watching us from the cliffside suite . . . and the peregrine, with those orbs of black encased in gold.

What did you see? I wondered.

*   *   *

I spotted Hux at the Bear Gulch Bar & Grille, nursing a beer under the vapid gaze of a mounted black-tailed deer. His waitress, a tall blonde wearing a tight black dress, laughed as she refreshed his bowl of nuts. I watched her pluck one out of the dish and pop it into her mouth.

"So, um," Vee said, clearing her throat. "Should I get us a table?"

I whipped my head around. "I'll get the table," I said.

"What about Hux?"

"He'll come over."

If Vee picked up on my slightly irritated tone, she didn't comment on it. I knew she probably had some questions about Hux and me, but, thankfully, she didn't ask them. She had caught me at a weak moment.

"I'm sorry," I said. "I'm just hungry."

Vee picked up a menu from the hostess stand and flipped it over, frowning when she saw that the back side was just drinks. None of the offerings were particularly cheap, either. Vee seemed oblivious to the fact that her deputy's uniform had drawn some eyes from the other diners. The hostess, who up until that point had been busy seating a large party, hurried over. Unlike the blonde, her attire was decidedly more conservative.

The hostess forced a smile. "Oh, um, hello," she said. "Are you looking for someone?"

"No," I said, returning her smile with a diplomatic look. "Are there any tables available in the back, by chance?"

"Of course." Her face brightened at the prospect of seating us miles away from other patrons. "How many in your party?"

"Three," I said.

She was reaching for a handful of menus when a voice behind us made her pause. "Make it four, if you would," came the cheery greeting.

I turned around to see my friend and former colleague Bodie Cramer, bearing a hearty smile that made his ruddy cheeks glow. Bodie was fair-skinned and perpetually sunburnt, and with his red hair, he looked like a drunken Irishman most of the time.

He was a hugger, too, and since we were friends, he didn't hesitate to gather me into his arms. His shirt was a little damp. "Sorry," he said sheepishly. "I really had to bust my butt to get here. I'm more of a sidewalk guy."

"Believe me, I understand," I said. "I hope you didn't push it too hard."

He waved me off. "Nah. I'm fit." He flexed his biceps.

A smile lingered on his face before he shifted his gaze to Deputy Vee. I made the introduction, which culminated in a crisp handshake and a few pleasantries. It was during this exchange that I saw Hux look up from his perch at the bar. He didn't get up, though, since he had multiple staff members in his orbit at this point, including two barmaids and the bartender.

Meanwhile, Vee, Bodie, and I followed the hostess to a cozy table in the back, a generous distance from the other diners. I wasn't worried about anyone hearing us back here, but I also wanted a *little* bit of visibility. It was important to me to be able to see out into the dining room, to watch the comings and goings of the other patrons. It would also help me recreate the scene as Chris Denton and Aria Privar had experienced it the night before.

"So, how was the drive?" I asked Bodie as we settled in around the table. He sat across from me, while Vee took the seat next to mine, facing the dining room.

"Oh, not bad at all," he said. "I was just happy to get out of my house, you know? I feel like I'm under house arrest."

"When are you cleared for field work again?"

He shrugged. "Any day now, I hope. I'm feeling pretty good."

Bodie's health struggles were well-known in the Bureau, in part because of Bodie's gregarious personality. He was very open about his "trash" heart and lousy genes, as he referred to his hypertrophic cardiomyopathy. He'd had two heart transplants, the last one only a couple months ago. Bodie wasn't the type to sit back and hope for the best; he had been working hard at getting clearance to return to work. I knew this because he texted me frequently about it, especially since he'd heard about my temporary relocation back to California.

"Well, we're glad you made it. You look good, by the way."

"Thanks, Harland." His gaze held mine with a surprising tenderness. "You, too."

I smiled back at him, suddenly aware of Vee watching the two of us, perhaps searching for a hidden meaning behind our exchange. There wasn't one, but she was a cop, after all. She was trained to look for it.

Hux was still at the bar, standing with his back to our table while he chatted with the bartender. I wondered if he had been keeping an eye on us now and then—Bodie and me, in particular. For Hux, knowing what was going on around him was second nature thanks to all the intense training he'd received in the navy. It served him well in this line of work, too.

Vee put the menu aside and said, "So, not to get too personal or whatever, but what's the story with you guys?" She folded her hands and looked from Bodie to me.

"What story?" I asked.

"Oh, um . . . I just thought . . ."

"Sorry," I said through gritted teeth that I tried to pass off as a smile. "Bodie and I used to work together out of the Chicago field office."

"Oh, yeah, no—I meant you and Hux."

I felt my mouth go dry. Bodie shifted in his seat.

"We, um—we're partners. Professional partners, that is. We have a professional partnership."

Vee lifted an eyebrow. "Uh-huh."

Desperate to change the subject, I blathered on. "Anyway, Bodie is going to help us with the forensics. The M.E. should have a preliminary report on the cause of death tomorrow, which will give us a clearer idea of what happened. Aside from that, we've got a lot of people to talk to on-site here."

"Wow," Vee said. "Tomorrow? That's fast."

"Out here, it has to be," I said. "The sooner we can get a handle on how the victim died, the better equipped we are to allocate resources. Chasing down witnesses is no easy task, especially when you've got wilderness all around you. Crime scenes and evidence tend to deteriorate quickly. Information is a precious commodity, especially early on when memories are fresh."

She nodded. "Yeah. That's why I tried to talk to Mrs. Denton as soon as Dunaway called me. But she wasn't having it."

"Well, she opened up a little," I said. "But no confession, so that complicates things."

Vee folded her napkin into an animal shape—an old habit, it seemed like. "Well, I'm hoping we get the full story when the girlfriend shows up."

"*If* she shows up," I said. "We still have no idea where she is."

Vee leaned back in her seat and sighed. "Could be Mrs. Denton killed her, too."

I decided it was best to let this go for now. Vee was a rookie, and there was no point making her feel bad. She had done her job keeping the suspect detained long enough for us to talk to her. That was a big win in my book.

A young server in a black cocktail dress—she looked like the other waitress's sister—came by to take our order. I ordered a cheeseburger, medium-rare with extra tomatoes, while Bodie went for a salad. Vee ordered a goat cheese appetizer of some sort, the cheapest thing on the menu. I lied and told everyone this meal was on the federal dime, and Vee upgraded to a pizza. No one ordered an alcoholic beverage, even though everyone was probably dying for one.

"So what's the one-liner on this case?" Bodie asked. "I've been hearing bits and pieces, but bring me up to speed."

I gave him a quick recap of the crime scene in the Peregrine suite and our revelatory conversation with Colleen Denton. Vee still seemed pissed about the fact that the woman had refused to confess. Vee kept shaking her head, muttering under her breath. When I talked about Colleen's decision to hire a hit man, Vee actually swore.

"Sounds like you think she's guilty," Bodie said to Vee.

"The lady hired a *hit man* to kill her husband," she said. "She followed him a hundred miles to a hotel that you have to hike over mountains to get to. She listened to him have sex with another woman." Vee lifted her hands off the table, as if to brace us for the dramatic denouement. "She snapped."

"And did what, exactly?" I asked. "How did she get into the room?"

"She got a key somehow. It's not that hard."

Bodie and I exchanged a glance. "Humor me," I said.

Vee leaned forward and grasped the glass of water in front of her. "She pretended to be Aria and asked the front desk for a key. She knew what room they were in, and she knew who had booked it. These places don't ask for identification because they don't want you to feel like a criminal or a liar. They want you to feel special."

She had a point there. The problem with this theory was that it could easily be disproven, especially when we talked to whoever was working the reception desk last night. In addition, key cards left a viable electronic trail, one that could be easily tracked.

Even aside from that, Colleen Denton and Aria Privar looked nothing alike, and I had a hard time believing that someone at the front desk was going to hand out an extra key to the Peregrine suite, *especially* if that person remembered Aria Privar or Chris Denton from hours earlier. And if for some reason Elizabeth or someone else working the desk *had* distributed an extra key, chances were good they would remember the exchange. It was just a matter of talking to those people and confirming the details.

The truth was, I didn't think that was how it had gone down. Mrs. Denton was smarter than that. She knew there were cameras, electronic key card records, and other ways of figuring out who accessed which guest rooms and when. According to her account of events, the door had been open when she got there fifteen minutes before seven AM. Not just unlocked, but ajar—and if true, that meant something.

"What do *you* think?" Bodie asked me. "Did she do it?"

"Honestly, I thought she did when I walked into that room," I said. "I wasn't so sure when I walked out again."

"Well, I'm hoping the forensics will clear it up for you."

"Me, too."

I watched a small smile curl on Bodie's lips as he reached for his Arnold Palmer. Hux, meanwhile, seemed to be wrapping things up at the bar. I was glad for it. He was a good devil's advocate, and I wanted to hear his take on Mrs. Denton's story.

After Hux had finally disentangled himself from his overly attentive waitress, he made his way over to our table. Seeing Bodie, he managed a half-hearted smile. I appreciated the effort, though. Hux wasn't one to be rude.

He stuck out his hand, which Bodie shook with the firmness that Hux demanded. "Good to see you, man," Hux said, which sounded at least partially genuine.

"You, too."

Hux settled into the chair next to Vee, directly across from mine. Vee handed him a menu. "We already ordered."

"Take your time," I said to Hux. "We're not in any hurry."

"We're *always* in a hurry," he said, laughing.

"True," I said, barely holding back a smile.

He scanned the menu and put in a quick order as the waitress brushed by our table on the way to the kitchen. I nudged an untouched glass of water in his direction.

"Thanks," he said. "What did I miss?"

I wanted to hear what Hux had gleaned from the bartender and the other staff, but I also preferred to do it when Vee and Bodie weren't listening in. It wasn't that I didn't trust them; I just liked to keep our investigation streamlined and efficient. For now, with the four of us here, it seemed like a prime opportunity to hash out what we had and see what stuck.

"Any word on Aria Privar?" Hux asked.

"Not exactly," I said. "But Griffiths and his team are working on the assumption that she's missing out in the park somewhere, and that it's her shoe they found. Dunaway also put out an alert here on the hotel grounds to keep an eye out for her."

Vee snorted. "I think she's long gone."

I turned to look at her. "You mean she ran off? Intentionally?"

Vee reached for a slice of bread from the basket and bit off a piece. "I just think she left in the middle of the night at some point. Otherwise Mrs. Denton would have offed her, too."

Hux leaned forward a bit, crowding the table with those giant shoulders of his that could have fended off a bear. "I tend to agree."

"Oh?"

Hux settled into himself a little bit. "I'm going with the theory they had a big blowout. My guess? Aria noticed that Colleen was on the premises. She realized Chris hadn't been completely truthful about the state of his marriage."

"That's possible," I said, warming to the blowout theory because it explained why Aria Privar wasn't in the room at the time of the murder. "What time do you think she left, then?"

"Had to have been after eleven, based on Colleen's account."

"But we're working on the theory that Chris Denton was asleep when he was stabbed. You think he had a blowout fight with his girlfriend and then just went to bed? I mean, she had nowhere to go—it's not like she could just drive out of here."

Hux was quiet for a moment. "I'm still working through the details," he said.

"It's okay. Keep going."

"Well, could be she got herself another room. Or maybe he paid for it, so she had a place to stay until morning." He ran his hand through his hair while Bodie asked the waitress for a beer. "I just think we would have found a suitcase, or clothes, or *something* that belonged to her in that room if she was there when Denton was killed. I can't imagine the killer taking the time to clear all that stuff out of there."

"Unless Aria did it," Bodie added. "Have you ruled her out as a suspect?"

"No," I said. "We haven't ruled anyone out yet."

The truth was, Bodie had a point. Aria absolutely was a person of interest. If she had killed Chris Denton, it would explain why she'd gone to such extreme lengths to remove all evidence of her presence from that room. It would also support the theory that she was on the run.

I was struggling, though, to establish a motive. *Love? Money?* Could things have gone bad between them, and Colleen was the obvious scapegoat? I had seen crazier things.

"I don't know what to say about what role Aria Privar played in all of this just yet," I said. "All we have is her driver's license and an eyewitness who claims she checked in."

"The bartender saw her, too," Hux interjected. "The description he gave matched the photo on the driver's license."

"Okay. Good."

Vee said, "Maybe Chris got rid of Aria's stuff for some reason. You know, like, he threw it over the balcony and then she carted it off later."

Hux leaned back and plopped his ankle on his knee. He seemed intrigued by Vee's theory. I wasn't so sure about it, though. It struck me as unnecessarily dramatic.

"Did anyone find anything down below, though?" I asked. "Even if it was late at night, I feel like someone would have reported that kind of thing."

"Not if you're on vacation," Vee said. "You wouldn't bother."

Hux said, "It could also explain why we found Aria's driver's license but nothing else."

I crooked my head at him. "And then what happened? It was still late, remember? It would have been pitch-black outside."

"She got herself a room. Or he got her one."

"But if that's the case, then where is she now?" I countered.

Everyone sipped their drinks. Was it possible that Aria Privar was hiding in plain sight? Or was she out in the park somewhere, on the run, or missing for some other reason?

"We'll look into any last-minute reservations made last night," I said. "If there aren't any, then I think we have to assume that Aria Privar has left the premises."

Our server came by with a tray of entrees that made my stomach rumble. Hux had ordered a burger, too; we both liked ours cooked the same way, with the same accoutrements that never, for any reason, included ketchup. Vee and Bodie dug in without a second thought. Between the four-mile hike and a hard day's work of investigating, everyone had worked up an appetite.

"Well, I'm hoping that didn't happen," Hux said, his tone somber. "The bartender said she'd had a few drinks. If she went out into the park for any reason, she could be in trouble."

I reached for my own burger. Hux was right, of course. Aria Privar was in trouble.

But what kind, exactly?

CHAPTER

9

AFTER DINNER, WE all gathered outside the lobby to review
the plan for the coming days. The inbound chopper that I'd
heard thirty minutes earlier lifted off the helipad, en route to the
morgue. I was glad to see things in motion on that front, since the
autopsy report was going to tell us a lot about Chris Denton's final
moments.

We stood a little way off the trail, but the people making their
way to the restaurant couldn't help but notice a group of law enforcement officials congregating on hotel property. I understood now why
Dunaway wanted to keep our involvement quiet. In the age of online
reviews, there was no room for error. Any whiff of a police presence
could put a big damper on the hotel's opening weeks.

"How long do you think you'll be up in Peregrine?" I asked
Bodie, who was rifling through his backpack on a park bench.

He shrugged. "All night, probably. It's not like I've got a place
to crash anyway." He forced a laugh that was met with tired
smiles. Vee looked at me like, *Are you kidding me with this guy?*
Then again, she always looked like she was on the verge of rolling
her eyes.

I said to Bodie, "Dunaway reserved some rooms for us in case
we needed them. Just let the front desk know."

"Really?" Bodie slung his backpack over his shoulder with a
grunt. "Good deal. Are you sure the big boys aren't going to crash
the party?"

All eyes landed on me. "The San Francisco Field Office is aware of the situation here," I said, which was the truth. I'd received a few texts from a member of the FBI's investigative team assigned to Pinnacles, but they were content to let me work it for now. *Sounds open and shut,* was their most recent message. *Just sit tight until we get there.*

I had no intention of "sitting tight," of course, since Hux and I had every right to launch our investigation as we saw fit, but I had long ago learned not to engage with my former employers. For the most part, it was common for law enforcement agencies to engage in turf wars, but the "open-and-shut" cases tended to be especially popular. Everyone wanted to tell their superior they'd closed a case and added it to their clearance record.

For a crime in Pinnacles National Park, though? Well, that was different. San Francisco was a world away from this desolate, scarcely populated stretch of the Salinas Valley, and it wasn't even accessible by car. I was glad to have this one all to myself, at least for now.

"I guess that's a maybe," Vee said with a smirk. "Well, look, I gotta get home."

Hux frowned. "You're hiking back to your car by yourself?"

"I'm a big girl," she said with a harrumph.

"You're not *that* big." The seriousness in his tone blunted the joke. "And there could be a killer on the loose."

"Psh. The killer's on her way back to San Fran. I'm not too worried."

"Look, you could get hurt, lost—it's just bad practice." Hux exhaled. "Why don't we walk you back?"

Vee shrugged. "No way. I'll be fine."

"Do you have a sat phone, at least?"

Another shrug. *So that's a no.*

"Take mine," Hux said as he bent down to grab the Iridium from his backpack.

"Don't you need it?"

"I'll use Harland's."

Playing the mediator, I cleared my throat and spoke to Vee. "Listen, we don't really know what we're dealing with yet. At the very least, take Hux's satellite phone."

Vee finally softened. She took the Iridium and powered it on.

"Do you know how to use one of those?" I asked.

"Yup."

After a round of good-byes, Vee walked off toward the trail-head. Bodie struck a stilted pose, hands in his pockets, eyes to the ground. The silence swelled, turning into something awkward and unwelcome. I knew Hux wasn't going to do anything about it, though; he actually *liked* painful silences. He told me once that silences gave him a valuable read on situations and the people in them. In this case, he was trying to get a read on Bodie.

Hux, after all, was a procurer of information: professional, criminal, personal, whatever. He always liked to know what and whom he was dealing with. I respected that about him, but it also made it nearly impossible to keep secrets from him. I honestly didn't know how to navigate this situation with Bodie; we all had to work together on this, like it or not. And it wasn't like I had a history with either of them. *So why are things so awkward right now?*

It was Bodie who finally broke the silence. "Well, I should be getting to it, then," he said. "I'll, uh . . . I'll check in with the front desk about a room."

I forced a smile. "Sounds good. Feel free to text me an update anytime."

"Will you two be around later?"

"We'll be talking to potential witnesses," I said. "That could take a few hours."

"Cool," he said—his favorite word for situations like these, I realized. It was a filler word, the kind you used to avoid having to say something meaningful. Hux didn't have any such words in his vocabulary. He seemed displeased at the moment, though, as he tilted his head to the sky.

I cleared my throat. "We'll catch up with you later, then."

"Right on." Bodie made a gesture like a mini salute, then seemed to think better of it and let his hand drop to his side. I watched him take out his map as he made his way down to the trail, folding and unfolding it while unsuspecting hotel guests walked past him.

After he was gone, Hux stretched out his arms and arched his back a bit as he watched the sky. I looked up, too, to see the distant galaxies on full display, the moon shining bright in pristine darkness. For him, the cosmos was relaxing. For me, it could be terrifying.

"Well, Harland, it's been a minute." Hux took his eyes off the stars and looked at me. "Has it really been a whole month since I saw you?"

"It *has* been a while," I said, pleased that he was keeping track, too.

"I was worried you'd picked up a new partner in crime."

"Nah," I said. "It's just a slow time of year. October rolls around and everyone in ISB takes a bit of a breather."

"Cold Case Sundays?" He knew about my current assignment and often checked in on my progress. Hux had a particular interest in unsolved missing persons cases. More than once, he'd gone looking for someone out in the wilderness, years or even decades after they disappeared. He had a few success stories to his name.

"Yep."

"Are you making any headway on any of those old cases?"

I shook my head. "Not really. I'm focusing on ones in California for now since I'll probably be here until the spring. I've got a Pinnacles case, actually."

"Well, you know I'd love to lend a hand," he said. "Once things slow down in Sequoia, I mean . . ."

"I know you've still got your Park Service duties," I said. "Which is probably for the best, since I can't really see you sitting at a desk looking at old crime scene photos. A lot of these cold cases don't have any photos at all—it's just scattershot witness interviews, bits and pieces of evidence . . . It's a shame, how little there is to go on." I picked my backpack up off the ground and tried to get it on gracefully. It always felt unbearably heavy at the end of the day.

"How are you feeling about *this* case?" he asked.

I thought for a moment. "Confused," I admitted. "What else did you learn from the waitstaff, by the way?"

"Quite a bit," he said. "The bartender's name is Timmy Jones. He was living in Fresno for a while before he took the gig here, which he said's been pretty good so far. Anyway, he was working last night from seven o'clock to close. He saw Denton come in with a woman who fit Aria Privar's description a few minutes after he started his shift. They sat at the bar for a while, maybe an hour."

"What did he say about them?"

"He said they seemed pretty into each other—a lot of physi-cal contact, touching and laughing, that kind of thing. Jones also noticed that Denton seemed a good bit older than her, which we already know. He carried himself like a confident guy . . . you know, never had a problem getting a drink, but he wasn't an ass-hole about it either. She was more reserved."

"What was Denton drinking?"

"Cranberry juice."

I was used to getting good information from bartenders, and Hux's account of his exchange with Jones didn't disappoint. As a rule, folks working the bar paid attention to their patrons. In part, this vigilance was a protective mechanism, especially as the night wore on. Heavy drinkers could get rowdy, even violent. Whoever was working behind the bar had to know what they were dealing with to avoid unpleasant surprises.

"What could they add to the timeline?" I asked. "It sounds like the couple arrived at the bar around seven and left an hour later?"

Hux took his phone out of his pocket. "I wrote it all down," he said. "I know how you are about timelines."

"*How* am I with timelines?" I asked.

"Obsessive," he said with a laugh. "In any case, yes, he thinks they sat down at the bar at around nineteen hundred. At twenty thirty or thereabouts, they were seated for dinner. He heard them talking about it."

"He never actually saw them sit down for dinner, though?"

"No. He assumes they were seated out on the terrace, which was pretty popular last night on account of the weather. But he also said the bar got kind of busy around twenty two hundred, so it's possible he missed them."

Twenty two hundred was 10 PM. I always had to do the conversion in my head, but I wasn't about to change Hux's mili-tary habit because of my mathematical shortcomings.

"Did he overhear any of their conversation?" I asked.

"A good bit of it, actually. Denton asked Aria a lot of questions—not the probing kind, but more of a genuine interest, it seemed to him. Jones got the feeling Aria was in the medical field. She talked a lot about a little girl with cancer she was caring

for at the hospital. Jones said Denton offered a lot of support . . .
held her hand, rubbed her arm and back at times. He got the feeling they'd been together a while."

"Anything else?"

"He said neither one of them seemed like real outdoors people.
He described her as 'delicate,' whatever that means. She was in a
cocktail dress and heels; Denton was wearing a suit jacket."

"No tie?"

"Nope."

"You know, we never got a detailed description of the shoe
they found on the trail. All Nate said was that it was a 'dress shoe'."

"It could be she packed more than one pair of shoes."

I shrugged. "Could be."

Overall, I would have loved an actual photo of that missing
shoe recovered on the trail, but that wasn't going to happen with
no cell service in the park.

"Hmm," I said, trying to picture Denton and Aria's intimate
moment at the bar. It wasn't difficult slipping back into the mindset of being with someone who you knew was into you. With
Kevin, there had never been any doubt that he liked me; he wasn't
the type to play it cool. Looking back, I wondered if the reason
he'd proposed to me so soon after we started dating was that he
wasn't sure I felt the same way about him.

Hux said, "What's on your mind there, Harland?"

I nudged the dirt with my hiking boot. "Nothing. It's just—
well, maybe Denton *wasn't* the huge asshole his wife made him
out to be."

Hux put his notepad back in his pocket. "Here's my take on it.
Colleen Denton hated her husband's guts, and she gave us all sorts
of reasons why. Maybe some of them are valid, maybe they all are.
Hard to say at this point. But he really touched a nerve there."

"I agree that Colleen hated him," I said. "But the line between
love and hate is a fine one, not to mention dangerous. Indifference
is much less volatile, in my experience. And marriage is always
complicated."

"Well, I can't speak to that," he said softly.

"Either way, it's looking like Colleen at least had motive. Her
husband fell for another woman, and not only that, he was wooing
her with the wife's money." I shifted my weight a bit and tried to

ignore the pain of my backpack pressing into my collarbone. "But we haven't really discussed how she felt about Aria Privar."

Hux seemed to consider this for a moment. "Don't women tend to blame other women in situations like these?"

"Some do. Some don't."

I checked my watch and saw that it was just a few minutes before seven. Marta would be coming on for her shift soon. She was first on our priority list of people to interview. After that, it was a bit of a crapshoot; I had no plan except to talk to as many people as possible.

A young couple in swimsuits and cover-ups breezed past us as they made their way down the trail toward the pool. At some point, it would be important for Hux and me to see the entire property, in part to figure out where all the security cameras were. There was a chance that some of that footage could make or break this case. *Add that to the task list,* I thought.

"It's almost seven o'clock," I said. "Let's head over to the employee lounge before Marta arrives for her shift. I don't want to miss her."

As we turned in the direction of the lobby, I remembered the other person Hux had connected with at the bar: his server. I was about to ask him about her when he seemed to read my mind, and he said, "Wait. Sorry. I forgot about the waitress."

"Don't be sorry."

"It's just . . . I could see it on your face."

"You could see what on my face?" I asked, reddening at the thought of a huge chunk of tomato in my teeth. I reisted the urge to reach up and pick it out.

"That I'd forgotten something."

"Oh." I didn't want to admit that the thought of Hux reading my mind and interpreting my expressions so handily made me uneasy. There were times I *really* didn't want him to know what I was thinking.

"Anyway, she was working last night, too—seven to close, same as Jones," Hux said. "But her memory wasn't as good as his. All she could remember about Chris Denton was that he left a nice tip."

"How much?"

He grinned. "I knew you'd ask. Forty bucks on a hundred-dollar tab."

"Not bad."

"Another strike against the asshole theory."

"Well, we know we can't trust Colleen," I said. "Her life is on the line here, literally. She could go to prison for a very long time if the circumstantial evidence continues to point in that direction. It's a long shot, but she knows she doesn't look good here."

"But do you think she did it?"

In my experience, this question could come back to haunt you later, but with Hux, I was willing to let it slide. I knew he was trying to learn when to trust your gut and when to question it in homicide investigations. To that end, he wanted to know what my gut was telling me.

"I think that when a cheating spouse turns up dead, it's always wise to take a painfully close look at the players," I said. "In this case, Colleen had motive and opportunity. She was emotionally invested to the extreme. She was there when the body was found, and she admitted to almost hiring a hit man."

"Uh-oh," he said with a smirk. "There's a 'but' coming, isn't there?"

I laughed. "Yeah, I guess there is."

"Are you thinking she hired someone to do it, then?"

"In my book, those are one and the same. In a court of law, they are, too. But no, I don't think it was a hit man, either."

"Why not, though?" He rocked back on his heels, striking a casual pose. "I'm not second-guessing you, Harland—I just don't see another possibility here. This woman really hated the guy, so much so that she wanted him dead. I think it's pretty likely she hired some goon to do the deed in some elaborate way and then showed up to watch the carnage. Then things got weird."

"Why would she talk to us, then? She had her attorney right there."

Hux shrugged. "Hubris."

My phone buzzed in my pocket; it was Bodie. I answered it while Hux ambled a short distance down the trail. I couldn't believe I had been navigating the worst of Bay Area traffic just a few hours ago. So much had happened since then.

"Anything yet?" I asked into the phone.

"It's a promising start," he said. "Plenty of DNA evidence here, that's for sure. It'll just take time to process it all."

"Can you place Aria Privar in the room?"

"There are a few different sets of prints," he said. "I've got nothing to match them to yet, but yeppers, I think she was here."

"What about the sheets?" I asked. "Semen? Anything?"

"I'm still working on that angle."

I knew DNA analysis could take weeks, but Bodie had his own way of doing things, and I wasn't about to question his methods. The real problem was that we still didn't know where Aria Privar was, and we had no solid leads on her whereabouts.

Hux was pacing the trail, getting antsy. He didn't like standing around, and I couldn't blame him. If our most promising witness went off and disappeared into a block of rooms for her night shift, it could be hours before we tracked her down again.

"Okay, thanks," I said to Bodie. "Do you want us to come up there?"

"I'm all good here," he said. "What time are you heading out in the AM?"

I glanced at Hux, who was looking off in the other direction. After years in the military, surviving in hostile territory, he had a knack for hearing things. Back then, that clandestine ability to pick up on stray sounds and conversations was about survival; now, it served him well when it came to staying in the loop on a case.

"Early," I said. "Probably five or so."

"Whoa," he said with a laugh. "Maybe I *won't* see you, then."

"Our plans could always change."

"Gotcha. Well, keep me posted."

"Will do."

I hung up. Hux stood with his hands in his pockets, watching the last vestiges of a golden sunset. He never hesitated to voice his opinion, but he also didn't like to rush me. In his mind, I was his superior—for the time being, anyway. ISB had yet to formalize our partnership.

"He's making his way through the crime scene," I said, getting Hux's attention. He walked back over to me.

"Well, I hope he finds something."

"He will," I said.

But the way the winds were blowing on this one, I wasn't so sure.

CHAPTER

10

*H*ER SISTER HAD *warned her about getting involved with a married man.*

She should have listened.

But Gabi didn't know Aria's struggles. Gabi was the youngest of four daughters, the baby of the family. She was coddled and spoiled and handled, endlessly, with delicate hands. Gabi had never understood the weight of her family's expectations, that punishing load of unfulfilled potential. Their parents were both well-educated, well-trained physicians who had come to the U.S. to give their girls a better life, but at great expense. Their father resented the restaurant he owned, the grease that stained his shirt and stank up his clothes. It was below him, this menial labor that required long hours and constant vigilance, as the world changed and their finances changed with it. There were bills to pay, mouths to feed. A wife and four daughters.

And her father never let Aria forget it.

It wasn't that Aria hated the man; she just couldn't seem to escape his influence. Starting from the day she stepped foot in a classroom, she had learned to fear failure more than anything—more than death, even. Anything less than an A was an embarrassment that brought harsh words and a weekend of detainment in her tiny bedroom, which she shared with her sister. There, she would do flashcards until her vision blurred and her head throbbed.

Somehow, though, she had survived those years of brutal edification. Her accomplishments had piled up, exactly according to the trajectory her parents had set out for her: valedictorian of her high school class, pre-med at a top college, admission to medical school, a coveted match at a prestigious residency program. Pediatrics, of course, was a disappointment to her father—it wasn't neurosurgery or orthopedics—so she'd gone on to do a fellowship in pediatric cardiology, a seven-year slog of eighty-hour weeks in the hospital. She had given up her childhood for her parents; she had sacrificed her twenties for medicine.

And then, at twenty-eight, she'd managed to step off the freight train for a precious twelve months thanks to a research year, which she had only ever dreamed about. It was, in every way, the realization of those dreams. She worked eight hours in the lab, left before the sun went down, ate dinner in her apartment, and watched Netflix before bed. On weekends, she went out with friends and sometimes splurged on a drink or two. She didn't have many friends, and she didn't drink very much, but for the first time in her life, she felt free.

It was during that period of personal freedom that Christopher Denton entered her life, and by then, she was too drunk on "the dream" to really see him coming. He was much older than she was, a middle-aged ex-surfer-type with a mischievous grin who owned his own company and seemed to relish the Silicon Valley lifestyle. He was also a welcome departure from the only world she'd ever known as an adult, which was medicine and hospitals and other trainees like her. She was desperate to get away from it.

He was good to her, too. He wined and dined her, offering her an escape from the cold Chinese food and cheap takeout that fit within her budget. He was always up for an adventure in the Bay Area, almost like he was discovering it for the first time, too. They ate at fancy places and drank beer at holes in the wall; they visited wineries and historic landmarks. They were native Californians who lived like tourists, and she loved it.

She loved him.

Was it worth it? *She wondered.*

A week ago, she would have recoiled at the ridiculousness of the question. Of course he was worth it! Love could be complicated, sure, but she was finally happy.

Now, though, with her leg badly broken and wilderness all around her, she couldn't help but feel that her answer to that question had changed. The events of the last twenty-four hours were like something

out of a dream—except this wasn't the Chris Denton dream, it was
a nightmare. The highs of a weekend getaway had spiraled so quickly
into terror that even now she struggled to make sense of it. She and
Chris rarely fought, but last night had been different. Aria had seen
his wife, Colleen, that fearsome tech executive who'd clearly had
multiple plastic surgeries on her nose, but to Aria, they weren't quite
enough to hide what must have been the woman's defining insecu-
rity: her obsession with Chris. Aria was angry because Chris had a
restraining order on Colleen; he just refused to enforce it. Not for the
first time, Aria had begged him to call the police.

He wouldn't listen. Chris had insisted that his wife was
harmless—jealous, but harmless. "She wasn't like this when we got
married," he'd said. "She was levelheaded, normal, totally cool about
everything. But then things just kind of changed . . ."

That change had come long before Aria met him, and, in fact,
Chris had confided in Aria that he had contemplated killing himself
after Colleen flat-out rejected the divorce papers. Not only that, but
she'd threatened his life when he insisted on ending the marriage.
"She kept telling me she knew a guy who was a fixer," Chris had told
Aria. "A guy who knew how to find people. And if I tried to fight the
divorce, or run, he'd find me."

At the time, Aria thought he was telling her tall tales, exaggerat-
ing the extreme characteristics of Colleen's personality disorder. He
had always been brutally honest when it came to his estranged wife.
Some of the stories he told Aria horrified her, especially the ones about
the things Colleen had done to become the corporate powerhouse she
was.

Now, though, Aria suspected that Chris had been telling the
truth. Colleen hated Aria for being the "other woman," but did she
hate Aria enough to kill her? Aria had never even met Colleen. To
Aria, Colleen's relentless pursuit of dominance was lunacy—or psy-
chopathy. Or maybe both. Aria had never taken much of an interest
in psychiatry because she couldn't sympathize with sociopaths. To her,
they weren't sick; they were evil.

Aria had seen Colleen in the lobby of the hotel right after Chris
and she checked in, and again out on the trail when they were walking to their room. It wasn't until later that Aria had seen "the guy."
Thinking back on it now, she supposed there was no way of knowing
that the broad-shouldered man with dark eyes and a mask was after

them, but she'd felt it deep in her bones, a primal response to a threat. There was something about him that unnerved her, and it wasn't just the fact that he was wearing a mask; a good number of the staff had them, too. It was something else.

She wished she had gotten a better look at his face, but of course, the mask got in the way. She didn't want to try too hard, either, because the last thing she needed was to spook the guy. A part of her had been holding out hope that he'd just go away.

He hadn't, of course. She remembered seeing him disappear into the shadows as they climbed the stairs to their room, twenty-six steps to the Peregrine suite. Aria had a habit of counting steps. It soothed her, somehow.

It had been late, almost ten o'clock, and she and Chris had grown weary of fighting about Colleen and the threat to Chris's safety. They'd fallen into bed, seduced by the fresh air blowing in through the window, desperate to forget about their problems back home.

Chris had sensed, though, that Aria was preoccupied about something. That was the thing about Chris; he listened to her. He saw her.

Aria had told him about Colleen, about the man out on the trail. After an emotional conversation, he convinced her to go down to the lobby and book a different room in the main building of the hotel, which he thought would be more secure than a cliffside suite with a balcony. Aria couldn't imagine someone scaling the cliff to get to them that way, but Chris wasn't taking any chances. Just talking about it made her uneasy.

"Shouldn't we both just go?" Aria had asked him, almost pleading with him. "We could just leave; get out of here. Maybe she won't even notice."

"Colleen doesn't do anything halfway," he'd told her. "I'm sure she's got eyes on us right now. That's what she does. She's like a dog with a bone."

"But how did she figure out we were staying here? I thought you said you reserved the room under a different name."

"I did." He paced the room. "Colleen knows some shady characters, Aria. I'm talking Secret Service, CIA-level operatives, defense contractors. All the big tech companies have international spies working for them; it's part of her world. You don't even want to know."

"But why does she care so much? Why can't she just let you go?"

By that point, Aria had been crying. It was pitiful, she knew, breaking down in front of a guy who himself had been living under an abusive regime for the last decade. She knew he was the one in danger, not her, but she was tired of living in this fraught, terrifying in-between. She just wanted the law, or a cop, or someone to step in and deal with this malevolent woman so that she and Chris could have a normal life, a normal relationship.

It wasn't going to happen. Not now, and maybe not ever.

Aria put her hands on the ground and tried to stand, but it was no use. Her femur was broken—the longest, strongest bone in the body, the one that forensic analysts so often used to identify human remains. She had fallen some twenty feet onto solid rock, and her only comfort was that she had landed in a dark, dank, bat-ridden cave that seemed to be closed to the public. She could hear those small, hairless creatures moving in the tiny crevasses above her.

On one hand, the cave felt like a sanctuary, but as the hours went by, she feared it might be her grave. Her leg was so badly broken that part of it was sticking out of her skin, ripe for infection. She couldn't put any weight on it at all, and she was pretty sure her pelvis was fractured, too. Aria specialized in hearts, not bones, but she had a good grasp on her body's physical limitations. There were so many ways she could die out here: hypothermia, starvation, pulmonary embolism from the fracture. Her only shelter was this ancient rock looming above her. The caves, she'd read, were known to flood, and when that happened, it could be months before anyone got to her.

And then there were the bats.

Their delicate, minuscule movements unnerved her. Aria respected bats, at least from a scientific perspective, but there in that cave, all she could think about was their beady little eyes and sharp teeth. What if one flew down and bit her? Would she live long enough to develop the clinical signs of rabies?

Would she go mad?

Aria feared that she was already losing her mind in this dark, otherworldly place. She tried to think about Chris, who had packed her things with meticulous care and handed her a wad of cash to get another room, just in case Colleen had access to his credit card account. Before Aria left, he had checked the closets, the bathroom, under the bed; he was determined to extirpate all sign of Aria's presence there, not to expunge her from his life but to protect her from

Colleen's wrath in case she somehow managed to get inside their room. Chris and Aria had decided, together, that he would tell Colleen that he had ended things with Aria and told her to leave, in the hopes that such a story might convince Colleen to go home.

And then, finally, Chris would get law enforcement involved. He vowed to call them as soon as they got back to San Francisco. He didn't want to live like this. He didn't want Aria to have to live like this. "You deserve better," he'd said. "I'm so sorry."

"Don't be sorry," she had said, just minutes before he sent her down the stairs. "This isn't your fault. It's hers."

He shook his head. "I should have done something about it a long time ago."

"Well, we're doing something about it now." She tried to project strength into her voice, but she wasn't sure she had succeeded.

He cupped her jaw in his hands and kissed her on the forehead. She loved his tender touch, the way he revered her and honored her. Aria had never known that kind of love before; in her family, love and obligation were one and the same.

Now, though, she questioned her naivete. Maybe Gabi was right—or partially right.

It wasn't the married man that was the problem.

It was his wife.

11

W ITH OLLIE CONTENT to wait outside, Hux and I showed up at the employee lounge at quarter-to-seven. To my surprise, it was a bright, spacious facility that had a couple of treadmills, a small café, and a pleasant view of the mountains in the distance.

A woman who fit Marta's description was stuffing her belongings into one of the roomy lockers. She looked about fifty, with a small frame and long graying hair that she kept back in a functional bun. Her uniform was a bland khaki color, designed to blend into the aesthetic. In that respect, it was effective.

After she had secured the locker with an electronic pin, the woman put her head down and moved quickly toward the exit.

Hux and I followed her out into a small hallway that bypassed the lobby, where employees could come and go without being seen. I didn't want to embarrass her, so we waited until we were outside before making our move. By that point, she must have known she was being followed, but she acted like she had no idea.

"Marta?" I called out, which made her turn around. The oversized bag on her shoulder slid down onto her arm. She eyed us suspiciously as she bent down to pick up the bottle of Windex that had fallen out of her bag.

"Hello," I said, offering a smile that I hoped might put her at ease a little bit. It was not returned, nor did it seem to put her at ease at all. "I'm Felicity Harland with the Investigative Services Branch, and this is my partner, Hux Huxley."

Marta glanced at Hux, who struck a friendly smile and a relaxed pose. She adjusted the bag of cleaning supplies on her shoulder, wincing as she pulled it up closer to her neck.

"Do you know why we're here?" I asked.

"Yes," she said, barely a whisper.

"Could we go somewhere to talk?"

"I only have a few minutes."

I couldn't help but wonder why she seemed so anxious to get away from us. She kept glancing at the trail behind us like it was tempting her with escape.

"This won't take long." I showed her my badge, which sometimes changed the tone of the conversation. It didn't seem to work on her, though. "We're investigating the death that occurred in the Peregrine suite last night."

She dropped her gaze to the ground.

"We understand you were the one who found the body?" I said, phrasing it as a question so as not to put her on the defensive.

She nodded.

"What time was this?"

"I don't . . . I don't remember."

I waited for Marta to look up again, but she kept her eyes glued to the ground. She shifted her bag on her shoulder, its contents weighing her down. She looked uncomfortable.

"Okay, not a problem," I said, deciding that maybe it made sense to take a more direct approach. "The hotel should have a record of everyone who accessed the room in the last twenty-four hours—"

"I was going upstairs to look for something I might have lost outside the Condor suite the night before," she said. "But the door to Peregrine was open. It worried me."

"Wide open?"

She shook her head. "Just a crack."

I glanced at Hux, who had his notepad out but was mostly just listening to Marta, studying her facial expressions. *Was she lying to us?* I didn't think so, but she wasn't our biggest fan either. She gritted her teeth as she tried a third time to reposition the bag on her shoulder.

"Do you want to put that down?" I asked her.

"No, no," she said. "I'm just in a hurry—lots of work to do tonight."

"We could talk another time, then," I said. "How about tomorrow? We could meet you wherever's convenient for you. Off the property, even. Would that work?"

"I live on the property," she said. "Most of the people who work here do."

"Where, exactly?" I asked, curious. Dunaway hadn't mentioned anything about employee housing, but it made sense that they lived close by. For most luxury hotels, the staff operated as invisible little fairies, doing work behind the scenes to make everything perfect, all the time. I had to admit that Dunaway had a good operation going here, especially for a hike-in hotel in its first week of operation. This was no Four Seasons in Maui.

"It's on the northern edge of the property," she said. "But I don't know that I'll have time; I picked up extra shifts this week."

I used the silence to refocus the conversation. "So what did you do when you saw that the door was open? I asked, opting to keep my questions open-ended. For now, at least; it was common police practice to dive into specifics later on.

"I tried calling out to whoever was inside, something like, 'Hello? Is everything okay?' but no one answered. I got worried so I called my manager, who told me to knock."

"And did you?"

"Yes. A few times." Her voice went quiet. "Then I heard something . . . disturbing."

"What did you hear?"

"Someone moaning . . . or, I don't know. A kind of weird breathing. I called my manager again, but she didn't answer—so I went inside. I thought maybe someone was hurt." She gripped her bag with trembling fingers. "That's when I saw the man. On the floor."

"Was he moving?"

She used a fingernail to scrape at her cuticles. "I—I don't know. Maybe. He was on his stomach. I thought I heard him take a breath . . ." Her voice broke as she wiped at her eyes. "But then I saw the woman . . . who I heard was the man's wife, just standing there. She told me to leave. She screamed at me. It was awful." Marta swallowed hard, burying a sob. "I ran out as fast as I could."

As she repositioned her left hand on the bag, I noticed a rather large abrasion on the palm of her wrist. She caught me looking at it and squeezed her fist. "I tripped on my bag and fell," she said. "I have some cuts on my knees, too."

"I'm sorry," I said. "Did you see a doctor about it?"

"No, no. It's not that bad."

Hux slipped his notepad into his back pocket, which was a signal that he had a question in mind. I took a step back and let him take it.

Hux cleared his throat. "Did the wife—Mrs. Denton—did she say anything else to you?" he asked in a soft, patient tone. By this time, Marta was sniffling. I felt sorry for her, but I also got the distinct feeling that this was going to be our only chance to talk to her. I was getting a squirrelly vibe from Marta but couldn't pinpoint why. I considered the possibility that she had a criminal record, but she sure didn't look the type. Then again, appearances could be deceiving.

Marta said, "Just that she was glad he was dead."

"Where was she in the room, exactly?"

"Right next to the balcony. She turned and looked at me when she heard me come in."

"I thought you told Deputy Vee that she was standing over the body," Hux said, more like he was seeking clarification than questioning her account.

She bunched her wounded hand into a fist. "Well, I don't know . . . she was right there."

"What was her emotional state like?" he asked.

Marta thought for a moment. "She seemed angry."

Not sad or grieving or shocked, but angry. It was hard to picture what Marta had seen in that moment, especially since she seemed to be implying Chris Denton might have still been alive when she walked in that room. In my experience, though, the sounds she was describing could have been anything from the HVAC (heating, ventilation, and air-conditioning) to her own imagination.

"What was she wearing?" I asked.

"I don't remember," she said. "Normal clothes, I guess."

"Pajamas?"

She thought for a second. "No, I don't think so."

"Where did you go after that?" I asked.

"To my manager's office. I guess she called you?"

"Mr. Dunaway called us," I said. This was the first I'd heard of a manager other than James Dunaway. "What's your manager's name?"

"Kelly Spier. She's in charge of the housekeeping staff."

Hux wrote down the name while I considered how best to proceed. Marta hiked her bag up onto her shoulder with a grunt. "That's all I remember," she said. "I'm sorry. I hope it helps."

"Just one more question."

A loud sigh. "Yes?"

"Do you know anyone else who might have interacted with the occupants of the Peregrine suite while they were here? Anyone who cleaned their room, brought them room service—anything?"

"I went right home after my shift, so no. Room service is delivered by someone on the kitchen staff, usually."

"Any chance you know who that person might have been last night?"

She looked down at her hands.

"Marta?" I pressed.

"I don't know his name. I saw him delivering trays to different rooms."

"What does he look like?"

"It was dark out. I couldn't really say."

"You never met him before?" I tried to hide my skepticism, but it wasn't easy. "Don't you all live in the same complex?"

"I only just moved in a couple days ago. I don't know anyone." Her tone was defensive, which took me aback. I could sense she was desperate to end this conversation.

"I understand," I said. "We're just trying to figure out who this person is."

"I would go down to the kitchen and ask them," she said. "Maybe whoever it was is working again tonight."

"Thank you; we'll do that. Are you sure there wasn't anyone else?"

She picked at her thumbnail, the worst of her ragged cuticles, the nail ridged and worn. "There are only two of us on the housekeeping staff who work at night. We do the turndown service together; one of us is in charge of guest rooms and the other stays in and around the main building—the lobby, bar, restaurant, and pool area—but Clarisse wasn't working anywhere near Peregrine last night."

"So you were on the guest room circuit?"

"Yes," Marta said. "I deal with any housekeeping issues that come up late at night."

"What kinds of issues?"

"It can be anything. Someone wants a toothbrush or an extra pillow. Things like that."

"Did anyone make any requests last night?"

She shook her head. "No, last night was quiet. I did the turn-down service for my block of rooms and spent the rest of the night helping Clarisse at the mothership."

Taking advantage of a momentary pause in the conversation, Hux said casually, "So what were you doing in the Condor suite on the night of the 26th, then? You said you might have left something behind. Was that room occupied?"

Marta shifted her feet, which made her bag of cleaning supplies slip down to her elbow. Exasperated, she let it drop to the ground.

"I was notified after midnight that there had been a very late check-in, but it was too late for turndown service. I went up there to leave the chocolate outside instead. I was only there for a couple minutes."

"What time was this?"

"Very late. Maybe two AM."

"Did you see or hear anything at that time?"

She shook her head.

"Who notified you of the late check-in?" Hux asked.

"Kelly, my boss."

Hux lifted an eyebrow as he noted the name. "Dunaway told us that room was part of the wedding block that was canceled," I said.

"I wouldn't know if it was or not," Marta said, bristling. "I just do what Kelly tells me to do."

"Were you supposed to clean the room that morning?" I asked.

"Yes," she said. "But Kelly checked it after the police came and said to forget about it; it looked like the room had never been occupied after all."

Could it be that Aria Privar had reserved the Condor suite late on the 26th? And if so, had something happened in there, too? The first step in answering those questions was to establish who exactly had reserved that room and when, and why Kelly Spier had deemed it unoccupied. It certainly looked and smelled pristine when we were in there interviewing Mrs. Denton.

"I see." I looked at Hux, whose expression was inscrutable.

"I really need to get going," she said. "I'm sorry."

I handed her my business card. "We'll be in touch."

"I really have nothing else to say. That's all I remember."

Grabbing her bag, she turned and made her way down a narrow, unmarked path that looked like the service trail. I decided that there was no point chasing her. If we needed to talk to her again, we at least knew where to find her. I wondered what had drawn Marta to this obscure hotel in a wilderness area, hours from any family or friends she might have had. Whatever it was, I didn't think it had anything to do with Denton's murder.

After she was gone, we went over to the bench that Ollie had claimed as his own. Hux rubbed the fur behind his ears. "Hm," he mused.

"She seemed a little nervous."

"Well, you do tend to have that effect on people."

"*I* do?" I broke into a smile. "You're literally twice my size."

"Yeah, but you're, well . . . intense."

"Thanks," I deadpanned. "In any case, I'm not going to peg Marta as Colleen Denton's hit man just yet."

"Hit woman?"

"Hit person. Sorry."

He chuckled as we stood there in the middle of the trail, debating our next move. I wanted to talk to Dunaway again, but he'd already let me know via text that he had gone home for the night and wouldn't be back until tomorrow morning. It occurred to me that he probably lived in employee housing, too, at least temporarily, but I wasn't about to go knocking on his door. There would be ample opportunity to talk to him again. So far, he had done his best to accommodate us, although Marta's account conflicted in some ways with what Dunaway and Colleen Denton had told us. I wondered what that meant.

Then again, humans were imperfect, their memories even more so, and time always made them hazier. It was important that we track down as many potential witnesses as we could while we were still on the property.

"It's seven thirty," I said to Hux, glancing at my watch. "What time did you want to get out on the trail tomorrow?"

"You know me," he said. "Oh four hundred sounds perfect."

I groaned.

He laughed. "You sound so damn excited."

"I'm a mere mortal, Hux. After a day like this, I need eight hours of sleep."

He looked off toward the lobby. "Well, I could go talk to the kitchen staff."

"I should go with you. It's important."

"I can do it, Harland."

He was right, of course. Hux could handle the interviews with the kitchen staff without my help. He knew how to talk to people.

"All right," I said. "You can brief me tomorrow."

He stretched his hands over his head and crinkled the joints in his neck and back. "It's a nice night, at least. Not too cold."

I rearranged the dirt underfoot. "What's your plan, then?"

"After I hit the restaurant, I'll find a place to camp, I guess. You?"

The truth was, I sometimes struggled to get excited about sleeping on the hard earth after a long day like this one, but I also didn't want Hux to think I was soft. At the moment, the rooms Dunaway had reserved for our investigative team were sorely tempting me.

"You should take one of the rooms Dunaway gave us," Hux said, reading my thoughts, or maybe just my general aura of exhaustion. "I won't tell anyone."

"Dunaway will know."

Hux laughed. "It'll make him feel better knowing you're close by."

I considered that for a moment, deciding that Hux was probably right. While we did have a prime suspect, we hadn't ruled anyone out either, and Dunaway had the hotel's reputation and a lot of high-maintenance guests to manage. This was still an open investigation with one person dead, another missing, and a lot of unanswered questions. If I were him, I would have wanted a police presence around, at least for a few more days.

"All right," I said. "I choose to believe you. Let's meet up tomorrow at four AM."

"We can push it to oh five hundred," he said.

"I can do four."

"Nah, let's do five. You'll be in a better mood."

As his teasing smile faded, I thought for a moment he might say something else, but a familiar silence filled the void instead. Hux called out to Ollie and walked, unhurriedly, toward the terrace entrance to the lobby. He held the door for a couple coming out and waved at me, catching my eyes briefly before he went inside. Ollie panted a good-bye.

I took the room key Dunaway had given me and checked the location on my map. The block of rooms he had set aside was part of the "Flora" cluster; mine was Manzanita. It was closer to the lobby than the Birds of Prey contingent, situated just beyond the pool and only one flight up a narrow set of stairs. *Much better than a grueling hike back to my car in the dark*, I thought.

At the top of the stairs was a platform that serviced five guest rooms: Buckeye, Chaparral, Manzanita, and then two others farther down the terrace that I didn't bother exploring. The hand-painted manzanita shrub on my door confirmed that I'd found the right place. It may as well have been a picture of the apple tree in Eden. There was nothing quite like retreating into a quiet, heated room after a long day in the great outdoors.

The accommodations did not disappoint, and I made quick use of the amenities, which included a walk-in shower with a bench, heated floors, and luxurious soaps and lotions. When my teeth were brushed and my backpack was all ready to go for the next day's adventure, I climbed into the plush bed with its pillow-top mattress and feather-down pillows.

But for all kinds of reasons, sleep didn't come easily.

12

I LAY ON MY *back, sprawled out, my bare limbs baking in the morning sun. At night, the temperature dropped, and as my body cooled, the pain would begin. The shivering was unbearable—the subtle motion like a thousand little knives boring into my spine. It was a miracle I could move my legs at all, since I knew my back was broken. I could feel it with every movement, every breath, every grimace.*

I stared at the sky, the stars glittering on a black canvas. In the early part of our trek through Australia's backcountry, the night sky hadn't looked diabolical at all; its expansiveness was hopeful, transcendent. Now, all I could see was an empty void, a deep nothingness that stretched back millennia, witnessing the dying of stars and the light they bore. I remembered seeing a picture of a dying star from the James Webb Space Telescope, a dusty exhalation of dust and light. That image haunted me now, a stark reminder of my own mortality, which would come at the hands of my own hubris.

We never should have come here.

"Filly?" It was Kevin, his voice hoarse and gritty, hardly any sound in it anymore. He hadn't had anything to drink since yesterday. We still had some food, but not much. He sounded weak. I knew we wouldn't last much longer out here. He should have left earlier—days earlier—but he was scared, and I was injured. I couldn't move.

I couldn't do a goddamn thing.

"I'm okay," I said, barely a whisper. It hurt to talk.

He was quiet for a while.

A long while.

"I'm sorry," I whispered.

"Don't be. I know you're hurting."

I had to bite my tongue to keep myself from lashing out at him. I hated that he kept coddling me like this, making me feel like I was completely blameless in this situation. This trip had been my idea, and never once had Kevin questioned my decision to take on Australia's Red Centre without a guide. It was a desert, for God's sake. A hot, ruthless, dangerous desert. I'd let my ego get the best of me and had managed to turn our international adventure into a nightmare.

I was too dehydrated to cry, but I felt the impulse to do so come over me again. This had become the cycle of my waking moments: anger, fear, despair. Sometimes I projected those emotions onto Kevin, who didn't deserve them.

Or did he?

I had begged him, time and time again, to go off and get help. To leave me here, alone. To try and find a trail or a road or even a watering hole to stave off the inevitable just a little longer.

But Kevin wasn't a survivalist; he was a computer nerd. He worked in the IT department at Northwestern and had never even gone camping as a kid. He was born and raised in the suburbs of Chicago, had gone to college in Chicago, had met his first and only girlfriend—me—in Chicago. His idea of adventure was watching a horror movie with the lights off.

There it was again: that anger, that resentment. If only Kevin had been the one to trip and fall down that ravine, we might have had a chance. I knew it was a dark and painful thought but was also true. Thanks to me, we were lost and stranded in some of Australia's most unforgiving wilderness. But thanks to him, we were going to die here.

"Filly?"

"You need to find help."

"What?" His voice was hoarse.

"Now. Not in a few hours or a few days. You need to go now. There's a watering hole not far from here; we passed it on our way in. Just go back the way we came. Use the compass and the sun to guide you."

"But we talked about this—"

"We're both going to die if you don't find help, Kev."

He was quiet again, but I could tell by his breathing that I had unnerved him. He wore his anxiety like a piece of clothing that didn't fit. It was obvious and ugly. He was good at providing comfort but terrible at being strong.

"I can't leave you alone here." His voice faltered in his throat so that I could barely hear the words, but I did hear them. I had heard them dozens of times in the last two days. He said he couldn't bear to leave me alone in the desert.

But the truth was a little different.

The truth was that he was scared of being alone.

He took a breath, this one so deep it seemed to keep going forever. When he finally exhaled, his voice sounded different. "I'd rather die with you than survive without you."

If this were a movie, I might have swooned at the tragic romance behind his words, but this was real life and I didn't want to die. This was no time for platitudes and good-byes. I wanted to go home. I wanted to see my parents and my sisters again; I wanted to watch their kids grow up. I wanted to rise up the ranks as a federal investigator, prove to everybody there that being a five foot tall female did not define me. I was better than this.

I was a survivor.

"If you love me, you'll go," I said.

I could see that I had wounded him, but my pleas weren't having any effect. He had to listen to me. We were out of water and nearly out of food. The dingoes were making noises in the brush; the vultures had picked up our scent.

He grasped my hands. "Filly, no."

Gritting my teeth to ward off the pain, I extricated my hands and squeezed his wrists. The sheer motion of lifting my arms almost made me black out, but I forced myself to ignore all that, to rise above the agony somehow.

"Just think about it," I said. "In an hour, the sun will be up. This is your best chance." I knew Kevin was afraid of the dark—of the dingoes, the snakes, the scorpions—but he wasn't so scared of the sun. He should have been, though. He wouldn't get far without water.

Unfortunately, we had no choice.

"Please," I begged him. "Please."

He squeezed my hand and put his head against mine. His breathing slowed. For the first time in years, I had no idea what he was *thinking. Was he going to deny me? Was his fear going to win the battle in his head? Did he even understand what love was?*

At last, he whispered, "Okay." And then: "I'll see you soon."

* * *

I woke with a start, drenched in sweat. *A Kevin dream*, I thought. These days, those were rare. I was glad for it. The dreams of my missing husband were always vivid, a replica of the events that had transpired in that desert. One therapist had referred to them as lucid dreams, in that my conscious mind knew they were dreams, but my unconscious controlled my body. I supposed that was true. In those dreams, I relived those last few moments with Kevin the way I remembered them, but the weight of those moments in the stupor of sleep was different.

It was heavier.

Unbearable.

My phone was showing 3:54 AM. It was early, but I could use the extra few minutes to get my backpack organized and reflect on the Denton case. My brain always worked best in the morning—my body, too. I wasn't feeling too stiff, even after yesterday's frenzied hike over rocky terrain, which was a good thing. I never knew how my back was going to feel after a day on a trail that was new to me. Some days, I could hardly walk.

My back hurt a little, as it always did, but maybe more so than usual because of the dream. I tried not to think about it as I picked out my clothes for the day: a UPF T-shirt, slim-fitting cargo pants, and my official ISB police jacket. I decided that on the off-chance Aria Privar was hiding in the park somewhere, she might feel comfortable making herself known if she saw a member of law enforcement on the trail. It was a long shot, sure, but being aware of the conditions out in the Pinnacles National Park, I knew that a person without a couple liters of water wouldn't last long in that hot sun.

I checked my cell phone and saw that Hux had texted me just minutes earlier. *I got us some breakfast. See you at the trailhead.*

Hux often texted me before a day out on the trail, which I appreciated because it got me over the hump of wondering if I could even handle being out there with him. It wasn't often we got assigned to a pleasantly easy part of the park with perfect weather;

if the circumstances called for it, we hiked in rain, snow, floods, sweltering heat, and high winds. Griffiths had warned us about the harder stretches of the High Peaks Trail, so I knew we were in for a physical challenge, too. That part, though, didn't worry me so much. I was focused on finding Aria Privar.

With my backpack on, I stepped out of my room and into the brisk pre-dawn air. I shined my flashlight on the trail as I made my way down to the trailhead on the south side of the property. At this hour, the cliffside suites were all dark, the hotel's muted lights twinkling behind the trees that populated the gulch. It smelled like damp chaparral, Pinnacles' signature vegetation. It was hard to walk five feet without tripping over it.

Hux was already at the trailhead, one elbow perched on a sign staked into the ground. He grinned when he saw me, his bright green eyes catching the white beam of my flashlight.

"Good morning," I said.

"Mornin'." He handed me a bagel with cream cheese, nicely wrapped in its waxed paper. Incredibly, it felt warm in my hands.

"Where the hell did you get this?" I asked.

"Don't worry about it," he said.

"Not from someone's old room service tray, I hope?"

He laughed. "Nah. I'm a little more discerning than that."

Ollie barked in greeting as I rubbed the scruff of his neck. It was good to have him back again. I could tell he was anxious to get out on the trail, too.

It was early, yet no signs of dawn on the horizon. These early hours were our best chance to cover some ground quickly, since we had both been warned by various sources that most of the trails in Pinnacles were completely exposed to the elements.

The hotel itself was south of the Chaparral Trailhead Parking Lot, at the end of a newly forged trail through rocky wilderness that cut west off Juniper Canyon. This was the way we'd both come in, and it was the only route off the hotel property without going into the backcountry.

At this predawn hour, the hike back out to the Juniper Canyon Trail felt like a stroll in a city park. We took advantage of the gentle conditions to talk about the case.

"How did it go with the kitchen staff?" I asked.

"Not great," he said. "I did find the guy who was on room service duty on the night of the 26ᵗʰ, but he said he never actually saw Denton or anyone else when he went to drop off the food at their room."

"No one answered the door?"

"He said there was a 'Do Not Disturb' sign on the door, so he assumed they were, you know—engaged in activities that were not to be disturbed."

"Uh-huh." I was glad Hux couldn't see me blushing in the darkness. "What time was this?"

"He pulled up the receipt for me; the order was placed at twenty two fifty five, and he delivered it just before twenty three thirty. I took a picture of it."

"Isn't that when Colleen Denton was staking out the room?"

"Probably just after she left," he said.

Ollie ran up ahead, exploring the hotel trail as it snaked around a boulder. I knew we were close to the intersection with Juniper Canyon, but this time, we'd be going south toward Bear Gulch and Monolith instead of north toward the parking lot.

"Did he see anyone outside the room? Or down below?"

"He did not." Hux looked at me over his shoulder. "It's notable that she didn't mention him, though."

"Well, it makes sense. If she was there, the last thing she needs is another witness putting her at the scene."

Hux paused on the ridge, which gave me time to catch up to him. "Well, he didn't remember seeing anyone near Peregrine or Condor at that time," he said, turning to me with an offering of some of his homemade granola. "He did say one interesting thing, though."

"What's that?"

"That he thinks he may have *heard* someone up in the Condor suite while he was outside Peregrine."

"Huh," I said.

Hux's eyes sparkled, even in the darkness. "Could be our killer."

"Or at least a valuable witness. It's worth a closer look, that's for sure." I munched on the granola, savoring its rich, nutty flavor. "Good work, Hux."

He smiled broadly. "Thanks."

Ollie barked to remind us we had places to be. As we hurried down the last stretch of the trail, Hux pointed at what looked like a broken sign poking out of the bushes. Standing in the pre-dawn stillness, he took out his topo map and used his compass to establish our location. I had my GPS-equipped sat phone handy, but Hux liked to keep things old-school when he could. He had also lent his sat phone to Vee, so he was without one at the moment.

"All good?" I asked.

"All good. We're just north of Scout Peak, which you can see right over there." He pointed with confidence at a hulking dark mass just over the ridge. "This busted sign here is for Juniper Canyon; that means we're only about a quarter-mile from the High Peaks Trail."

"And what's the plan from there?"

"We'll head south on High Peaks for one-point-six miles, and after that we'll pick up Rim Trail for about a half mile to end up at Monolith."

"Then what?"

He grinned. "Then the real fun begins."

13

OUR BRIEF STINT on the well-maintained Juniper Canyon Trail took us through dense shrubs, rocky outcroppings, and rolling hills. The weather forecast was calling for clear skies and temperatures in the low seventies, which was about average for this time of year. At night, though, the higher altitudes turned cold quickly; right now my smartwatch was showing an ambient temperature of forty-two degrees.

The chief ranger hadn't called off the search for the presumed-missing Aria Privar, which meant there was still hope of finding her alive. Hux, for one, was feeling optimistic. Ollie, too. I could tell by the excited tenor of his bark that he was thrilled to be out here.

As we hiked around another rock formation, my sat phone chimed with a new message. I liked to keep my Iridium on standby mode to preserve battery, but I also didn't want to miss something important from the chief ranger. Griffiths had promised to send an updated set of coordinates to my satellite phone by six AM.

Sure enough, there they were: *36.467012, -121.184804.*

Hux had paused his relentless push forward and turned around to face me. He watched me enter the coordinates into my GPS device, a painstaking process that never seemed to get easier. I missed having a functional cell phone at times.

"You got 'em?" Hux asked.

"Yup."

"Where?"

"On the Chalone Peak Trail," I said. "About a half mile south of Monolith."

Hux put his hands on his hips and looked southward. "Huh," he said.

"What's wrong?"

He took his map out again. "That's pretty much the middle of nowhere."

I peered over his shoulder at the map. "It's close to Mount Defiance, looks like."

"Yeah, but there's no maintained trail to Mount Defiance."

Hux liked to study the topographic details of a park before venturing into it, and I trusted his knowledge of the area. This latest development, however, was unwelcome news. If the search-and-rescue squad was exploring the Mount Defiance area, then we were in for some aggressive bushwhacking. I would have preferred Chalone Peak, which would entail more mileage, but it at least had a maintained trail leading all the way to the summit. Defiance wasn't going to be an easy hike, and I doubted the search conditions out there were very good, either.

"What time should I give him as our ETA?" I asked.

Hux looked from his map to his watch, which he had taken to wearing when he'd realized that people were always waiting on us in our line of work. It was important to give them reasonable estimates so they weren't stranded on a trail for hours at a time.

"It's oh five fifty now," he said. "I think we can be there by oh seven thirty, easily."

Easily. Despite Hux's casual comment, I knew this wasn't going to be an easy hike. The High Peaks Trail featured a number of specialized elements, including footholds, Inca-like stairs built into the rock, and an abundance of elevation change. The only easy thing about it so far was the lack of scorching sunlight, but in a few hours, we'd be in for that, too. At least the temperatures were mild, and we had plenty of provisions.

I didn't voice any of these concerns to Hux, though. Instead, I tightened the straps on my backpack, straightened my shoulders, and took a breath. My stomach was a bundle of nerves, roiling with fear of the unknown.

"You good to go?" Hux asked, as Ollie whined at his feet.

"Yup."

We started back up again, taking the trail at Hux's brisk pace, or at least the pace he thought I could handle. Unlike the relatively flat nature of the Juniper Canyon Trail, High Peaks lived up to its name. The Civil Conservation Corps had outfitted this and other trails with metal catwalks, footholds, and handrails back in the 1930s, all of which still served the hikers traversing the route through Pinnacles' rocky landscape. Hux, for one, was delighted.

"You seem pleased by the accommodations," I said, remarking on the smile on his face as he gripped yet another handrail and leveraged himself over a rock.

"Oh, yeah." He smirked. "I like the change of pace."

"I think I prefer just basic dirt and rock, that kind of thing."

"You mean sidewalks?"

I rolled my eyes at him. "Oh, come on."

"You know what they say: variety is the spice of life."

"So says the guy that lives alone in the woods."

"I'm not always alone," he countered. "And every day is different."

Hux had a point. To his credit, he had found a way to shun the nine-to-five lifestyle while doing something that he loved. Park rangers spent their days in the great outdoors, which could mean doing anything from field surveys to rescue missions. As an ISB agent, Hux would get to keep the lifestyle, but the work was different. He seemed to enjoy the investigative process; he said it gave him purpose, similar to what he'd had during his time in the military. It was the perfect marriage of a wilderness setting with a civilian job.

I loved that aspect of it, too, but the physical demands of being an ISB agent taxed me on a daily basis. As we navigated a tricky switchback, I couldn't help but think of how much my life had changed since my outdoor adventures with Kevin. Back then, we used to plan our hikes based on our moods, and we never ventured into the backcountry.

Well, except that one time . . . in Australia. I recalled meeting one park ranger there who had remarked that rescues were rare in that region because the conditions in summer were so dangerous; most people didn't go out at all. He'd found our situation *so* unusual, in fact, that he asked me if it was possible my husband had *planned* to abandon me there. *What if there's nothing out there to find?* He had asked.

"What's on your mind there, Harland?" Hux asked.

It took me a moment for his question to jar me back into the real world. "Not much."

"You're not thinking about the case, then."

"What makes you say that?"

He picked up a rock, studied its contours, and tossed it back into the brush. "If you were thinking about the case, you'd tell me exactly what was on your mind. But when you say 'not much,' I know it's something else."

I stared at the ground, debating what to say to him. The fact that no one had ever found Kevin's body sometimes haunted me, even all these years later. In my heart, I knew that he was dead. My rational mind told me that he *had* to be; he'd gone off into a hostile wilderness with no water, a day's worth of food, and no real outdoor experience. He had taken the map and compass, but we both knew he wasn't very good with either. By that time, we had waited days before deciding that someone had to go for help. He had left me not in prime physical condition, but tired, hungry, and weak.

And so, I had come to the same conclusion time and time again: he was dead. That didn't mean I didn't wonder about his final moments, though. *What was he thinking before he succumbed to the elements? Did he hate me for sending him out into the desert when he knew he had no chance of making it? Was his last breath a peaceful one or filled with terror?*

I usually found a way to deflect Hux's questions about this topic, but right then, with a stretch of flat ground spilling out in front of us, I felt compelled to give him a truthful answer. Maybe it was because he'd alluded to this subject a couple times before, and at some point, he just deserved to know. Perhaps it was that I trusted him, and I didn't see the point in lying to someone who had never once tried to deceive me.

"Australia," I said.

He slowed his pace a bit until I was standing right behind him, breathing in the heady scent of his backpack and gear. He turned around and looked me in the eye. I knew he wasn't going to press me for information; he was leaving it to me to continue.

With that dream of Kevin so fresh in my mind, I figured now was as good a time as any.

"I never told you the whole story," I said.

"No." Hux's tone was pleasant, no judgment in it at all. He reached around his backpack for a piece of beef jerky. "I don't believe you did."

I straightened the brim of my hat and looked out at the forbidden landscape. The sky had gone purple with dawn, casting a tepid light on the jagged peaks. No matter where we were, it was always cool, peaceful, and quiet in this elusive predawn hour. I relished it.

And yet, as I knew better than most, daylight could also mean searing sunshine and the threat of heat stroke, dehydration, and other maladies. That time Kevin and I had gone to Australia, it was early fall, but the weather had been unusually hot, up into the triple digits. In hindsight, we should have changed our plans.

But you didn't, and Kevin paid for it with his life.

I started walking. "The trip to Australia was my idea," I said as Hux fell into step beside me. "The Red Centre, specifically. I thought it would be a challenge—you know, something exotic and different." Ollie trailed behind me, sensing my conflicted mood. I reached down and scratched the fur behind his collar. "Anyway, it was definitely more than we bargained for. I could tell Kevin was nervous from the get-go . . . the flight, the rental car, the hotels. By the time we got to the campsite, he was practically shaking."

"Did he say anything?"

"No, not really. He said it was just the logistics that were stressing him out. We'd done plenty of outdoorsy stuff in the States, including some backpacking trips. But this was different, for some reason. Even though the Red Centre is a popular wilderness attraction there, it had that vastness to it, you know? 'The Australian outback.' I'm not sure it ever held any appeal for Kevin at all." I cleared my throat, catching myself on a sudden surge of emotion. It was hard to admit to Hux how selfish I'd been.

"You can't blame yourself for not reading someone's mind, Harland."

"I was *married* to him, Hux. I should have listened to his signals." I tried to reign in the disgust I felt for myself by taking a breath. "That was always Kevin's problem—he never challenged me, even when he should have. I think in some ways he was intimidated by me, his own wife." I shook my head, tormented by the ugliest part of our relationship. "Looking back, we didn't have the healthiest dynamic, but I was young and so was he."

Hux and I navigated onto another switchback in the trail as a brisk wind rustled the low-lying trees. The starlight was holding on to that last gasp of darkness.

"Well, I've never been married, so I'm no expert on that front," Hux said. "I can't say I ever met your husband, either."

"I know what you're trying to say," I said. "And I appreciate it. I just . . . what happened to him didn't need to happen. The way I planned that trip, organized it, convinced him we didn't need a guide. I know you've never been there, but it's not much different than the mountainous desert in Afghanistan. It's hot, it's dry. If you get stranded out there for much longer than a day or two, you're in trouble."

"But you fell, Harland," he said. "That was just bad luck."

I shook my head, suddenly unable to lift my gaze from the ground. "Luck is preparation meeting opportunity," I said softly, quoting my grandmother, who loved self-help books almost as much as she enjoyed her garden. "And I prepared poorly for a bad opportunity."

"You're too hard on yourself."

I tugged on the straps at my chest, the ones that kept my backpack secure on my tiny frame, feeling them cutting into my shoulder blades. My right clavicle had a titanium plate in it that felt like a knife was being twisted into bone with the wrong kind of pressure on it. In that moment, though, the pain felt good, a distraction from the agony of losing Kevin in that desert.

"I have no idea how we went off the trail," I continued, comforted by the rhythm of my own strides. "I've gone over it a thousand times in my mind, but the truth is that I still can't believe it happened. Kevin put me in charge of the route, so he never knew anything was wrong until I told him we might be lost."

"He couldn't read a map?"

"No," I said. "He had no real sense of direction."

"Did you have a sat phone?"

"Yes, but we couldn't get a signal in the gorge, and our battery was low. By the time Kevin agreed to hike out on his own, the phone was dead."

Hux sighed. "It sounds to me like he wasn't prepared for things going wrong." Hux wasn't being glib; he was just stating the facts. Kevin rarely planned for worst-case scenarios because he wasn't a risk-taker—that, and he trusted me to worry about the logistics.

"He was in over his head," I admitted. "After we realized my back was broken, Kevin panicked. He knew he was never going to be able to go off and find help on his own. He couldn't read a map, had no knowledge of the terrain . . . he was also scared and tired and dehydrated. If he had left right then, or at least tried harder to get a signal, who knows. But I couldn't convince him to go until we'd been out in that gorge for two days."

Hux was quiet as we began our ascent onto another stretch of trail outfitted with a crooked set of metal railings. I hoped that maybe this treacherous portion might distract Hux from the conversation, but once we were back on flat ground, he gazed at me with an expectant look. "You don't have to talk about this, you know," he said. "No pressure from me."

I knew that of all people, Hux understood the dangers that came with venturing into the unknown, especially when you had no way of knowing what was really out there. He had experienced all kinds of things during his time as a SEAL (sea, air, land) operator, things he couldn't talk about, even now. The truth was, though, that Hux never would have left one of his men behind. That was the whole point of his specialized training: you learned to trust each other in the absolute worst of times. Hux, in my situation, would have made a different decision. There was no doubt in my mind about that.

"I sat there for a while after Kevin left," I said. "Being alone forced me to really think about my situation, which was only getting worse."

"Did you think he was going to make it?"

I shook my head. "No," I admitted. "It occurred to me not long after he left that I was going to die if I didn't figure out a way to save myself."

I learned later, at the hospital, that one of my thoracic vertebrae had all but shattered in the fall, the kind of fracture that paralyzes most people. The pain in my upper back had been indescribable—terrifying, too. I'd worried that the slightest movement might have severed my spinal cord and left me defense-less against the outback's predators. For the time being, though, my legs still worked.

It was move or die.

"With Kevin gone," I went on, "I didn't know what was worse: dying or becoming paralyzed. Moving any part of my body was excruciating. I crawled on my hands and knees, or sometimes upright, trying to keep my back still. I worried that my spine would just suddenly shift out of gear like a rusty old bike, and I'd never get up again."

"You dug deep," Hux said, with genuine approval in his voice.

"I had to. There was no one coming to help me. I thought I might at some point find a rancher's fence, or even a road, but the longer I was out there, the more desolate it felt. I started to hal-lucinate. For a while there, I was convinced I was on Mars."

"How did you decide which direction to go?" Hux asked. "Was there a trail?"

"I never found the trail we'd come in on. I tried, but the brush was so thick, and that gorge . . . I was just completely disoriented."

"Did you ever see any signs of Kevin?"

I shook my head. "No. Nothing."

"What did the rangers think of that?"

I thought back to that one park ranger, the sinewy olive-skinned man who'd seemed convinced that Kevin had left me out there to die. *So he can start a new life*, the man had said, like that was something that actually happened to real people in real life. I supposed it *did* happen, once in a rare while, but only to other people.

Not to us.

"They said the conditions were always changing there," I said. "Even their canines struggled with search-and-rescue operations in that area."

"Hm," Hux mused.

"What?"

"I thought you said the terrain out there was pretty exposed."

"In some areas it was, but the rangers said the wildlife in that part of the wilderness is always quick to scavenge remains." Anx-ious to change the subject, I said, "In any case, I didn't see any sign of him. After two whole days, I finally managed to get out of the gorge. Just as the sun was starting to set, I spotted some tire tracks in the dirt. But here's the thing—there was no road. It was just the tracks. I had no idea which way to go or if it was even worth following them."

"I bet you had some idea," Hux said, briefly making eye contact. "You've got good instincts, Harland."

"Not back then. It was just a hope and a prayer, like that watering hole I found. I ended up going south, towards the mountains." I swallowed a lump in my throat. "It felt like the better place to die."

"But you didn't," Hux said—with sympathy in his voice, yes, but also a clear-edged matter-of-factness. *You're a survivor.*

I slowed my pace a bit as we made our way around a large rock formation that jutted into the trail. "I had no way of knowing how far that vehicle could have gone, or even how old the tracks were. But the next day, just as the weather was starting to turn bad, I spotted an old Jeep. I couldn't believe it—finally, a bit of good luck."

He cracked a smile. "That's not luck."

Hux was giving me too much credit, but he was right in that I hadn't just flipped a coin when it came to deciding which set of tracks to follow. I'd gone south because there were trees in those mountains, and trees often meant a water source. I knew that even if I got there and saw no sign of a vehicle at all, I might last a few more days with a fresh supply of water. By then, someone back home might have contacted the authorities in Australia to alert them that Kevin and I hadn't returned on time. At some point, a call like that would trigger a rescue effort.

"Well, the guy who owned that Jeep sure didn't think much of me," I said. "I thought he was going to leave me in the desert to teach me a lesson."

Hux laughed. "He sounds like my kinda guy."

"No doubt."

"A real bogan, eh?"

"Yeah. Too bad I didn't know what that meant at the time."

Hux's laughter faded as his expression turned serious. "So what happened with the search for Kevin?"

What had *happened with the search for Kevin?* I wondered—and not for the first time, not by a long shot. The Australian Park

Service had given me its official report, but their conclusion that he was "presumed dead" didn't help me sleep at night. The search, in fact, had simply ended when it became clear that a man like Kevin couldn't have survived for weeks in the outback—nor was he the type to *want* to spend weeks out there alone.

As for Hux, though, I assumed that his interest in the outcome was more of a professional one. He was an expert tracker, after all, trained by the world's elite. He was fascinated by stories of those who had gone off the grid, never to be seen again. While he, like me, suspected that the vast majority of those people had died from exposure or other natural causes, he also believed that some of those cases could still be solved. In more than one instance, he'd gone off into the Sequoia backcountry on his own and discovered human remains based off his own search tactics.

"The search went on officially for ten days, but unofficially, it lasted for weeks. The story of the missing American made a lot of headlines, really brought out the woo-woo's. I couldn't help with the search effort, but the fact that I knew exactly where I'd last seen him gave a lot of people the misguided sense that they could just go out there and find him."

"What was their search radius?" Hux asked.

"I think it was twenty miles."

Hux thought for a moment. "What was he carrying?"

"Not much. He had his backpack, but there was hardly anything in it: a couple snacks, a pen-knife. He didn't have any camping gear. His plan was to move as fast as he could with what he had and hope for the best."

"Twenty miles might not have been enough, then, especially if he managed to find water. I might've gone with thirty."

I shook my head. "Not Kevin," I said. "He wasn't in tip-top physical condition. Even if he'd had a straight line to follow in the sand, with perfect weather to boot, he never could have gone thirty miles in a day."

"But you were out there without him longer than a day. By the time they started searching for him, he could've gone a hundred miles or more."

Hux's line of thought made me the slightest bit uncomfortable, in part because it raised questions that I didn't like thinking about. Could Kevin have hiked a hundred miles in a week even in the *best* of conditions? Well-nourished, well-hydrated, and well-conditioned? I honestly didn't think so. He just wasn't made for that type of expedition.

I learned later that while the Northern Territories (NT) in Australia had its issues with crime—both within and separate from the Aboriginal communities that lived there—the NT police never found any evidence to suggest that a crime had occurred in or around the part of the Red Centre where Kevin had gone missing. Unfortunately, there were no witnesses who came forward, either; no one hiking in the area during that crucial time period had seen someone who matched his description. At least, this was what the investigators had told me.

"I was with him, Hux," I said. "I knew his limits better than anyone."

"What about abduction? Homicide, even?"

The Park Service had raised those possibilities—for instance, that he'd been killed for his supplies. The abduction theory didn't make sense to me since it required a series of things to happen: first, Kevin had gone far enough to reach a road; two, he had successfully hailed a ride; and three, the driver had nefarious intentions. As for supplies, he hardly had anything of value.

"The Northern Territory police never found any evidence to suggest it."

"Yeah, but it's not like they've got cameras out there. Isn't there a large Aboriginal population in that part of the country? It could be that they didn't talk to the right people—or the right people wouldn't talk to *them*."

I stopped and put my hands on my hips, both to get a breather and to scrutinize Hux's expression. He didn't shy away from my gaze.

"What are you getting at, Hux?"

"I'm just wondering if they missed something."

"They told me they didn't."

"Haven't *we* been told that more than once?"

He had a point, of course. I just didn't like it.

Because here we were, looking for Aria Privar, holding out hope that she was still alive, the same way I had hoped that Kevin would one day show up on my doorstep. Even though Aria had only been missing for thirty hours, her odds of survival were dwindling fast. The nights were cold and windy, the days hot and dry. Everything we'd heard about her so far indicated that she was neither experienced nor prepared.

Just like Kevin—and Kevin was dead.

Wasn't he?

14

Aria languished in the murky bowels of the cave. She wished she had taken the time to change out of her skimpy cocktail dress. At least she had traded her heels for a pair of tennis shoes after dinner, but she wished she'd changed into pants, too.

What worried her the most was how cold she was after running all night on trails that were sun-exposed in the daytime but unprotected after nightfall. Without the flashlight, she surely would have lost her way on the trail. She'd heard stories about people getting lost in national parks, never to be seen again. Stories about people whose bones were found months or years later, less than a hundred feet from where they were last seen. She knew it could happen to her.

Aria had always been the practical type, maybe too practical. As a resident physician, she worried constantly about making a mistake. One time, she'd missed something small at rounds—a lab value, not even relevant to the patient's current condition—and her senior resident, a dark-haired New Yorker who was only a year or two older than Aria but reminded Aria of her father, had taken her into an unoccupied room and chewed her out until she cried. "You're not smart enough to be a doctor," the woman had said. "You couldn't even handle one admission. You're going to kill a kid if you don't get your shit together."

Aria had tried to take it in the way she'd been raised to respond to conflict—dutifully, stoically, apologetically—but to hear these things from a peer, a person who should have been an ally, shook her resolve.

She remembered the look of disgust on the third-year's face when Aria broke into tears. Later that day, she cried in the cafeteria, tears streaming down her cheeks while she ate a stale sandwich in silence. On the way home, riding the shuttle back to her apartment, the tears came a third time as she pressed her face to the window and watched the city spring to life as darkness fell.

The next day, she woke up determined to go back to work and act like nothing had happened. She would be more meticulous, even if that meant waking up at four AM to round on her patients at 5, these sick, tiny children who needed their rest more than they needed her pointless questions. But such was life as a resident, and she didn't question it. One day, she would finish the program and be out on her own, unencumbered by the expectations of others.

But was that really true? Aria wondered. Her parents would never let her do or be anything else. They were counting on her. Their three other daughters had gone on to do fun, unusual, exciting things; it was Aria they were counting on to restore pride to the family.

Chris, of course, was the escape she'd been looking for, the small act of rebellion that even her sisters disapproved of. Aria's parents didn't even know about him, but she figured that one day, after she'd finished her training and was working as a pediatric cardiologist at some academic monstrosity, she would tell them. By then, Colleen would be a distant memory—hopefully in jail, or even dead. Aria hated herself for thinking it, but she honestly wished the woman would die in a car crash or get cancer. As long as she was alive, she was a threat to Chris and everyone in his life.

Now, though, it didn't matter. Chris was dead. Aria had watched it happen. She'd also seen Colleen, hiding in the bushes like some low-rent spy. Her hit man, though, wasn't low-rent. He had stalked Aria in the Condor suite, the room she had reserved in cash under a fake name. Somehow, he managed to get in. She had even told the person checking her in to please not give out any extra keys or provide any information about her to anyone who asked; the woman reassured her that it was "hotel policy" to protect the privacy of their guests at all costs. Even now, Aria struggled to make sense of what had happened. It was painful to think about, the trauma of it all. It all felt so personal.

And then came the knock at the door.

She closed her eyes and willed it all away.

15

IT WAS BARELY seven AM when Hux and I arrived at the designated location on the Chalone Peak Trail. Chief Griffiths was standing in the middle of the dirt path, squinting at the sky. He had a sat phone in one hand, a walking stick in the other.

Standing at least six feet tall, Griffiths was burlier than most men who held his position, but his ruddy, suntanned face gave him away as a genuine outdoorsman. When he heard us coming down the trail, he gave a wave and started in our direction. Hux and I waved back. "Hope this goes well," I said to Hux, keeping my voice hushed so Griffiths wouldn't hear.

"You worried?" Hux asked.

"A little."

We all shook hands. Griffiths seemed a little taken aback by Hux's size, maybe because the chief ranger wasn't used to meeting people who matched him pound for pound.

Hux and I introduced ourselves as a formality. In my case, it wasn't really necessary, since I was wearing my badge and a dark green jacket with the word "AGENT" stitched on the back. As a general rule, I didn't like to advertise my occupation to every single hiker on the trail, but Griffiths would have understood the reasoning behind it.

"You made good time," Griffiths said, and I could tell he meant it. Hux responded with a perfunctory smile, while I did my best to look nonplussed. Deep down, though, I was proud of myself for making what the chief thought was good time.

"Any update on the missing person?" I asked.

"Well, we found that shoe on High Peaks Trail, as you know—size six and a half, a black satin shoe with a two-inch heel. The brand name's worn off, unfortunately."

"You only found the one?"

He nodded. "Just a little ways north of Monolith, right smack dab in the middle of the trail. We kept our southward bearing on Chalone because that's where the dogs took us."

"They were going off the shoe?" Hux asked.

"Yup."

"We could always do some DNA testing on it to confirm it belongs to Aria," I said, speaking to both Griffiths and Hux.

"Have you contacted the family?" Griffiths asked.

"Not yet. To be honest, no one's reported her missing."

Griffiths frowned. "Well, I know you've got your protocols and all, but I think we oughta reach out. Don't you?"

I wasn't sure what to tell him. In the vast majority of missing person cases, it was a family member who reported their loved one missing. In Aria's case, no calls had come in, which seemed strange, but not unheard of. I had put Vee on the task of contacting the family, but that was mainly because my sat phone service was somewhat spotty.

"I've got an officer on it," I said. "Unfortunately, the hotel has no formal record of her staying there. She never checked in with her name or used a credit card."

"But you found her driver's license?"

Hux pulled the license from a side pouch on his backpack. The little plastic card was still in the evidence bag, but Aria Privar's name and identifying information were clearly visible on the front.

Griffiths squinted at the photo through the crinkled plastic. "Too bad it doesn't have her shoe size on there," he harrumphed.

"I'm not worried about confirming that detail," I said. "Aria Privar is missing, and we have reason to believe she's out here somewhere."

Griffiths looked conflicted. "So was she staying at the hotel or not? I'm confused."

"We confirmed that Ms. Privar was definitely on the hotel property on the 26th between the hours of five PM and eleven o'clock," I said. "Several witnesses confirmed it. Outside of that window, we can't say for sure where she was. All we can say is that she wasn't with the victim when he was found."

"But she was romantically involved with the dead guy?" Griffiths asked.

"From what we know, yes," I said.

"Huh."

Hux and I exchanged a glance.

"Sorry?" I asked.

Griffiths rubbed the scruff on his chin. "It's just that, well, could *she* have done it?"

While Griffiths had seen Aria Privar's photo, he couldn't have known much about the nature of the homicide—unless, of course, Nate Horvath had filled him in.

Either way, Griffiths had a point, and it was one that Hux and I had already considered without ruling it out. "We haven't found any evidence to suggest that," I said. "But we're investigating every angle."

"Okay, but she's the one who's gone missing after her boyfriend turned up dead. Just flat-out disappeared off the face of the earth, seems like."

"That's not entirely true," I said. "You found what you believe to be her shoe."

His lips curled in a wry smile. "Now I'm not so sure. It could be completely unrelated."

Griffiths was right, of course, especially since we hadn't even had a chance to lay eyes on the object in question. Hux took his hands out of his pockets and shifted his feet. Up to that point, he had been taking notes on his phone, but now he turned his attention to Griffiths.

"Can I ask a question?" Hux interjected.

Griffiths nodded. "Sure thing."

"Are you thinking we're not going to find this woman?"

Griffiths grunted in response, but the lilt in his smile told me that Hux had hit on something important. "You know, I'm not so sure what we're looking for at this point," Griffiths said. "We've got the shoe we found out in the middle of a remote trail, but it backs up to a couple of homesteads that have their own roads outta here."

"You think she hitched a ride out?" Hux asked.

"I don't know what to think. But I'll tell ya, our dogs are mighty confused."

"About what?" Hux asked.

"Even with that shoe, they've got nothin'."

"Who's your handler?"

"Dirk."

"Can I talk to him?"

Griffiths nodded. "Sure thing." He looked off at the mountains, the feathery white clouds swirling around the peaks. When he turned back to face me, the lines in his brow cut a little deeper than before. "Here's the thing. I don't want my volunteers out here for that long. They've got jobs, families—the last thing I need is to round up the calvary for a wild goose chase."

The skeptical look on Hux's face mirrored my own. "Explain what you mean by that," I said.

"I used to work search and rescue up in Maine, covered the borderlands next to Canada, mainly, but it was a huge area. I remember this one lady, family reported her missing from somewhere in New Hampshire, then she turned up in a little town called Fort Kent in the North Woods. An old lumberjack had seen her on the news and called it in. When I called the family, they refused to believe it was her. They'd already had the funeral and everything."

"Why?" I asked.

"'Cause they said she wasn't the type to pull a stunt like that. Weeks earlier, her car had been found in a used car lot next to a river. She left a note and everything. The local police ruled it a suicide, but a man came forward and said this gal, who was supposed to be dead, had killed his wife in a hit-and-run. He said he had camera footage to prove it."

"Okay, but if her death had been ruled a suicide, then why all the theatrics to cross the border? I'm not seeing it."

"The dead lady's husband had contacted this gal right before that, apparently. Asked for a personal apology before he took it to the media, but she denied everything. She refused to admit she'd even been in the same town at the time of his wife's death."

I had a feeling Griffiths had gotten this whole story second-hand, but I wasn't about to interrupt him. I wanted to hear where he was going with this, even if it meant we had to listen to some Maine lore to get there.

Griffiths went on. "Turns out she *did* hit the lady, though, because the camera footage checked out. The widower was a cop; he tracked her down from a partial plate. Had her dead to rights." He tucked his thumbs in his belt loops. "Alls I'm saying is, you can't judge a book by its cover. This lady who we caught trying to cross the border was a goddamn dance teacher. But there she was, thigh-deep in an icy cold river. Only reason we caught her is 'cause she stopped at a convenience store and paid for a bottled water in cash. From the retired lumberer. Who saw the news." He seemed amused by the memory. "So you just never know."

I could tell that Griffiths enjoyed this story, and probably told it often. Then again, I understood the appeal; I had misjudged a number of covers in my day. One of them had almost cost me my life.

"Here's the thing, Mr. Griffiths," I said. "We haven't collected any evidence to suggest that Aria Privar killed anyone, so it's hard to believe she's en route to Mexico to start a new life."

"What evidence *have* you collected?" Griffiths asked.

Even though the directness of his question ruffled my feathers, I worked hard not to show it. "Right now, we're waiting on the report from the medical examiner," I said. "Our timeline of events is coming together, though."

"There's actually something else," Griffiths said. "Last night we went and surveyed all the vehicles parked at the west and east entrances, which we do as part of our protocol when we've got an overdue hiker. We found your victim's yellow Jeep in the hotel lot at the west entrance."

"Registered to Christopher Denton?"

He nodded. "Yup, that's the one."

I looked over at Hux, who was typing on his iPhone, adding these details to the case file. When we had a free moment, we'd go over them together.

"What else came up on that search?" I asked Griffiths.

"Nothing of interest at the east entrance parking lot . . . no stolen vehicles, no late registrations. No abandoned vehicles, either, from what we could tell. But we didn't run the search until last night around six PM, so your killer could've been long gone by then."

"Could we get the names and addresses from those plates at some point?" I asked.

"Sure thing."

Hux had put his phone away and was looking out at the landscape. A jagged canyon cut into the mountain range before spilling into a valley that baked in the California sun. A hundred miles east was Sequoia National Park, its snow-capped peaks barely visible in the distance. It was easy to forget how vast this state was.

"That to the east there is Frog Canyon," Griffiths said, pointing to the canyon that dissected the earth just over the ridge from where we were standing. "And over there is Mount Defiance, the most underrated peak in the park." He gestured to a gentle giant nestled in the mountain range that shaped Pinnacles' topography. "I don't get called out this way very often; folks tend to stay on the north side of the Chalone Trail, especially the day hikers. Bear Gulch is a real popular destination right up into November."

"Because of the caves?" I asked, referring to one of the park's most popular attractions. I had overheard one guest back at the hotel talking about a guided tour.

"Yup, especially this week," he said. "Usually the entire cave's open the last week in October, which only happens once a year. But there was a disturbance in the upper cave just yesterday, and we had to close it down."

"What kind of disturbance?"

"Hard to say, but these kinds of things happen all the time. Usually it's a hiker who gets a little too curious, but our chiropterologist told us to close it immediately."

I almost laughed at the expression on Hux's face—one eyebrow raised, his brow furrowed, like, *Huh?* For me, too, "chiropterologist" was new territory.

Griffiths saw the expressions on both our faces and chuckled. "Apologies. Our bat expert."

"What's the chiropterologist's name?" I asked.

"Betsy Friedlander," Griffiths said. "But don't worry, I already talked to her about our missing person. She was a hundred percent sure the cave was vacant."

"She checked it?"

"She knows our caves better than anyone. Betsy practically lives in there."

I couldn't imagine a worse place to spend my free time, but to each their own. "All right," I said, making a mental note to follow up with the bat expert if Aria Privar didn't turn up soon. "Where else do people tend to go in this part of the park?"

Griffiths thought for a moment. "Well, most visitors to Pinnacles actually park at the east entrance. From there, you've got the Bear Gulch Caves, the reservoir, and some real nice scenic trails that are good for beginners. Monolith is a big destination for climbers."

"How hard is it to get from one side of the park to the other?"

"Not terribly hard, assuming it's a nice day and not too hot. It's about a ten-mile loop to cover the whole park, depending on which route you take. But there are a couple of interconnecting trails—High Peaks, Juniper Canyon, Balconies, Tunnel. The average hiker could do the full loop in about ten hours."

Ten hours was a lot of time to be out on the trail in these conditions, especially for a woman in heels. "I assume your team searched the whole loop?"

He nodded. "We have a small crew out on the north side right now, but our dogs don't think she went that way. I wanted to rendezvous here because it's got lost of visibility. This ridgeline here gives you clear views of Frog Canyon and Defiance to the east, High Peaks to the north, and Chalone to the south."

"You mentioned the dogs," I said. "Did they alert around here?"

Ollie barked, perhaps sensing that we were talking about his competition. I was anxious to introduce him to the shoe the other canines had used to guide their search, but I had no idea where it was at the moment. I assumed the canine handler had it.

"They did," Griffiths said. "To a point. We got to Monolith and they lost the scent, so here we are."

I rubbed the scruff around Ollie's neck, doing my best to comfort him. *You'll get your chance*, I wanted to tell him. *Just hold on a little while longer.*

Griffiths seemed to notice my Shepherd mix, who was finally starting to show his impatience. "Is this fella search-and-rescue trained?" he asked.

"Yes, sir," Hux interjected. "Trained him myself."

"You're a canine handler?"

Hux said diplomatically, "When the situation calls for it."

Griffiths crossed his arms over his chest and looked up at the sky. Ominous-looking clouds were moving in from the east, casting long shadows over the sand-colored farmland. I remembered the snowy forecast for the Sierras. While I wasn't exactly looking forward to a drenching downpour, I much preferred it to a scorching hot sun.

"Something doesn't feel right here," Griffiths said.

"How so?" I turned away from the sky.

"Pinnacles is a newer national park, as you know. We've had folks run into problems with exposure . . . heat stroke, dehydration, you know the drill. People don't bring enough water." He took a swig from his own canteen. "But we've recovered everybody; no deaths since I started here. This isn't Acadia or Yosemite, if you know what I'm saying."

Griffiths spoke from experience, that much was clear. In the Sierras and other wooded wilderness areas, you could go just a few feet off the trail and risk never finding it again. Pinnacles, on the other hand, was a gentler beast. The trails were well-maintained and clearly marked, even though the going wasn't always easy. The Chalone Mountain Trail, in particular, had its share of steep ascents, harsh switchbacks, and punishing conditions. The real danger on a trail like this wasn't getting lost, it was succumbing to the elements.

It stood to reason, then, that if Aria Privar *had* died of heat-related illness, why hadn't we found her body? The search dogs should have picked up on the scent of decay, especially in these dry, windy conditions. It hadn't rained in at least a week.

"Have you called in any air support?" I asked. "To canvas the area?"

Griffiths chuckled. "You say that like it's no big thing. Well, this isn't Yosemite; choppers are hard to come by."

"I can call one for you," I said.

"You sure about that? I hear your people are swamped at the airport."

I no longer thought of the FBI as "my people," but a lot of park rangers did. In my early days with ISB, I used to spend a lot of time spelling out the distinction between the two federal agencies. Now, I realized my time was better spent elsewhere.

"I'll work on air support," I said.

With that settled, Hux interjected, "I got a question, Chief."

Griffiths looked at him.

"Where's that shoe?"

"Dirk's got it. I can call him up on his sat phone if you want."

"We'd appreciate that, sir. Thank you."

Griffiths nodded as he went off to make the call to his canine handler. Hux and I idled on the trail, surveying the landscape from this unique vantage point. Temperatures had stalled in the low fifties. I zipped my jacket up to my chin and mourned the decision to wear short sleeves when I got dressed this morning.

Hux, on the other hand, wasn't even wearing a jacket. Complementing his green Park Service pants, his non-descript gray collared shirt functioned as his uniform of sorts when we were out in the field on official business. On unofficial business—or, really, when we weren't expecting to deal with any Park Service or law enforcement agents out in the wilderness—he usually wore a plain T-shirt and a casual jacket. Hux had admitted to me once that he hated collars, but he wasn't about to sacrifice professionalism for comfort.

"What do you think about all this?" I asked Hux.

He looked at me with a crooked grin. "About what?"

"About Aria Privar being all the way out here in a cocktail dress and one shoe?"

"I don't buy it."

"I don't, either."

He crouched down and smoothed the fur around Ollie's neck with both hands. "Do you think their dogs are confused?"

"Look, all credit to their handler, but Ollie seems to think we're in the wrong place."

Ollie whimpered as he tried to nudge me back in the direction we'd come. I pulled a treat out of my backpack and offered it to him. He licked it off my hand, but I could tell he wasn't happy.

"I'm not sure what we can contribute out here," I said. "I think we're better off canvassing the hotel, talking to witnesses there."

"Can we look at the shoe first?"

I nodded. "Yes, absolutely. If it's a dead end, we need to figure that out now."

Standing out here on a ridge miles from the hotel, I couldn't figure why Aria Privar would have come this way. South of Monolith, there was nowhere to go except Chalone Peak, for which there was precisely one route to the summit. If she was looking for a road or other egress point, she wouldn't have found it in this part of the park, unless she'd picked up a private road on a homesteader's property. That felt like a long shot to me, though. She would have been better off taking the hotel trail back to the parking lot.

Then again, I wasn't sure *what* Aria Privar's intentions were, assuming she had even left the hotel property in the first place. We still couldn't say for sure that she had. Was the shoe even a clue? Or was it completely unrelated to the case? Was it possible that another hotel guest, her high heels packed away in a hastily zipped side pocket, had lost it on the trail? The only way to answer that question was to confiscate the shoe from this guy Dirk and lay eyes on it ourselves.

Griffiths was having a disjointed conversation with someone on the phone. When he finally hung up, he wandered back over to us.

"Dirk is on his way here," he said. "I've got to meet up with two of my rangers at the reservoir. They think they might have found something."

"They called you?"

"Sent me a message. I'm gonna head back that way now; I'll let you know what we've got when I get there."

I didn't relish the idea of waiting for Canine Handler Dirk while the chief ranger went off to investigate a new development, but we had to get our hands on that shoe.

"All right," I said. "Thanks."

After Griffiths was gone, Hux and I wandered over to one of the many rock formations in the park and sat on its smooth surface. He offered me some of his homemade granola.

"One of these days," he said as we munched on ample and delicious handfuls, "you'll have to try it right out of the oven."

I nodded, unsure what he meant by that. I'd only been to his cabin once, back when we were working our first case together. While Hux had said I was welcome anytime, the truth was that I hadn't been able to come up with an excuse to go back to Sequoia. Another agent was stationed there for the foreseeable future, and I had no reason to be there.

"It's pretty good just the way it is," I said.

"It's not hot, though. When it's fresh, it's crackling and crispy. Nothing beats it." He pinched the Ziploc bag to seal it. "I'm telling you, it's a whole different experience."

I managed a polite smile. "Someday, then."

"How about this weekend?"

His question took me by surprise, startling me with its earnestness. While I thought about his cabin from time to time, I never expected to be invited back there. The reason was simple: there was no *reason* for Hux to invite me back there. His cabin was way off the grid.

"I don't know," I said. "I've got those cold cases to work on . . ."

"The cabin's got good internet," he said. "And you wouldn't have to work in some dusty cubicle at the San Francisco field office. The coffee's bad there, I bet. And the granola, it's probably that Costco stuff that comes *in a bag*." He spoke with feigned disgust, which made me smile.

"Yeah." The cubicles *were* dusty, and the air tasted stale, like it hadn't been ventilated in months. The last time I spent a whole day there, I'd returned to my hotel covered in red welts. *You've developed an allergy to the FBI*, I had decided.

"See?" Hux said with a smirk. "You know you can do better. Come on out to my redwood wonderland."

"Is that really your best pitch?"

He laughed. "I forgot how picky you are."

"I'm good with redwoods. It's just . . . I'm not sure what you were going for with 'wonderland.'"

"You're right. It was stupid." He rubbed his chin, the tips of his ears turning pink. Then he said, "How about 'my granola paradise'? Or 'the cabin of intellectual excellence'?"

I laughed. "You really think quite a lot of yourself, don't you?"

He sighed good-naturedly. "Look, I'm not much of a salesman," he said. "I was just hoping you'd take me up on the offer."

"Are you off next weekend?"

He nodded. "Yes, ma'am."

"Your chief finally gave you some time off?"

"He's trying to get used to life without me."

"Well, that's good news for me. I could use your help this winter."

"On the cold cases?"

A brisk wind gusted over the mountain, blowing wayward strands of hair across my face. Hux kept his short, blondish locks tucked under his hat. "On whatever comes our way," I said. "The national parks are only getting more popular. You know that."

He offered me a hand as we hoisted ourselves off the rock. A little way down the ridge, coming from the east, was a young man being trailed by a handsome Malinois. Ollie watched the pair like a soldier at attention, nothing moving in his body except his eyes.

"Uh-oh," Hux said.

"What?"

"I have a feeling this guy is gonna be trouble."

CHAPTER

16

DIRK BEASLEY, THE canine handler, introduced us to Mollie, his search-and-rescue dog. She had a powerful, muscular build, which was standard for her breed. Ollie and Mollie, as it were, sat facing each other and hardly moved an inch. They both had nerves of steel and made a handsome couple, in a way.

"Huh," Dirk said after we'd made all our introductions. He bent over and studied Ollie's haunches. "Is that a *mutt*?"

"Shepherd mix," I said. "But his mother was well-bred—Czech working line GSD."

"So what happened? She got busy with Fido next door?"

I felt my lips twitch with a smile. "Actually, yes, that's the story I heard."

Dirk bent down and studied Ollie's face: his bone structure, his build. Dirk rubbed Ollie's coat and inspected his coloring, which I had always thought was the loveliest dark brown. Dirk spent a good while studying Ollie's physique before asking my poor dog to get up and walk.

What is this? I thought. *Westminster? Christ.*

"Sorry," Dirk said, maybe because he had caught a glimpse of my expression. "I'm just obsessed with *canis lupus familiaris*." He smiled, perhaps thinking that he'd win me over with his scientific knowledge, but I had other things on my mind right then, and *canis lupus familiaris* was not one of them.

Hux cleared his throat. "So, Dirk," he said. "Can we see that shoe?"

"Oh, yeah." He reached into his pocket for the critical clue we'd all been hearing about for hours now. To my horror, the shoe wasn't even in a bag. At this point, there wouldn't be much of a scent left on it at all, other than whatever was emanating off Dirk's butt. It surprised me that a canine handler would be so careless.

The shoe matched the description the bartender had given about Aria's heels the night she went missing, but at the same time, there was nothing distinctive about it. Black high heels were a staple in most women's closets.

Wild goose chase, I thought, while fighting to keep my expression neutral.

I reached into my backpack for an evidence bag and handed it to Hux, who already had his gloves on, ready to accept the transfer. "Why isn't the scent article in a bag?" I asked Dirk.

"Scent article," he said, mildly amused. "You mean the shoe?"

"It was supposed to be used as a scent article, wasn't it?"

"Well, sure, that was the hope. But it was marinating out there in the hot sun for who knows how long. I let Mollie take a shot at it, but she wasn't interested."

I sighed. "Hux will take the shoe, if you don't mind."

Hux grasped the dusty high heel between his thumb and forefinger. As Griffiths had said, the shoe was in excellent condition, hardly any scuff marks on it at all, which meant it probably hadn't been out in the elements very long.

Hux held it out for Ollie to sniff, which seemed to agitate Mollie a little bit. Dirk flicked a finger at her. "Just wait a second there, girl," he chastised her.

Ollie sat on his haunches and barked at Dirk, his signal for a hit—confirming that the shoe did, in fact, smell like Dirk's butt. Then Ollie looked at me like, *Is this a joke?* Hux fought back a smile as he dropped the shoe in an evidence bag.

"We're going to have to keep this, actually," I said. "It could be an important piece of evidence."

"Or it could be nothing," Dirk countered.

I caught myself gritting my teeth. "We can't say for sure either way at this point."

"I heard about the business back at the hotel." Dirk snorted. "The wife did it, eh?"

Don't let him get to you, I reminded myself. "We're still investigating."

Dirk shrugged. "Either that, or it was the jealous girlfriend." He pointed a finger at me. "You know what they say about women, don't you? Most of 'em are batshit crazy."

He laughed, a high-pitched gargle that made Ollie whine. I could see that my dog wasn't excited about the shoe or any other facet of this tracking expedition so far—except maybe Mollie. They both looked frustrated with their humans at this point.

"We'll take the shoe and be on our way," I said. "Thanks."

"You don't want to link up for a bit? My bitch against your mutt?"

"No, thanks."

Before Hux could manhandle Dirk for being a pompous little prick, I stepped down off the ridge we were standing on to diffuse the situation. Hux said something to Dirk that I couldn't hear, but it didn't matter; we had gotten what we needed from him.

As Hux and I hit the trail, leaving Dirk to lick his proverbial wounds, Hux said, "I feel bad for Mollie."

"Me, too."

"He was kind of a weird guy."

"He wouldn't be the first."

I looked over my shoulder, relieved to see that Dirk had moved on to greener pastures. A lilting breeze picked up the faint scent of vinegar weed. I tried to savor the wildness of this place, the brute origins of a landscape that had literally molted into existence.

"I'm not sure what to make of this shoe," I said. "Is it normal for a high heel abandoned on a trail to trigger a search-and-rescue operation?"

"Not necessarily," Hux said. "But I get the feeling they're all on edge with this new hotel in their backyard. I think Griffiths is just playing it safe."

"I'm not at all convinced it's Aria Privar's."

"Me, neither."

I sighed, doing my best to cope with the frustration of potentially wasting hours out on the trail. Hux chewed on a piece of grass, which told me he was feeling the same way. He liked to chew on things when he was feeling crabby or impatient.

I pulled out my map to have another look at the network of trails that crisscrossed and looped between the east and west entrances of the park. The east entrance wasn't actually the last stop for vehicles heading into the park; Highway 146 continued west another mile or two to the Old Pinnacles Trailhead, which tracked north and ultimately diverged into two routes: a southerly one to the popular Balconies Cave, and another that went further north, seemingly toward nothing at all. On my map, this was the North Wilderness Trail.

I hadn't heard much about that one, but seeing it there, stranded in the northern territory of the park, I got the impression that the Wilderness Trail was one of those long hikes that appealed to solitary hikers and pretty much no one else. The entire loop, which covered a large swath of the park's northern region before coursing down past the west entrance and back up again, was nearly ten miles long. It didn't have much in the way of tourist attractions, either—no lakes, reservoirs, or caves, at least according to the map. On a hot day, there wouldn't be much shade either. I could tell that much from the topography.

Hux looked at my map over my shoulder, undoubtedly anxious to get out there and canvas the park. For me, the thoughts running through my mind were, *How many miles am I going to have to cover today? Can I actually do this? Am I going to be able to keep up with my superhuman partner, or am I going to embarrass myself?*

I suspected that Hux's calculations were quite different. For one thing, he was always thinking like a tracker, and trackers liked to put themselves in the mindset of whoever had gotten lost out on the trail. Where would Aria Privar go? Where would a *killer* go?

"What's on your mind there, Hux?" I asked, suddenly desperate to know.

He backed off the edge of the dirt-packed trail, which offered an unobstructed view of the mountains to the east. "I was just thinking that I underestimated this park," he said. "I mean, yeah, you've got lots of exposed areas, good visibility, but that makes it easy to overestimate your abilities." He turned and met my gaze. "Nate told me that the North Wilderness Trail is a beast, especially in summer. The rangers put a sign up there in summer advising hikers to turn back because they've had so many heat-related rescues.

"It looks remote, too," I said. "A good one for loners."

"Yep. It's the one I'd choose if I were trying to make a quiet getaway out of the park."

"Is that what you're thinking Aria Privar did?"

As the wind kicked up, I wondered if Hux had even heard me, but then he said, "Not really, no. Griffiths may have found a dance teacher trying to jump the border in Maine, but every ranger's got a story like that. I'm not saying it's *not possible*, I just don't think it's *likely*."

I agreed with him on that front, but it didn't explain why we hadn't found any trace of Aria Privar in the park. While I didn't fault Griffiths for calling us all the way out here, I also felt strongly that our time was better served back at the hotel.

Hux held up the shoe in the evidence bag. "Well, too bad this isn't the break we needed . . . unless you're in the mood to track Dirk."

"No, thanks," I said with a wry laugh. Ollie whimpered at the suggestion as he rested his head on his paws. Hux reassured him by rubbing the fur behind his ears.

Hux said, "I feel bad leaving Griffiths in a lurch."

"We're not leaving him in a lurch, Hux. He's welcome to call off the search anytime."

He nodded. "He's the chief ranger, after all."

"Yes, and you're an ISB agent. I need you with me at that hotel."

Ollie, intrigued by our conversation, sat on his haunches and whined. Hux looked out at the rocky vista, cased in shadows from the approaching clouds.

"Understood," he said. "Let's get going, then."

Ollie barked in excitement as he took off ahead down the trail.

* * *

By the time we were back on the property of the Pinnacles Grand, Hux had spoken with Griffiths several times about their search-and-rescue plan. He suggested that they shift their efforts north, in the direction of the Chaparral Parking Lot. That route, at least, would have felt familiar to Aria—or anyone else coming from the hotel. Hux also offered to verify the guest list with Dunaway, just to make sure no one else was unaccounted for.

After Hux had made his peace with the chief ranger, we decided to meet up with Dunaway at his office, which was located down a small hallway behind the reception area. Ollie cozied up under his favorite bench outside, content to wait for us to return.

I knew Dunaway would be anxious to hear any updates, but I also wanted to see what we could get from the hotel's technology, including its security cameras and key cards.

The door was open, so Hux and I walked right in. Dunaway put his mask on and coughed into his hand. His eyes had that red, rheumy look.

"Hello, Detectives," he said. "Please, have a seat."

While we took the pair of chairs across from his desk, the beleaguered hotel manager watered a lefty green plant that sat atop his desk. After he had sated the plant, he plucked his reading glasses off the desk and sighed as he sat down.

"Have you found the woman who's missing?" he asked.

"No," I said. "How is the search going here?"

Dunaway had vowed to conduct as thorough a search as possible; after all, it was bad for business to have a missing person associated with his hotel.

"We haven't found anything of note, nor do we have any guests unaccounted for."

"Have you searched the guest rooms at all?"

"For the most part, yes, but we can't search any that have been continuously occupied since the 26th. Those aren't my rules; that's according to the Fourth Amendment. We couldn't conduct a search without a warrant, in any case, and not until the guest has checked out."

"There are exceptions to that," I said.

He sighed, his glasses slipping down his nose. "Yes, of course. Peregrine and Condor are fair game, as are the unreserved block of rooms in the main building here. But you've seen Peregrine and Condor; they're clearly unoccupied."

"What else can you tell us about your census on the 26th?"

He slid a piece of paper across the desk. "This here is a list of unoccupied rooms as of four PM of the 26th, when Mr. Denton checked in. As you can see, it's limited to a block of rooms on the third floor in the lodge here, plus Peregrine and Condor. Now, late on the 26th, shortly before midnight, Condor was sold to a guest who paid in cash."

"Almost certainly Aria Privar," I said. "Based on what we know so far."

"It was a late check-in. So yes, I would assume it was for someone already staying on the grounds. No one hikes in after sunset."

"Tell us about the wedding party that canceled," I said. "Was Denton on the guest list, by chance?"

He rubbed his eyes. "No. That block of rooms was canceled around noon by the bride's mother, who said that her daughter was too sick from her chemo treatments to get married that day."

"Oh, man," Hux said. "I'm sorry to hear that."

"You haven't heard the whole story. She wanted a full refund on the entire block—several thousand dollars, as it were. I politely declined, given that the deadline had passed; this is very clearly stated on our website. I also knew there was no way we would be able to fill those rooms on short notice."

"You filled one room," I pointed out.

"Just barely," Dunaway muttered. "In any case, the woman was lying." He must have caught the skeptical look on both our faces because at that point he shifted his laptop screen in our direction. "See here? This is the name on that block of rooms." He pulled up the internet browser and typed in the same name: Holstenberger-Berger. A list of social media accounts popped up. He clicked on the Instagram profile that matched the bride's name on the reservation.

"Here we go," he said, rather spitefully. "You can read it for yourself."

It was a black-and-white selfie of a young woman standing alone on a grassy field. She had been crying recently; the tears had ruined her mascara, leaving dramatic black smears on her cheeks. In the background was a hilltop view of San Francisco, with the Golden Gate Bridge spanning the bay in the sunset.

The caption was a doozy. In it she ranted about her cheating fiancé, his diabolical mother, and his crazy sister who had turned the entire wedding party against her. The diatribe was colorful but poorly written. It made me wince.

"See?" he said. "Liars."

I caught a smile twitching at Hux's lips, but I couldn't tell if he was amused by the wedding drama or Dunaway's reaction to it.

"Well, yes," I said, pandering to Dunaway's ire. "It does seem that you caught someone being dishonest here. Good work."

He pushed his glasses up higher on the bridge of his nose. "Anyway, here's the booking list." He went back to the reservation with the bride's name on it. There were a total of six rooms that had been booked for the 23rd to the 27th. Pretty small for a wedding party.

"Only six rooms?" I asked. "For a wedding?"

"I assume it had something to do with the room fees."

"Is that common for weddings? To have so few rooms reserved?"

He nodded. "We have several weddings already booked for the winter, but it's hard to predict how many rooms someone will want. Some weddings are small, some people don't want to spend the money, some folks don't mind getting married on a Monday when the room rates are lower. This was a Saturday night in our opening week; there were no discounts."

I scanned the sheet. "Okay, so six reservations were made and then canceled. Were you able to fill any other rooms on the 26th? Even last minute?"

He turned the screen in my direction. I was no tech expert, but the program they were using for reservations seemed straightforward. There had been several phone inquiries on that day, but according to the log, the only reservation had been made at 11:42 PM for the Condor suite, booked over the phone and paid for via credit card. *Chris Denton's* credit card.

"Who was working the desk at that time?" I asked.

"Elizabeth."

"Does she recall seeing the person who took the room?"

"No. It was a special circumstance since the reservation was made from a guest already staying on the grounds. The key cards were delivered to the Peregrine suite by one of our housekeeping staff."

"What time?"

"Clarisse hand-delivered them that evening just before midnight."

"Did she ever see Aria? Or Chris Denton?"

"No.

"Can we speak with her?"

"You certainly can, but Clarisse had a family emergency and went home this morning. I'll give you her number."

I gritted my teeth, doing my best to accept yet another obstacle to information in this case. "Thank you," I managed.

"My pleasure. In any case, it's very rare for someone to check in after hours. It's strenuous hike to get here, as you know, and we make it very clear on the website that guests should plan to arrive at the parking lot in the morning so they can take their time on the hike in. In fact, the trails are all closed after dark."

Dunaway's landline started blinking with an incoming call. He glanced at it but made no move to answer it.

"One clarification," I said. "So it appears that Chris Denton reserved Condor very late on the 26th, but Colleen Denton was being held there on the morning of the 27th. Had that room been vacated by then?"

He seemed confused by the question. "The guest in Condor requested an early checkout at six AM, which is not uncommon for avid hikers. We provide water and trail snacks for those folks."

"Who requested it?"

"I assume Mr. Denton, since he made the reservation."

"Could Aria Privar have made that request after she arrived in the Condor suite?"

He thought for a moment. "If she did, I would have no way of knowing for certain."

Was that Aria Privar's play, then? An early checkout with food and supplies?

"Was the room cleaned?" I asked.

"Housekeeping was dispatched early on the 27th, but the room looked like it hadn't been used. You would have to talk to Kelly Spier for more details on that front. I don't interface with the housekeeping staff on a daily basis. Kelly is in charge of our personnel."

Reaching for his Pinnacles Grand coffee mug, Dunaway said, "Agent Harland, I trust my staff completely, especially Kelly. She inspected the rooms personally." He scribbled a number on a notepad. "Feel free to give her a call."

I pocketed the scrap of paper as the phone started ringing again. I could tell Dunaway was getting antsy with all these incoming calls. It was getting close to check-in time, after all, and he had a hotel to manage.

"One more thing," I said. "What can you tell us about who might have come and gone in the Peregrine suite on the 26th going into the 27th? Does the key card store any data?"

Dunaway's lips curled in a wry smile at the question. When his office phone lit up again, he ignored it, which confirmed that I had hit on a topic he liked.

"I'm glad you asked," he said. "One of the reasons I accepted this job was because of its emphasis on modern hotel technology. As you may or may not know, the hotel industry has been slow to adapt to changes in how its guests access rooms—which for me, honestly, has been a real sore spot. In some hotels, particularly the older 'relics' that refuse to adapt to the twenty-first century, brass keys are still the norm. Some of the investors in the Pinnacles Grand wanted to go that route, opining that real keys are 'charming' and 'classic.'" He snorted, making clear his thoughts on the matter. "As you would know, brass keys might be nostalgic, but they aren't secure. And so, the next best option has always been key or swipe cards—you equip the door with an electronic device that controls the locking mechanism. To gain entry, you use a key card equipped with either a magnetic strip or a chip."

"Isn't that what you have at this hotel?" I asked.

"Yes, but only temporarily. The Pinnacles Grand is planning to launch a hybrid app-based entry program in the spring, where guests will be able to use their cell phone to gain entry if they wish. It's extremely secure, not to mention convenient and personalized."

Hux leaned back in his chair and crossed his ankle over his knee, like he was preparing himself for a grand ol' tale.

"Now, I know what you're thinking," Dunaway went on. "That this is a national park with limited cell service, but people carry their phones no matter where they are these days. I suspect the app-based system will be the norm in just a few years, and not just in luxury hotels. I'm talking Hiltons, Motel 6s, everywhere."

"It seems like it could be a privacy issue, though," Hux said. "Not everybody goes to hotels for a family vacation, if you know what I mean."

Dunaway folded his glasses and put them down on the desk. "The app is encrypted, for one thing. And the locking mechanism on the door itself doesn't store personal identifying information; it never has. If you wanted access to the app, you'd have to get a warrant for that person's cell phone."

"But the lock must have *some* smart features," I said. "Especially if it's an integrated system."

"Yes. The lock stores information that can be communicated to hotel staff in real time about occupancy, check-in, checkout, and other needs the guest may have. Some of these features are still in their earliest stages, but we're excited about them."

"But it's not online here yet?"

He shook his head. "Unfortunately, there was some pushback from the investors. For now, we just have the key cards."

"Do they store any useful information?"

"It depends on the type. In general, a key card used by hotels does not store any identifying information as required by law. A unique code that links to the guest's account is reset after checkout. The only other piece of information on the key card is a chip technology that integrates with the lock on the door so that it opens when activated."

Hux asked, "What about time stamps?"

"The locks don't record the time. We use occupancy sensors for that—well, we will, once they're up and running."

Occupancy sensors? That could have been a real win for us. Instead, we were battling the newness of the hotel, where some things were functional but others had yet to be activated. I was losing hope that technology would be able to help us here.

Dunaway pointed at the display on his laptop. "This is the entry-exit data from the Peregrine suite. It's not much, I know." He leaned back in his chair. "I'm sorry."

Hux and I scanned the spreadsheet on the screen, which was called a room audit in hotel lingo. It had logged all activity involving Peregrine's door lock from three PM on the 26th to eleven AM on the 27th.

The first key card user in the log had engaged the lock to the Peregrine suite shortly after check-in. There were no times listed, just the user ID number next to the first entry. That same ID number had accessed the room again later on.

In the interim, though, a different user had accessed the room. "Who was this?" I asked.

"Clarisse Hammond," Dunaway said. "She's one of our house-keepers. She was on turndown service duty for that block of rooms. Her keycard logged the entry, after which the door locks automatically. When she went out again, the lock recorded it as an 'egress.' The key card wasn't used because she was already inside the room."

I pointed at the screen at the next number in the log. "This user here is Denton, I assume?"

"This was the card linked to Denton's account, yes."

I scanned the data. "It was only used twice."

He nodded. "Yes, the card was used to gain entry in both instances. He wouldn't have needed it to exit the room."

"But it looks like the door locking mechanism was engaged two more times that night, since there are a total of seven 'actions' on the lock here." I looked back at Hux. "Hmm. So what's the occupancy story there? Denton and Aria go inside, they leave for dinner. They go back in later, and Aria leaves close to midnight. That's four."

"Clarisse went in and out for turndown service," Dunaway said.

"So that's six. Someon else left the room at some point, then—the killer, perhaps?"

Dunaway shook his head. "Most likely, a room occupant opened the door for some reason—to receive room service, per-haps, or to check on a disturbance outside. It does not necessarily mean that they left the room. As you can imagine, this happens all the time."

"The room service attendant said no one ever answered the door," Hux said, more to me than to Dunaway. "It couldn't have been him."

Dunaway cleared his throat.

I leveled my gaze at him. "Yes?"

"Well, if I may, our room service attendants are instructed to go inside the room and arrange the platter to the guest's liking."

"The tray was outside the room."

"Perhaps Mr. Denton put it there when he was finished."

Hux shook his head. "It wasn't touched."

Dunaway sighed. "That isn't protocol. I should talk to our kitchen staff."

"Okay, we can come back to that," I said. "The last egress was recorded at 11:52 PM, which had to have been Aria."

Did the killer leave with her? How is it that the door was ajar seven hours later? I had hoped that the room audit would give us some answers, but for me, it just muddied the picture.

Dunaway tapped his fingers on the desk with polite gentility. "May I posit a thought?"

"Yes, please," I said.

"What if *she's* the killer? Wouldn't that make the most sense based on this audit?"

He asked a valid question. Aria was still a person of interest, of course. I just wasn't ready to commit to her as our prime suspect."

"It's certainly possible, but I just feel like we're missing something here," I said. "This data suggests that only three unique users accessed the room on the night of the murder: Clarisse and Denton himself, twice.

"That doesn't leave much room for a hit man," Hux remarked.

Hotel technology wasn't my specialty, but I could see now how much an app-based system would have helped us. This audit was like staring at a bunch of random puzzle pieces with no clear picture to make it whole.

"There's also the balcony," Hux said.

"It's forty feet off the ground," Dunaway said.

"I know it's implausible, but it's not impossible," Hux said. "Colleen Denton knew a bunch of super spies, apparently."

"I think you've got your answer right here on this audit." Dunaway pointed at the screen. "Someone who was already staying in that room killed Mr. Denton."

Dunaway was starting to sound a lot like Deputy Vee, except with a different working theory. As I tried to reconcile the audit with what we knew about both Dentons and Aria Privar, my phone chimed with a new message. I glanced down to see that Ray had texted me a link to what looked like an encrypted document. *FYI Privar*, his message read.

"Pardon me a moment," I said, both to Dunaway and to Hux.

I clicked on the link.

"Harland?" It was Hux.

I tried to answer, but the words wouldn't come. Hux's voice sounded far away, even though he was sitting right next to me.

According to Ray's background check, Aria was no stranger to law enforcement.

So much for a damsel in distress.

17

O N OUR WAY out the door, Dunaway let us know that the hotel was now fully occupied except for the Peregrine suite, which remained an active crime scene, and Condor, which he had reserved for our use. He handed me a key card.

"This is for the Condor suite," he said. "It's yours for as long as you need."

"We appreciate that," I said.

He used a Kleenex to wipe his nose. "How long do you think you'll be here?"

"A couple days, most likely. It depends on a few things."

His phone started ringing again. After a diplomatic good-bye, we parted ways—Dunaway back to his desk to run the hotel, Hux and I off to the network of hotel trails. I figured Condor was as good a place as any to stage our headquarters, so we decided to head in that direction.

As we made our way out to the lobby, I navigated to Ray's text about the unwelcome news concerning Aria Privar's criminal history, which included a charge for attempted murder in juvenile court. I logged into my inbox on my phone and saw the email from Ray with Aria's file attached to it.

"What's that?" Hux asked over my shoulder.

"A wrinkle," I said. "I'm forwarding it to you now."

Hux reached into his back pocket for his phone and navigated to his inbox. "Whoa," he said, clicking on the link. His eyes widened as he scanned the screen.

"I know."

"I thought this woman was a pediatrician."

"Well, she might not be if the accusers had pursued the charges."

"Huh," he said, still reading. "Says here she assaulted her parents, but the charges were dropped. *Yikes.*"

"It could mean anything, Hux. We don't know her side of the story." I peeked out at the lobby as we rounded a corner. The hotel's luxe interior was mostly empty, maybe on account of the lousy weather or the mid-afternoon hour. A bespectacled old man sat by the hearth reading a newspaper, but aside from him, the only person in view was a hotel staff member, sweeping the floor by the bar, which was closed, along with the restaurant.

Hux handed me his phone, where he had pulled up a file with a link to the police interviews that had occurred at the time. The first one was with Mr. Privar, Aria's father. "Check this one out," Hux said. "I just skimmed the transcript."

I took the phone and clicked on the link. The file was dated the day after the incident, a little over ten years ago now. The audio quality wasn't spectacular, but I could make out the exchange: Mr. Privar's gruff, accented voice, the detective's pointed tone. His name was Smith.

Privar: Aria confronted me in the kitchen. I was there with her mother, having a coffee.

Smith: What time was this?

Privar: Late. Around ten o'clock.

Smith: What was the confrontation about?

Privar: Her future. The pressure we put on her. It was something we argued about often. Aria was under a lot of stress at that time. We suspected she was using Ritalin to keep up with her studies, doing all she could to be valedictorian. She hardly slept. Her mother suspected she was depressed, but depression doesn't run in our family. I told her to be strong.

Smith: I see. What was different about this time?

Privar: She wanted to move to Africa, do some kind of charity work there. She wanted to put her life on hold at our expense.

Smith: And Aria's mother was there, too?

Privar: Yes. She was involved in the discussion.
Smith: So what happened with the knife?
Privar: When I told Aria that she brought shame to our
*   family, she reacted badly. She grabbed a knife from the*
*   drawer. I think it was a steak knife, but I can't be sure. It*
*   had a long blade. She held it out in a way that made me*
*   and my wife feel threatened.*
Smith: What did you do?
Privar: I told her to put it down.
Smith: Did she?
Privar: No. She came at me.
Smith: With the knife?
Privar: Yes. I told my wife to call the police while I tried to
*   get away from her.*
Smith: Were you able to get away?
Privar: I was able to get the knife away from her.
Smith: I see those cuts on your arms there. Did she do that
*   to you?*
Privar: Yes, she did. I put my arms up to defend myself.

I paused the interview and said to Hux, "Well, that part of the story checks out. Did you see the photos of his arms in the file? The defensive wounds?"

Hux nodded. "They looked genuine to me."

I navigated to a different part of the file containing the photos. There was one of Mr. Privar, dated the day after the incident took place. The photographs of his forearms told a particularly compelling story, as both arms were covered in scratches, cuts, and fresh bruises. It certainly *looked* like someone had attacked him, although none of the wounds were especially deep. At the time these photos were taken, he had already received some medical attention, since one of the lacerations had been bandaged.

Some of the other photos showed a rather large scrape on his left collarbone, but his face and neck were unharmed. I could tell from these images that he was a tall, solidly built man, with a thick neck and broad shoulders that struck an intimidating pose. The lines in his brow cut deep, complimenting the hardness in his glare. His expression wasn't neutral; it was furious.

I couldn't see how Aria ever would have stood a chance against him, even armed with a knife. She might have gotten lucky with one damaging blow, but even then, I had a hard time believing her frenzied swipes would have incapacitated a man of his size.

Were the wounds faked, then? Was the whole thing staged? And if so, why? I could feel my own biases creeping in, wanting to defend Aria Privar, even though I had never met the woman.

There were other questions to consider, too. Even though the charges had been dropped, that didn't mean Aria hadn't attacked her father in exactly the way he had described. I wondered if they had reconciled, somehow, or if Mr. Privar had, in some way, changed his story. *What was their relationship like now? Was Aria still capable of violence?* I could also picture a seventeen-year-old kid weighed down by her parents' expectations, pushed to the brink. It wasn't hard to imagine how a tense conversation could have unraveled.

Hux and I took the first door on the left to exit the lobby, where Ollie had been waiting for us. A light rain fell, casting a pall on the colorful shrubs that lined the hotel's network of trails. Hux put out some food for him.

"It just gets worse as it goes on," Hux said, going back to the file on his phone. "Aria's mother gave an account supporting her husband's testimony."

"It sounds like there were some serious tensions in the family, that much we can say for sure," I said. "But Aria was, what, seventeen at the time?"

"Yup. Almost eighteen."

"Well, that's important, because Aria would have been charged as a juvenile. Had she assaulted her father just a month later and been charged with the same crime, she probably never would have gotten into medical school. Not with a felony on her record, or even an arrest."

"So who dismissed the charges?"

"The prosecutor did, ultimately, but the file doesn't say why— at least I'm not seeing it. We'd have to do some digging to find out."

Hux scrolled to another photo. "Here's her mug shot."

I looked at the face of young Aria Privar on Hux's phone, trying to decide if this doe-eyed teenage girl was capable of aggravated assault—or, in Denton's case, murder. In some respects, her police photograph could have been one of those forgettable school portraits: the bland white background, the terrible lighting. Her long black hair was parted in the middle, and she wore a dark blue sweater that looked a little bit like a school uniform.

But it was her eyes that stood out to me—dark, wide, and haunted by an unspeakable emotion. I could see rage in those eyes, flickering behind an otherwise stoic gaze.

Was I wrong, though? Could it be that I was projecting my own biases about Aria's role in her parents' attack onto an innocent mug shot? Maybe. Though something about this chapter of Aria Privar's past wasn't sitting right with me. *What drove her to attack her father?* I wondered. *Had that same impulse come over her in the Peregrine suite?*

The rain picked up a little bit, turning the rust-colored dirt at my feet a sopping brown. I slipped my hood over my head and looked out at the tasteful rock garden that complimented the trail. A quaint little koi pond completed the aesthetic.

"Well?" Hux asked. "Does this change things for you?"

"A little," I said, suddenly feeling unsure of myself. "But it doesn't change the fact that we need to find Aria Privar to hear her side of the story."

"I think Griffiths is ready to call it. He thinks she's gone, living the life in Mexico."

"Do *you* think that?"

Hux was quiet for a moment. "I don't know."

While Ollie finished up his meal, I shivered in the rain as the wind kicked up and lashed my face. I cinched my hood around my face, not that it did much good. Out in the wilderness, it was common to see hikers braving the elements, but the hotel was a different story. The quaint little trails illuminated by tea lights were deserted.

Hux looked up at the cliffside suites in the distance. With more resources, I would have pushed for a search of the whole property, but that just wasn't going to happen.

"You feel that?" Hux asked.

"Feel what?"

"That draft—it's the cold air sinking into the canyon."

I groaned. "Am I about to get a lecture on geothermals?"

Hux laughed. "Not right now, but let's save it for later." He took a few steps down the trail, toward the pool complex. "Anyway, I'm just saying that with the way the air is flowing in this canyon, I think it's worth talking to whoever was hanging out by the pool on the 26th. We're downwind from Peregrine and Condor."

"I thought you were a math guy, not a physicist."

He looked at me out of the corner of his eye and smiled. "As you must know, Harland, there's some overlap."

"Look, I'm all for it. You lead the way."

With Ollie at his side, Hux walked down to the pool, which was a lovely cerulean blue lit by tea lights and surrounded by luxurious cabanas. It was empty, though, on account of the rain. Hux dipped his hand in the water and shook out his fingers. He seemed pleased.

"Up to your standards there, Hux?" I chided him.

"Oh, you bet," he said, smiling.

"Did you see the water slide?"

"What? Where?" He looked over both shoulders.

I laughed. "Sorry. No water slide. It's not that kind of place."

"Well, it *should* be that kind of place," he said. "Who doesn't like a good water slide? I'll take a slide over a lazy river any day."

I folded my arms over my chest and looked up at the hotel's sprawling façade as the rain tracked down its glassy windows. "I'll make note of that next time we need to book a hotel."

"Psh," he said. "Forget those plastic tubes. You ever been to Tenaya Creek?"

"No." I couldn't help but admire Hux's encyclopedic knowledge of notable natural landmarks. "Where's that?"

"Yosemite. It's a hundred-foot slide on granite—a real thrill ride. You'd love it."

"Sounds like an injury waiting to happen."

Hux muttered, "Lame."

"I'm sorry." I laughed. "Look, if we ever get assigned a case in Yosemite, we can hit up Tenaya while we're there, but don't hold your breath. Ben Sojez has been the agent there since Half Dome was formed."

Hux gave me the side-eye. "He's gotta retire at some point."

"Like I said, don't hold your breath."

As we walked past the row of cabanas, Hux and I came upon an older gentleman languishing in the hot tub. Steam rose up around him, mingling with the fog and rain. He sat with his head tilted toward the sky, the rain pouring down on his cheeks.

"Hello, sir," I said, deciding, *What the hell*. Maybe he had seen or heard something. He brought his head back down and gave me a startled look.

"Um, yes?"

"I'm Felicity Harland with the Investigative Services Branch, and this here is my partner, Hux Huxley. We were just surveying some of the hotel patrons to see if they'd heard a disturbance of any kind on the night of the 26th."

"The 26th?" He crinkled his brow. "What day is it?"

"Today is the 28th, sir. So it would have been Saturday night."

"Oh." He frowned. "Nope, don't recall. It was quiet. Every night's been quiet. That's the whole point, isn't it?"

"Yes, sir," Hux said cheerfully.

He sat up on his chair. "Is this about that fella that had a heart attack?"

"Pardon?" I asked.

"That's what I heard: a man died in his room."

For the moment, I decided to dodge the question, although I was relieved that the general public had gotten wind of a death on the property. Ray had nixed my calls to shut down the hotel for a few days, since he shared the Hollister Police Department's view that there was no threat to the public. To him, it sounded like a domestic dispute gone bad.

"We're investigating an incident that took place in one of the cliffside suites," I said. "We're just gathering information at this point."

"Ah." The man leaned back again. "Well, let me think for a minute." He paused. "Actually, well . . . ah . . ."

"What is it?"

"You were asking about Saturday night?"

"Yes, sir."

"Well, the café was open awfully late Saturday night because they had an event going on. Music, drinks—that kind of thing." He frowned. "It annoyed me, to be honest. I didn't come all the way out here looking for a party."

In some respects, this was bad news; an event at the pool would have drowned out any noise coming from Peregrine. "How late?"

"I didn't leave until midnight. It was still open then."

"What time does the café usually close?"

"Ten o'clock or so. At least, that's when it closed last night."

"I see," I said, exchanging a glance with Hux. "Thank you."

The hot-tub enthusiast went back to indulging in the steam as it dissolved into the cool, rainy mist. I couldn't help but feel a little jealous of this contented stranger, even though my hot tub time tapped out at about five minutes. After a long hike in the rain, though? Nothing better.

Hux pointed at the small café parked between two cabanas. "Should we check it out?"

"It's worth a shot," I said as Ollie darted ahead, sniffing hot dogs.

When we approached the café, a young woman popped up behind the counter and settled herself on a stool behind the register. She placed her paperback book on the counter and flipped the pages to her spot. I figured employees at the Pinnacles Grand weren't allowed to use their cell phones while at work, but that restriction appeared to be testing her resolve. She yawned.

"You can order something if you want," I said to Hux. "I know it's been a long day."

Hux brightened. "Are you sure?"

"Yup."

"What about Bodie?" Hux asked. "Have you heard from him?"

I suddenly remembered my colleague, who was probably still up in the Peregrine suite, entrenched in his part of the investigation. He had actually called a couple of times while we were out this morning, but his calls had gone straight to voicemail, failing to show up as new notifications on my phone. He hadn't tried my sat phone for some reason, but I figured he was waiting for me to let him know we were back on the property.

After all that had happened, I was eager to touch base with him about the forensic analysis, since we had some tough decisions to make about which leads to pursue while we were still here. I took my phone out and typed a quick text to Bodie.

Meet us in condor when you're free.

Barely a second after I hit "Send," I saw those three little dots blinking on the screen, indicating that he was typing a response.

Be there in a jiff.

I couldn't think of a single person in my professional orbit who used the word "jiff," but Bodie was a rare breed. In any case, I didn't have time to wrestle with Bodie's diction at the moment. Ollie was getting antsy, too.

"Okay," I said. "He's going to meet us at Condor."

"When?"

"In a jiff."

"Uh-huh," Hux said with a grunt.

The girl working the café had stopped yawning to ogle my partner, offering a wave and a smile as Hux walked up to the counter.

"Hiya," Hux said, then went on and introduced us. The girl closed her book hurriedly and stuffed it under the counter. "We're going to order some food, but we also had a couple questions for you, if you don't mind."

"I don't mind," she said pleasantly.

"Well, we're here investigating a crime that occurred at this hotel on the night of the 26th. Are you aware of what happened?"

"Um, yeah," she said, gulping. "I heard about that."

I glanced at the name badge on her shirt: "Sue Lynn." Underneath her name was what I assumed to be her hometown: Dubois, Wyoming. I had heard of the place; it was a tiny little town just outside of Yellowstone National Park. "What did you hear, Sue Lynn?" I asked her.

"Well, my friend's on the waitstaff here. He was on room service duty that night."

"What's his name?"

She pulled her sleeves down over her hands and fidgeted with them as she stared at the countertop. I could tell she was nervous. "Dave," she said.

Dave was the room attendant Hux had talked to the night before, the one who had claimed that no one in Peregrine had answered the door when he had gone up there to deliver the food.

"What did Dave tell you?"

"That, um . . ." She glanced at Hux, who tried to encourage her with a smile. I wasn't sure it was working; his size and scope made some people uncomfortable.

"It's okay," I said. "No one's in trouble."

Sue Lynn picked at her cuticles. "He said he saw the guy that was killed. He talked to him."

Hux and I exchanged a glance. "He did?"

"Yeah. He, um, rang the bell or whatever, which is what he's supposed to do when he's delivering an order, and the guy answered. He said he thanked him for the food and then went back inside."

If this was true, then the seventh "hit" on the locking mechanism was Denton, answering the door when Dave rang the bell. I wasn't sure what to make of that yet.

"And this guy . . . the victim . . . you're sure Dave actually saw him? Because he told my partner here that he didn't."

She looked at the backs of her hands and nodded.

"Well, Sue Lynn, here's the thing." I spoke in a didactic tone that I hoped reminded her of a no-nonsense high school teacher. "Dave claimed he never saw the victim, or anyone else inside the Peregrine suite. He said that when he knocked, no one opened the door for him."

"Yeah, well . . ." She finally managed to look up. "Dave got fired from his last job at a hotel for reporting workplace non-compliance. Now he's afraid to say anything at all."

I stole a glance at Hux but was unable to get a read on his reaction. I hoped he didn't blame himself for not getting the truth out of Dave. A lot of witnesses didn't cooperate.

"What time was this?" I asked Sue Lynn. "Did he tell you?"

"Yeah. It was like eleven forty five."

"Did he see anyone else inside the room?"

She shook her head. "He didn't look. You're really not supposed to do that."

Sensing her unease, I stepped aside to let Hux redirect the conversation. Our dynamic had an easy flow to it now, and he knew exactly what to do.

Hux asked, "Sue Lynn, how late is the café usually open?"

She looked up at him, relaxing a bit at the change in his tone. "Oh, um . . . it's open from noon to ten PM every day, sometimes later on weekends if there's an event."

"Was there an event last Saturday?"

She thought for a moment. "Um, yeah. That was our opening weekend, so we had a band and special drinks and stuff."

"How late was the café open?"

"Like midnight, maybe twelve fifteen."

"Were you working here by chance?"

She nodded. "Yeah, I was closing."

"Did you happen to see anything unusual? Either at the pool or up in one of the rooms?"

"My manager already asked me all those questions," she said. "I said I didn't see anything."

Hux put one hand on his hip and leaned back a bit, keeping one hand on the counter. "Did you turn all the lights off after your shift?"

"Yeah, I did."

"And what time was that?"

"Like, twelve thirty. We closed up quick."

I turned to see Ollie circling a cabana next to the pool. He was up on the cushions, sniffing around, thrusting his nose into the crevices.

"What about after the music ended?" Hux asked. "Did you hear anything?"

She shook her head. "Look, I was tired. And I was pissed, too, because somebody had loaded the freezer in here with bags of ice, so I had to bring all the ice cream and frozen stuff back to the kitchen. It sucked."

Hux and I exchanged a glance.

"What freezer?" I asked.

"The one back there." She jutted her thumb over her shoulder. "Kelly told me I could use it for the event, but it was full."

"Had you used it before?" I asked.

"Well, no. I just used the small one under the counter. Every-thing's so new; we haven't really gotten our protocols down yet . . ."

"Could I see the freezer?"

Sue Lynn lifted an eyebrow. "Um, okay. Why, though?"

Ollie trotted over to us and sat between Hux and me, his tongue lolling. Sue Lynn cocked her head at him.

"He's cute," she said.

As she leaned forward to admire him, Ollie leaped up and put his front paws on the counter. He barked once, startling Sue Lynn, who nearly fell off her stool. I gently admonished Ollie to get down, but he clearly wanted a view of the café's interior.

"I'm sorry," I said. "We'll have him wait outside while we have a look around."

She still seemed uncertain, though, so I said in a gentler tone, "We can call Mr. Dunaway or your manager if you'd feel more comfortable."

"No, no," she said. "I'll just . . . um, I'll open the door for you." She got off her stool and made her way toward the shelves in the back. Hux and I went around the exterior, past the pavilion for towels and linens, to a small service entrance. Ollie sat by the door.

While we were walking, Hux asked, "What's the deal with the freezer?"

"I don't know that there *is* a deal," I said. "But it's always a good idea to take a closer look at anything that seems out of the ordinary, especially on the night of the murder."

Sue Lynn opened the door and stepped aside to let us enter. Hux went in first, while I followed behind. It was quiet except for the soft, familiar drone of tropical music.

The interior had a pleasant, tangy smell, like fruity cocktails and crisp liquor. There wasn't a hint of decay or anything else sinister, at least not to my nose. If there was a body in the back somewhere, it wasn't lying under a bag of old chicken bones. It wasn't *in* a bag, either. I had encountered perpetrators who tried to conceal the scent of decay that way—with not just one but dozens of bags, each one stuffed inside the next one.

Ollie, who was usually content to wait, started whining as we made our way toward the back of the café. Unsurprisingly, the brand new facility was fully stocked with beverages, food items, perishables, and a large refrigerator.

Hux had propped the café door open, which made it hard to ignore Ollie's escalating whines. When I turned around to quiet him, he bolted over the threshold and ran into the café.

What's going on with you? I wondered, worried that Kelly Spier was going to show up and issue a health code violation.

Right as I was about to discipline Ollie, I saw my dog head for the corner of a deep freezer that was bolted to the floor behind one of the large shelving units. The freezer was stainless steel, not white, to match the aesthetic of the other appliances. I felt that familiar shiver roll through me just the same, though.

Ollie sat in front of the freezer and barked.

It was a hit.

On *what*, though?

Sue Lynn shifted her feet, shivering a bit thanks to the draft from outside. "Um, what's going on?" she asked.

"I'm sorry," I said, suddenly remembering her presence. "Why don't you go wait outside for a minute?"

Hux went over to the freezer, but when he tried to open it, it wouldn't budge. He looked over his shoulder at Sue Lynn. "Is the freezer usually locked?"

"No," she said. "It wasn't locked the other night."

"On Saturday?"

She nodded.

"What was inside?"

"Just, um . . . bags of ice, like I said." Her eyes darted from Hux to me. "What's going on?"

I said to a nervous Sue Lynn, "Why don't you go outside and call your manager? Maybe she can help us get it open."

"Um, okay." She grabbed her phone off the counter and hurried out the door.

The freezer had a lock on it, but it wasn't a rusted old padlock with a tiny keyhole. Instead, securing the lid to the frame was a slender electronic fixture that engaged with the locking mechanism. I couldn't see any aperture for a physical key, so I assumed the lock was activated by a card or app, just like the other doors and appliances in the hotel.

Hux got down on the ground and used his flashlight to inspect the locking mechanism. He put his key card up against it, which would have been my next move, too, but the lock chirped in protest. A tiny red bulb flashed.

Hux pulled out a pair of gloves and his Swiss Army knife—it had an array of tools on it, including a screwdriver, a wrench, and some other doodads that I basically never used—and went to work on one of the hinges. Hux was always fiddling with some random tool. At the moment, his handiness was paying off; he'd already gotten one of the hinges off.

The next few hinges came off easily, and Hux stood back, proud of his handiwork. Ollie paced the area in front of the freezer, whimpering and whining as he often did when he was relying on a human to finish a job for him.

"All right," Hux said. "Time for some muscle."

Working together, we pushed the lid off the freezer onto the floor. It landed on the linoleum with a deafening thud that made Ollie scamper backward. The tall shelves blocked much of the overhead light, but Hux and I wasted no time peering inside with our flashlights. Sue Lynn had told us to expect bags of ice, but I was prepared for something more sinister. After all, Aria Privar was still missing.

But just as Sue Lynn had said, the freezer contained dozens of bags of ice. Hux exhaled, clearly a little disappointed. We went to work removing the bags.

There was nothing at the bottom, either.

Ollie whimpered.

Something wasn't right.

The open door ushered in a constant draft of cold air. I went over to close it, flipped the light switch, too, but the recessed lighting refused to cooperate. Rain battered the roof, but that wasn't what was bothering me. It was the music. I couldn't hear anything but Bob Marley.

I finally found the sound system and shut it off. The counter had a rolling door that came down, so I closed that, too, sealing us inside.

Finally, it was quiet.

"Harland?" Hux asked.

I put my fingers to my lips.

Everything was quiet, even Ollie.

The freezer gaped open—empty, eerie. Melting ice bags littered the floor. I walked over and climbed inside. Sometimes being on the small side had its advantages.

I put my ear to the bottom of the freezer and listened.

Ollie started barking. He had heard it, too.

Something—or *someone*—was down there.

18

I CALLED BODIE, WHO came down from Peregrine and helped us move the freezer, which wasn't an easy task on account of the bolts. I knew the café had a false floor, though; I could tell by the way it reverberated ever so slightly under my feet.

At last, we freed the freezer from its infrastructure and accessed the floor beneath it. Hux had to first peel off the carpet, and then use his versatile Swiss Army knife to chip away at the paint that covered the floorboards.

When that was done, we were rewarded with a welcome sight: a latch.

Hux yanked it open using brute force—no tools needed. I held my breath, expecting the fetid scent of decay, but the secret compartment beneath the freezer smelled like damp earth and musk instead. I shined my light into the shadows that filled the space.

We saw it at the same time.

A person, curled in the fetal position. Unconscious or dead, it was hard to tell. But he looked to be a male, maybe forties or fifties, dressed in a black sweatsuit. A purplish-yellow bruise accompanied by a great deal of swelling distorted his facial features. He wasn't wearing shoes.

Hux scrambled down into the makeshift cellar. I held my flashlight overhead so he could see.

Bodie called out, "Is he alive?" The fact that he had even asked the question gave me reason to hope. Bodie, after all, was an expert in dead bodies.

"He's alive," Hux confirmed, as he crouched over the man's neck to feel for a pulse. "We've got to get a MedEvac up here—*now*."

As Hux hoisted the man over his shoulder and carried him out of the cellar, up onto the floor of the café, Sue Lynn came back inside.

"Oh my God," she shrieked, repeating the words until they lost their meaning.

* * *

Hours later, after the paramedics had arrived to take the unidentified man to the hospital, Hux and I convened in the poolside café. Bodie was doing his best to get a print or DNA evidence, whatever he could find to shed some light on the victim hidden away under a bolted-down freezer. So far, though, it wasn't looking good.

I bent down and rubbed the fur behind Ollie's ears with one hand while offering him a treat with the other. "Good job, boy," I said, which made him tilt his snout up with pride.

Hux peered down into the shadowy hole. "How long do you think he was in there?"

"Not long," I said. "The ice in the bags looked fresh—no freezer burn. I'm inclined to think the freezer was loaded up right after he went down there. It would have been a good way to deter anyone from using it."

"Or the ice was just coincidental." Hux picked up a bag, which by now was just water. "He wouldn't have lasted too long in that cellar. I didn't see any food or water down there."

I thought back to the man's black sweatsuit, which was rather odd attire for a visitor to Pinnacles National Park in October. He could have been a guest at the hotel, since there was no way to account for everyone staying on the premises. For reservations with two people, only one was required to give their name.

Then again, if he *was* a guest, why hadn't anyone reported him missing? Especially with the obvious police presence on the grounds? It seemed odd.

Hux said, "So who is he?"

I sighed. "Let's hope he wakes up so he can tell us."

"Did you notice what he was wearing?"

"Yep. The sweatsuit."

"It was more than that. We used to wear that same brand on our night ops—you know, for acquiring human targets in hostile territory."

I didn't like the sound of that. Was Cellar Man a victim—or a trained killer?

Or both?

"Wait a second," I said. "Are you thinking he's our hit man?"

"I'm just saying he's dressed for the part."

It unnerved me to think that someone with a stealth get-up wasn't even at the top of the food chain here, especially since the hotel was still open and operating. Even if this man was Chris Denton's killer, who had gotten the best of *him*?

As I reached for my phone to notify Ray of our latest discovery, a hard knock came at the door to the café. I had already put police tape there to keep out the curious passersby, but I knew by the authority of the knock that this wasn't some nosy hotel guest.

When I opened the door, Dunaway was standing under an oversized umbrella with a well-dressed associate at his side. He pinched the bridge of his nose to secure his mask, while his colleague—"Kelly Spier," it said so right there on her name badge—put hers on.

"What happened here?" Dunaway asked, though he made no move to come inside. "Kelly told me you found another victim?"

"Unfortunately, yes," I said. "We found a man in this small compartment here under the freezer."

Dunaway rubbed his temples while Kelly squeezed his arm to comfort him. They both stood with their heads bowed. "This is awful," Dunaway murmured.

"Do you know how long the freezer itself has been here?" I asked him.

"I'd have to pull up the installation records. Most of the large appliances were delivered about six weeks ago."

I saw Hux pull out his phone, adding to the growing case file. He never missed an opportunity to take notes.

"When was this café built?" I asked.

"Only about three months ago. The pool was the last part of the hotel to be completed."

"Who worked on it?"

"The same people who worked on the hotel, I imagine. I had nothing to do with its construction; I was hired only about a month ago."

I walked over to the ruined freezer—its hinges broken, its door cast haphazardly on the floor. The sight of it made Dunaway sigh; he was probably thinking about the cost to replace it. *Add it to the endless list of tasks*, I thought. I knew the feeling.

"Are you aware that this freezer had a lock on it?"

"A padlock?"

"No, an electronic lock."

"Oh." He took a tentative step inside. "Well, yes. All of our appliances are equipped with these app-based locks. It's part of our enhanced security protocols."

"So who has access to this one?" I asked.

"Technically, anyone who has a phone. The locks are brand new, but they haven't been activated yet. For that reason, the password for all the appliances on the property are the same: 7-7-7-7-7."

"Lucky number 7," Hux remarked.

"I figured it would be easy for people to remember," Dunaway explained. "I wanted our employees to get used to the app-based systems before the system goes live." He glanced at the dismantled hinges. "It looks like you broke into this one?"

"Yup," Hux said. "Sorry, but you never gave us the password."

"I most certainly did," Dunaway said, pinching the bridge of his nose again. "I gave you a file containing all of our passwords, protocols, blueprints—you name it."

I cleared my throat. "Actually, sir, you sent *me* the file. It's my oversight. I never forwarded it to my partner here, nor did I happen to see the part about the passwords." What I did recall, however, was that the pdf file Dunaway had sent me was 455 pages long, and some of the pages were handwritten. It didn't have a table of contents, either. It would have taken me hours to plow through that thing while Ollie barked himself hoarse and Sue Lynn had a panic attack. Sometimes brute force was the answer.

"We'll replace the freezer," I said. "But is there any way to know who might have accessed it since it was installed? Either using the lock or some other mechanism?"

Dunaway looked at me like I had insulted him with a stupid question, but I didn't care. My specialty was dusty trails and mountain lakes, not app-based electronic locks.

"Not unless you have access to the user's phone," he said. "That data isn't stored on the lock itself—for privacy reasons, as I mentioned. I can't even say for sure that the freezer was locked before this happened."

"It was definitely locked when we got here," I said.

"Like I said, I was not the one who signed for this appliance at this location."

"Who did sign for it?"

He glanced at the woman standing in the doorway. "Kelly can speak to that."

Kelly was a stout woman with big shoulders. She crossed her hands in front of her waist and spoke in a voice that seemed a little louder than necessary. "I interfaced with some of the construction crew," she said. "But I have no idea who put it here."

"Sue Lynn said it was open two days ago when she was working the event."

"That's certainly possible," she said.

"What about cameras?" I asked. "Do you have any in or around the pool area?"

Dunaway sighed. "They've all been installed," he said. "They were installed very early on, in fact, for insurance purposes. But they aren't live yet, either."

"They aren't working?"

"They aren't turned on."

Another dead end. On the whole, modern technology should have made my job easier, but for the most part, it only made things more complicated. These locking mechanisms and security cameras were an example of so much potential, but here we were, with nothing to show for it.

"We can talk to the construction company later," I said. "For now, we have to ask you—do you have any idea who was in that cellar?"

Hux produced a photo he had taken of the man after he had lifted him out of the hole and showed it to Dunaway and Kelly Spier.

Kelly flinched and turned away.

"No," she said. "I have never seen that man in my life."

Dunaway peered at the photo for another beat, his jaw working as he studied the man's swollen face. My hope was that he had gotten wind of a missing or disturbed employee, or maybe an intruder who was breaking into rooms.

"No," he said. "I'm sorry."

"You're sure it's not one of your employees—"

"I'm sure," he said. "I'll circulate the photo to our staff, but I don't recognize him. I'm sorry."

I decided to try a different tact. "Have any of your guests reported a theft?"

The question seemed to surprise Dunaway. "No, nothing." He grabbed a random dishtowel off one of the shelves and patted his face with it. His white dress shirt clung to his chest, matted and wet. He looked like he hadn't slept in a week. "Why?"

"I'm just trying to understand who this man is—an intruder, maybe, or an opportunist. It could be he came here to rob your guests."

"That would be difficult," Dunaway said. "Our security personnel is top-notch."

Is it, though? I wondered. One person was dead; another in dire condition. I wasn't going to make any headway on that theory, though—not now, and not with Dunaway.

Hux was scrutinizing the hinges he had broken. I noticed that the shelves were tucked in close to the freezer, leaving barely a foot of space between them. Whoever had put the man in the cellar could have moved them after the fact to discourage use of the freezer until they had time to dispose of its contents.

Bodie popped his head out of the hole. He was taking his time processing it.

"Oxygen supply is pretty good down here," he said.

I peered over the edge at him. "What do you mean?"

"It's well-ventilated. He could have survived pretty much indefinitely with food and water and some temperature control."

"Hmm," I mused aloud. It struck me as an especially cruel fate to go into a cellar like that alive, only to starve to death days or weeks later. Had the captor planned to return?

And if so, why?

I turned back to Dunaway. "You've got a serious situation on your hands here, Mr. Dunaway. At this point, I need to call in the FBI to assist, and I strongly suggest you close the hotel for at least a few days."

He kept his head bowed.

Leaving Bodie to process the scene, I said to Dunaway, "Let's go outside and talk for a bit." I shot a glance at Hux to let him know I wanted him to be a part of this conversation.

While Bodie descended into the cellar, Hux and I walked outside with Dunaway and Kelly. We sat at one of the tables outfitted with an oversized umbrella, but it did little to dampen the chill. The hotel's seductive lights glittered in the darkness.

"We should just close the hotel," Dunaway muttered. "Permanently."

"Let's not go there just yet," I said. "It's going to be a painful couple of days, yes, but people have short memories."

"Have you ever tried to run a business in the social media age, Agent Harland?"

"No, I haven't. But there is some good news—for you, at least."

He looked up.

"Because of the terrorist incident at the airport, the FBI has no agents to spare. I will say, though, that sometimes a major investigation in one place can compromise a smaller investigation elsewhere. That could end up being the case at your hotel."

"I want a thorough investigation for the safety of our guests," he said. "That is my priority."

Ray had already sent me texts letting me know that at least one agent from the San Francisco field office was on his way down to the Pinnacles Grand. A potential double homicide at a brand new national park had caught their attention.

Right then, another text from Ray lit up my phone:

Granger wants to talk to you.

Granger was an FBI special investigator who handled violent crimes. I had worked with him a couple of times, and I knew how he operated. He liked to get in, get out, and push me to the side wherever he had the opportunity. His clearance record was over 90 percent, and he liked to keep it that way.

In some respects, though, Granger's involvement in the case was good news for Dunaway. Granger hated fanfare and loathed inefficiency. He did things by the book, and he did them at record pace. I understood, too, that the situation at SFO meant he'd be even more time-strapped than usual. This was not going to be a protracted affair; if the man in the cellar woke up and told us everything he knew, Granger would take the case and arrest a killer.

But would it be the right resolution . . . or the convenient one?

19

SPECIAL AGENT ARI Granger arrived within the hour with two forensic analysts in tow. Hux, Bodie, and I got him up to speed on the case so far, which we did inside the pool café. The Peregrine suite had already been processed, cleared, and cleaned, and Granger had no interest in camping out there. He had done his own walk-through, of course, but now he wanted to focus on the evidence already collected to put the case together.

As for Cellar Man, Granger and his team were optimistic that he was going to pull through and tell them what they needed to know. Granger wanted Bodie's assistance processing the scene, but Bodie seemed reluctant to join forces with Granger's team. In the end, though, he was on their payroll, and he was anxious to move on from his medical leave.

After a brief conversation that ended with Granger pretty much telling us to take a hike, Hux and I decided to make our way up to Condor to get some room service and debrief the case.

As we climbed the stairs to the familiar bird-themed suites, I was ready for some downtime. I reached into my back pocket for my key card, which had "Pinnacles" emblazoned on the front. It made me feel like a VIP—right up until it didn't work.

"Uh-oh," Hux said, as the light flashed red with each swipe.

"Is it just me?" I handed the card to him. "You try it."

He did.

No luck.

"Maybe Dunaway forgot to activate it," Hux said.

"I'll text him."

Hux leaned over my shoulder as I typed out the text. Dunaway's reply was immediate.

My apologies. The FBI requested a new key for the room since they will be using it.

"Shocking," I deadpanned.

"But you told Granger we were working up here."

I shoved my fancy, useless key card back into my pocket. "Yeah, well, it's his way of saying we aren't welcome here anymore." I tried to muster a smile. "Get used to it, Hux. We're like the guy in that cellar: we may think we're at the top of the food chain, but we aren't."

Hux shrugged. "I'm cool with it."

"You are?"

"Yeah. I work better at home anyway."

Home. I knew he meant his cabin in Sequoia.

"We could be in Sequoia by midnight if we left now," he said. "What say you?"

Every part of me was screaming inside, *Yes, go!*, but I didn't want to put Hux in an awkward position. "We still have some people to talk to here," I said. "Maybe another time."

"Not with Granger in the neighborhood," he said. "You said it yourself."

Hux was right. Granger wasn't going to appreciate our presence here. He was a lone ranger, always had been. If he handed the case back to us, we could come back after he'd completed his part of the investigation. I also knew that for as particular as Granger could be about his procedures, he wouldn't have any problem sharing his case file with me once he got back to San Francisco. In the end, we'd probably end up working this one together in some capacity, especially if we uncovered a definitive link between Cellar Man and Chris Denton.

For now, though, I felt like a third wheel with Granger on the case. Hux's cabin in Sequoia held much more appeal than a hard patch of dirt at some lonely campsite, with a cold, hard rain seeping through the canvas. *No, thanks.*

Hux could handle those kinds of conditions without a second thought, but I didn't do as well sleeping on the ground after a long day on the trail. My back ached and my shoulder felt stiff. Ray had called a couple times, but I already knew what he was going to say: *Give the FBI some space and get back to your cold cases.* We were so short-staffed that he always liked for his agents to hand things over to the big boys when we could. I didn't feel the same way, but this wasn't the time to engage in a turf war. There came a time in every case when Hux and I could do better investigative work behind a computer.

"Well?" Hux raised an eyebrow as he waited for my answer.

"All right," I said. "Let's get some food to go."

* * *

No one was sad to see us hit the trail back to the parking lot, except maybe Bodie, but Granger refused to let him head out with us. The situation at the airport had really strained Granger's resources, not that he'd ever admit as much.

"Sucks," Bodie said as he walked me over to the trailhead. "Any chance we could grab dinner next week, maybe? I know you're busy, but . . ."

"Um, sure," I said, acutely aware of Hux standing just a few feet away from me, minding Ollie while Bodie made his awkward pitch to meet up later. The truth was, I liked Bodie—he was a little nerdy, maybe too earnest, but overall a solid guy. He didn't intimidate me like Hux sometimes did, even though I knew Hux wasn't *trying* to intimidate me. It just came with the territory. Bodie, on the other hand, reminded me of Kevin—average height, average build, no impressive military history whatsoever.

Was Bodie *boring*, though? Maybe a little. I wasn't going to fault him for that, though. My day job was exciting enough. In my life, "boring" could be an asset when it came to romance.

"Awesome," Bodie said. "I know a great spot. Just call me when you're back in town and we'll make it happen."

"Will do."

Bodie offered a half-wave, half-salute for Hux that struck me as unbearably stilted, but Hux let it ride.

"Good seeing you, man," Hux said. "Take it easy."

"You, too."

As Bodie made his way back to the café, which was drenched in the eerie glare of spotlights in the rain, Hux and I hit the trail alone. Ollie hardly noticed the bad weather as he ran up ahead. He had done his work for the day; now it was time to stretch his legs.

For me, though, all I could think about was the case and the endless number of loose ends that we had left unresolved. Aria Privar was the most significant one; she still hadn't been found. Griffiths continued to text me updates on my cell phone, but the SAR team hadn't found any trace of her. I could tell by the tone of his updates that he thought she was long gone. Even Hux felt that we should leave the search to Griffith's team for now. He sensed from the chief that our services weren't wanted, and that we'd be questioning his authority by going out on our own.

I wasn't so sure. We had several witnesses placing Aria Privar at the hotel prior to midnight on the 26th, but *someone* must have seen her after that. It was just a matter of finding that person. As for whether she was missing in the park somewhere, I wasn't the one to make that call. It was Griffiths, who had the knowledge and experience to decide if an ongoing search-and-rescue mission was warranted or not. After all, those efforts put his volunteers at risk.

"You're quiet tonight," Hux said, his voice barely carrying above the pitter-patter of the rain on the rocks. "Thinking about the case?"

I nodded. "There's a lot to think about."

"Well, let's talk about it."

"I'm not even sure where to begin," I said, a little out of breath as we made our way up a small hill. Hux was hiking at a pace that he reserved for leisurely jaunts; he must have sensed that I was dragging a little bit. At the moment, though, I couldn't bring myself to care. It had been a long day, and I decided to give myself some grace.

"Good news is, I took over a thousand photos," he said. "And we've got Bodie's analysis we're waiting on, right? Fingerprints. DNA. Plus, there's the M.E.'s report on Denton, and Cellar Man could come around and tell us what happened . . ."

"All good points." I curled my fingers around the straps on my backpack and hiked them up a bit, wincing as the weight settled on my shoulder. "It's just a lot to put together on what seemed like an open-and-shut case at the outset."

"Maybe it still *is* open and shut."

I noticed a mile marker up ahead, signaling our arrival at the Juniper Canyon Trailhead. From here, it was another two miles north back to the Chaparral Parking Lot. Hux shined his flashlight at the trail, parts of which were flooded from the day's rain.

"Which part?" I asked him.

"Let's say Cellar Man was Colleen Denton's hit man. Maybe *he* killed Chris, and *she* put him in that hole to keep him quiet."

"Then why not just kill him if she's going to go through all that trouble? I mean, even assuming she lured him into that café, which seems like a stretch, I can't figure out how she coaxed a full-grown man into an underground tomb. I'm sorry, but I don't see it."

"Maybe she had help."

"From who?" I scoffed. "Another hit man?"

Hux was quiet for a moment. "Well, she had that private investigator on her payroll, right? She'd been in communication with him right up until she made the drive out here. And, yeah, she mentioned a hit man. So that's two people with at least some knowledge of tactical weapons who were directly associated with Colleen Denton. Maybe they had a run-in that wasn't supposed to happen, and one of 'em got trigger-happy."

I cursed under my breath as my boot landed in a deep puddle. "Why, though? How?"

"No idea. These lovers' spats get complicated. Maybe Colleen was sleeping with the hit man, and the PI got jealous."

The wind picked up, blasting my face with a sheet of rain. A chill coursed through me, rattling my bones. I liked hiking in the rain during the summer months, but as soon as the weather turned cold, I tried to avoid it at all costs.

"Here's a tip for ya, Hux," I said. "Don't let things get away from you."

He laughed. "Is that what I'm doing?"

"I'm just saying that these kinds of crimes don't tend to be complicated. They tend to be simple. Think about motive: most people tend to kill for one of two things."

A smile tugged at his lips. "Love or money."

"Right. In Chris Denton's case, we have a jealous wife who openly admitted her hatred for her husband. She resented him for cheating on her and spending her hard-earned money on his new girlfriend. Colleen Denton also doesn't have an alibi, remember? No one recalled seeing her in the lobby when she said she was there, and the security cameras aren't up and running yet." I sighed heavily. "Another bad break for us."

"You hate technology," he remarked.

"I hate being disappointed by it." I adjusted the beam on my flashlight on account of the darkening skies. "Okay, back to the basics. Let's say for now that Mrs. Denton killed her husband, either by her own hand or with the help of a third party. We have decent evidence so far to support this theory, and that evidence could get even better once we get the forensics back. We also have Mrs. Denton's interview—which, I'll admit, didn't do her any favors. It wasn't a confession, but it made her sound guilty."

"Is it enough to arrest her?"

"No," I said. "Not even close. But let's move on to Cellar Man; what if this guy is completely unrelated to the Denton case?"

Hux stopped on the trail, turned, and looked at me. He towered over me, our size mismatch almost comical, but he never made me feel small or powerless. I could see, even in the driving rain on this remote mountain trail, that he viewed me as an equal.

"But you *know* they are, Harland," he said. "You're a lumper, not a splitter."

I laughed, lingering a bit on his gaze before he turned and started walking back down the trail. "That's a true statement," I admitted.

"And we know he was no random Joe wandering the hotel property. He was dressed like a goddamn special operator. He was here to kill someone."

"So you think Cellar Man killed Chris Denton?" I asked, leading him on a little bit.

"I think he was the hit man, and Colleen hired him to kill her husband. That makes her guilty by association."

"So who tried to dispose of *him*?"

"She did, with the help of her PI," he said. "Maybe he had something on her—blackmailed her, even. I can't quite figure why they didn't just kill him, but that's for Cellar Man to tell us when he wakes up."

"This is quite a complicated web of lies and betrayal, Hux," I teased him.

"Not really," he countered. "I mean, it's a little complicated, but marriage is complicated. People are complicated. But like you said, they're simple, too. Colleen was jealous . . . wealthy *and* jealous. She had the means to eliminate someone without having to do the dirty work itself."

"This is getting pretty dirty, Hux."

His lips curled up in a smile. "Yes, ma'am."

I admired Hux's conviction, but I wasn't quite on board with his theory. While I *did* think that the man in the cellar had something to do with the Denton case, it wasn't obvious to me that Colleen's hired assassin or private investigator were the missing link. One thing we could do, however, was to track down the name of her private investigator using her cell phone or email records. I was also holding out hope that we'd get our hands on Chris Denton's phone at some point.

"I just wish we didn't have to hike four-and-a-half miles to the parking lot in the rain," I said. "I really wasn't in the mood for this."

He laughed. "Don't worry, Harland," he said. "I've got some more homemade granola in my car. You'll feel like a new person."

I hoped he was right.

20

A FTER A MUCH-NEEDED change of clothes before tackling the drive back to Sequoia, I did, in fact, feel like a new person. Hux changed clothes, too—on the other side of the Hyundai, in the dark. I made a point of keeping my eyes to myself.

Hux offered to drive; he knew I didn't like driving tired. Since Josh had taken Hux's Jeep, we had no choice but to carpool.

The truth was, I missed Hux's company. The hardest part of my transition from FBI to ISB had been the isolation of the job: the long hours on the road, the uncertainty of assignments, the wilderness excursions to places that, by definition, were inhospitable to people. I wasn't sure I would have made it a year if Hux hadn't joined me on that first case in Sequoia.

That was also the last time I'd seen his cabin. His cozy abode was smack dab in the middle of the woods, a mile off a mountain road that saw hardly any traffic, even in peak season. Hux liked being out there, though. He claimed that after all his years overseas, navigating difficult personalities and hostile places in the military, he relished the solitude.

Hux had linked his phone with Hyundai's CarPlay system, and the display flashed with a new incoming call: *Josh Huxley.*

He flicked his gaze in my direction. "Okay if I answer that?"

"Of course."

He tapped the button to accept the call. "Hey, man," he said. "Everything okay?"

"Yup, all good. I decided to drive up to San Fran to see some friends." Josh's voice came through loud and clear despite the spotty service. "Are you headed home?"

"For now, yeah."

"You bringing a girl back?"

Hux tightened his grip on the steering wheel. "I'm with Harland to work on the case. She's between apartments right now and needs a place to crash. Just wanted to give you a heads-up so we don't surprise you." His lengthy explanation about our circumstances made sense to me, but I wondered how it sounded to Josh.

"Oh, yeah, don't worry about that. I'm crashing at a friend's place."

"You are?" Hux put his hands back in the ten-two position.

"Yep. The cabin's all yours."

"What friend? You don't even know anyone in San Francisco."

"It's, uh—Ginny from high school. You remember her, right? Red hair, cute smile, ran cross-country . . ."

"Nope."

"Oh, come on, Hux. You took her to prom when she was a senior and you were a freshman. You were the only guy to pull that off, as I recall."

Hux moved one hand off the wheel, clenching his fist as he reached, habitually, for the gear shift. Remembering that the Hyundai was an automatic, he put his hands back on the wheel and flexed his shoulders. "Um, yeah . . . I might remember that . . ."

Josh laughed. "Hey, come on. You always had a thing for older women."

"Okay, I'm hanging up now," Hux muttered. "Call me when you're on the road. I need my Jeep to get to work."

After he ended the call, Hux said under his breath, "He's always been a pain in my ass."

Turning my head toward the window to hide a smile, I said, "I wasn't listening."

"I'm going to choose to believe that," he said, a bit of amusement shining through in his voice. He turned and looked at me. "You're a lousy liar, Harland."

"Older women, huh?" I couldn't help myself.

"I was *then*, maybe. My high school had, like, a hundred people in it. Slim pickings."

"Now *you're* the bad liar." I knew we were verging into unfamiliar territory. I could hear it in his voice, and mine, that delicate but unmistakable note of flirtation. I could feel it in my gut, too, those tiny flutters that made me feel a little bit out of sorts.

I needed to get back on track—a *professional* track, that is. "I've got my cold case files in the backseat there," I said. "Care to take a crack at them?"

"While I'm driving?" He lifted an eyebrow. "How does that work?"

"I give you the summary of the case, the evidence, the list of suspects. You tell me who you think did it."

"This feels like a game show."

"It's not that," I said. "These cases are very much open—cold, but open. I think what helps to crack them is a fresh perspective, and nothing works better than a rapid-fire opinion on the case as it stands. I want your emotional reaction, not a logical one."

Hux shrugged. "I'm game."

"Great."

I started with the oldest case in my stack, an unsolved murder in the Colorado Rockies from 1934, and we proceeded from there. Hux was most intrigued by the missing persons cases, most of which he had already read about, and a few of which he had considered taking up on his own. He wasn't alone in that endeavor, either; there were several groups across the country that specialized in mobilizing resources to solve missing persons cases that had long since gone cold.

Hours into the drive, as darkness settled in thick and foreboding over the Sierras, I felt my eyelids getting heavy. After making little progress on eleven cases, it was starting to feel like a futile exercise. But Hux, the eternal optimist, wanted to do one more.

"You mentioned that there was a Pinnacles case," he said. "Let's tackle that one."

"That one's ice cold," I said. "It's a 'no body' case."

"Even better," he said, smiling. "I like a challenge."

I removed the thin manilla file folder labeled *Cox* from the stack; it was the thinnest of them all, only about twenty pages. Every criminal case in the FBI's storage facility had long since been digitized, but I liked to have the hard copy on hand, especially cold cases. There was something about handling the original, crinkled documents that had collected dust. They smelled old and foreboding. It motivated me, in a way.

I shined the beam of my flashlight on the first page in the file. The crime scene photos were sparse, captured by a low-rent camera the detectives had used back in 1994. I could tell from the first few that this crime had occurred in a cave, and that the "no body" label on the case probably had something to do with the fact that none of the crime scene photos had a body in them.

For a cold case, this was a bad sign. For *any* case, this was a bad sign, since it meant law enforcement had to prove that a crime had occurred without the most critical piece of evidence. In these cases, the investigation relied particularly hard on forensics; failing that, witness interviews were used to fill in the gaps. A confession could help, too, but most suspects who had gone through the trouble to dispose of a body knew better than to confess to a crime that police were already hard-pressed to prove had occurred.

In any case, no one had confessed to this particular crime, but law enforcement had called it a double homicide based on several factors. First was the significant pool of blood in the cave, which was captured in several photos. The specific location was Balconies Cave, a popular tourist destination not far from the park's west entrance. These days, at peak season, Balconies Cave saw a few dozen visitors daily. Back then, it would have been much less, in part because Pinnacles hadn't achieved national park status until recently.

"Well?" Hux said. "What's the one-liner?"

I read the top sheet, doing my best to summarize it in my mind before relaying the information to Hux. "A couple of teenage boys were exploring Balconies Cave near the west entrance of the park when they found a large pool of blood a little way off the trail. They assumed it was an animal attack until they found a small die-cast train at the scene, which was also covered in blood."

"A toy train?"

"It appeared that way," I said, my voice softening. "Two days later, the Park Service found a four-year-old boy wandering one of the trails. He identified the train as his, and from there they learned that the boy's parents were missing."

"Jesus," Hux whispered. "That's sad as hell."

I flipped through the thin pages. "The boy was too traumatized to speak in initial interviews. Weeks later, a child psychologist got him to say that the 'bad man' did it; there's an affidavit here with that interview."

"How long is it?"

"Not long. The relevant portion is highlighted; the rest is just a lot of gentle prodding by the child psychologist. She basically asks him what he remembers about the day he went to the park with Mommy and Daddy; he says the 'bad man' did it."

"Did what, though?"

"That's all he said, Hux."

Hux shook his head, releasing a slow exhale. "Poor kid."

"Ultimately, the child could not speak to the details of the presumed murder or the whereabouts of his parents, despite several attempts by police and the child psychologist. Their bodies were never found."

"The police assumed they were dead at that point?"

"They didn't 'assume,' Hux. They deduced as much by the volume of blood found in that cave." I took one of the photos out of the file as Hux turned onto the mountain road that led to his cabin. "You can have a look at this one when we get there, but suffice to say, it was a tremendous amount of blood."

"What were their names?"

"Leland and Joy Cox. They were both twenty-four years old. High school sweethearts."

"Was there any trouble in the marriage?"

I put the photos aside to get to the documents that contained all the interviews that police had conducted at the time. Instead, I found a page with one line on it that made my heart sink: *Please note that the interviews recorded in the course of this investigation were destroyed in a flood in the storage facility in December 1998.*

"The police interviews were lost," I said. "So I can't speak to that."

"They were *lost*?"

"In a flood, yes."

"Could we re-interview the witnesses?"

"It's always an option." I picked up a photo of Leland and Joy Cox standing outside their modest home. Leland was holding his infant son in his arms, while Joy stood proudly next to a "Sold" sign out on the front lawn. All three of them were smiling.

Sad, indeed, I thought, recalling my own memory of our first house, the walls bursting with the constant activity of four sisters. A new home represented hope and promise, at least at first.

"It says here that the couple had had their son while they were still in college, but at the time of her death, Joy was studying to be a nurse. Leland worked as an electrician."

"Maybe there was trouble in paradise."

"Maybe." I put the pages back in order as I worked my way through the file. "I don't think so, though. This one feels random to me."

"How so?"

"The location, mostly. The fact that this young couple was slaughtered in a cave; to me, it feels like a random act of brutality and violence. I don't think it was personal."

"Were there any suspects?"

"Not that I can see here." I closed the file. Of the twelve cases we had covered on the ride, this one felt the most unsolvable. A good number of the cold cases, in fact, had a prime suspect, or even decent forensic evidence; it just hadn't been processed by the FBI's lab yet. Forensic genetics was an emerging field, too, but it wouldn't do any good in a case like this. I couldn't even think of where to start, the file was so damn sparse.

"This feels like the coldest case ever," Hux remarked.

"Yes," I said.

"Hyperborean, even."

"Sorry?"

"My mom had a particular affinity for thesauruses."

I tried to hold back a smile. "Sounds like a rip-roaring good time."

He laughed. "It was better than Dictionary Night."

As the clock on the dash turned to 12:02, Hux made a right onto the gravel road that marked his address. At this hour, the sequoia forest was pitch-black, the darkness steeped in a fragrant dampness that marked the recent rains. Tree branches curled over the road in a menacing pose.

Up ahead, Hux's cabin came into view, welcoming us home with its white tea lights and homey red shutters. Hux parked out front and killed the engine. I opened my door and stepped out onto the gravel, which crunched underfoot. Otherwise, it was quiet.

Hux popped the trunk and grabbed both our backpacks before I could argue with him, and since it was his house, and his rules, I decided *not* to argue with him. Ollie bounded up onto the front porch like he lived here. To some extent, I supposed he did.

It was late for me, well past the time I liked to be in bed. Then again, tomorrow wasn't a trail day; we were in a holding pattern until we heard from Granger and his team. After Granger was done with his investigation, I figured we'd head back to the Pinnacles Grand and talk to a few more people before hooking back up with the Park Service in their search for Aria Privar.

Hux put on a pot of coffee while I excused myself to use the bathroom. After a quick shower and a much-needed hair-washing, I rummaged through my backpack for something casual and warm. For me, that meant a pair of leggings and an oversized FBI sweatshirt that fell past my thighs. I never backpacked with it because it just wasn't practical, but I kept it in the trunk of the rental car for chilly nights at a hotel. This wasn't that, but Hux's cabin was better than just about any hotel. Spending all day with the likes of Granger and Dunaway had put me in a tense mood, and all I really wanted to do was unwind a bit.

"You can hit the hay if you want," Hux said as I emerged from the cabin's only bedroom—the one he insisted I sleep in because he couldn't cope with me being on the couch. I really didn't *mind* the couch, but he knew I had a bad back, whereas he could sleep on the surface of the moon if he had to. It wasn't worth the argument.

"That's okay," I said. "I'm not that tired."

"Have a seat, then." He gestured to the kitchen table, which had a nice leafy plant as the centerpiece and a pair of checkered green placemats to complete the aesthetic. I sat on one of his cushioned wooden chairs. He handed me a cup of coffee.

Hux joined me at the table, and for a moment we indulged in a natural silence. I noticed he had put something on the stove to warm, and after a minute of pretty much just staring at each other, he stood up to mix it with a ladle.

"Let's go back to the old Pinnacles case for a minute," he said over his shoulder.

"Okay."

"You said this was a 'no body' case—which, I gotta say, blows my mind. All that blood in the cave, a traumatized four-year-old boy, and nobody ever found a body? That's just crazy to me. Pinnacles isn't even that big."

"It's big enough," I said. "Especially back then, when the area was more of a local attraction. At that time, a lot of the valley was overrun by feral pigs."

Hux poured out a generous helping of tomato soup into a matching pair of bowls. "Hmm," he said. "Maybe that's a clue."

"How so?"

"Pigs eat everything," he said. "I wonder if the blood was just what was left over after the pigs got to them."

I had brought the stack of case files inside, and once Hux had finished serving the soup, he went and grabbed the Cox file off the couch.

He sat back down at the table. With his coffee in hand, he opened the folder and immediately noticed the first photo in the stack. I could see the shock in his eyes, the sudden tension in his face. He tried to unload it with a lingering exhale, but the fact of the matter was the same: something unspeakable had happened in that cave, and no one had ever been held accountable for it. A killer had gone free.

In the light of Hux's kitchen, the grainy photos seemed to reveal themselves a little bit more. It was clear by the sight of the blood-drenched toy train that the boy had likely witnessed a terrible act of violence. Maybe it was a small blessing that he hadn't remembered anything.

"I don't know," Hux said as he scrutinized a photo of the entrance to the cave. "You know, looking at this, I'm not sure a pig would have ventured in there." He met my gaze across the table. "What do we know about Balconies Cave?"

"Well, it's a talus cave—you know, where the boulders fall into the canyon and create a ceiling of sorts. So it's not a true cave."

"Didn't realize you were a geologist," he said with a straight face.

"Har-har," I shot back. "It was the WiFi password that inspired some research. In any case, Balconies Cave has its share of nooks and crannies, but for the most part, you can walk from one end to the other without any special equipment. It can flood in heavy rain."

"Was it raining around the time this happened?"

"The weather wasn't mentioned in the report, but I could check."

He laced his fingers together and looked at me. "I'll wait."

Rolling my eyes, which was part of our usual shtick, I pulled up the weather archives from Pinnacles National Park on my phone. It took less than a minute. *See, sometimes technology actually works*, I reminded myself.

"It was clear the whole week before," I said. "But it rained the day the blood was discovered in the cave."

"Did they bring some canines out there, at least?"

To answer his own question, Hux reached for one of the loose pages in the file. "It says here they had a human remains detection dog on the case, but there's no follow-up on it." He put the page down. "Could we talk to the detective that worked this case?"

"We could try."

"Where is he now?"

I entered the detective's name into the FBI database and came up with a hit—on a guy who had died ten years ago.

"He's six feet under, I'm sorry to say."

"Damn."

"I'm not sure that conversation would have gone very well anyway," I said. "I feel like this case didn't get the attention it deserved."

"What happened to the boy?"

"No idea. His name was redacted from the file."

"Why?"

"Any number of reasons. I assume the family didn't want him to be contacted about this case. It's possible he was adopted. Who knows."

Hux frowned. "That's not fair to him. I, for one, would want to know what the hell happened to my parents." He studied the part of the file that contained the first and last interview with the orphaned child. "He doesn't say much."

"No."

"Just that the 'bad man' did it."

"Yup."

"Could that be his dad?"

"I can't imagine a four-year-old referring to his father as anything other than 'daddy,' can you? Young children aren't that sophisticated."

Hux dunked a piece of bread into his steaming bowl of soup and popped it into his mouth. He chewed slowly. "What if it's a trail name?"

I put my coffee down, captivated by the sudden intensity in Hux's gaze as he watched me from across the table. "What do you mean?"

"What if it's *Batman*, not 'bad man'?" He pointed to the piece of paper on the top of the file. "In this part of the interview here, he leaves out the word 'the.'"

"That could be a typographical error."

"Yeah, but it could also be intentional. There were a bunch of Batman movies that came out around then. Plus, you've got Bear Gulch Cave, with all those bats."

I tore off a piece of bread while my gaze drifted to the window. Outside, the darkness was absolute, not even a hint of starlight.

"I'm just saying it's an angle worth exploring." Hux sounded a little sheepish, like he had taken my silence as a bad sign.

"I agree with you," I said, looking back at him. "But if this kid knew his trail name, that could imply that he knew his parents' killer."

"It's not that much of a stretch if they were regulars out on those trails."

I thought for a moment. "It's a viable theory, that's for sure."

Hux exhaled, giving in to a smile. "It looks like they interviewed a few people they saw out on the trail, but I'm not seeing any names." He scanned through the pages of the file, handing them off to me so I could review them a second time, just to make sure we hadn't missed anything. "No Batman, unfortunately." He sounded deflated. "That's a bummer."

"These old-school cops weren't going to document a trail name," I said. "Hell, they didn't bother to document *any* names. But it only takes one."

"One name?"

I nodded. "If we can track down a frequent hiker from that time period, I bet we'll know pretty quickly if there was a Batman hanging around Pinnacles National Park in 1994. And if we can find *that* guy, well . . ." It was hard to resist Hux's boyishly eager expression. "You may have just broken this case, Mr. Huxley."

21

IN THE THREE days that followed, Hux and I dove into everything we had: the interviews, the photos, the timeline, and forensics. Cellar Man was recuperating at a hospital in San Jose, where he had awakened from his unconscious state but could not recall anything that had happened to him. The guy couldn't even remember his own name. The neurologist on staff there told us it might take a little while, but that he was optimistic that the man's memory would return. In the meantime, the FBI up there was working on his dental records to assist with the ID.

The next task was working things out with Granger, who seemed anxious to dump the Cellar Man case. That Thursday, five days after the Denton murder, we met in the lobby of the hotel, which was currently closed to guests at the FBI's directive. Dunaway planned to reopen for the weekend, but for now, he was working on damage control.

Bodie was in the lobby, too, his usual enthusiasm tempered by Granger's gruff presence. The seasoned federal investigator shifted his bulk in one of the lobby's oversized chairs while reading off an iPad. His team had already uploaded all the photos to the device, along with any pertinent forensic analysis. Bodie had already texted me that the pool café hadn't yielded any forensic information that could help with the investigation. The freezer had been wiped clean.

"Good news is we got into Colleen Denton's hard drive," Granger said. "Turns out she was in communication with a man named Derek Hassan. He's ex-Army, military police; for the last ten years, he's been working as a private investigator in the Bay Area."

Hux and I exchanged a glance. "Where is he now?" I asked.

"Is that a serious question?" Granger scowled. "He's in a hospital in San Jose."

"No one has confirmed that, sir. The patient can't recall his own name."

"Because he was drugged."

This was the first I had heard of any intoxication. I felt myself leaning forward. "What?"

"The prelim tox screen revealed a cocktail of drugs known to cause memory loss. We suspect that Colleen Denton drugged him before she put him in that cellar."

"And then she moved a two-hundred-pound freezer on top of the door?" Hux asked, dryly. "Was Sue Lynn her accomplice?" His unabashed sarcasm made me smile.

Granger moved his upper limbs to the armrests. "Look, this Denton lady has connections up the wazoo. She first got into contact with Hassan two years ago—said she wanted him to look into her husband, who she thought was cheating on her."

"Which he was."

"Which he was. And, you know, that's usually enough for most folks, since these PIs ain't cheap, but Mrs. Denton kept him on the payroll. Him and probably a team of guys just like him."

Hux furrowed his brow. "Why?"

"I had my team do a full-on forensic analysis of Mrs. Denton's communication with Hassan over the years. Early on, they were in touch pretty often—every couple days, that kind of thing. He sent her the photos proving the affair, yada yada." Granger cleared his throat. "But then it stopped."

"Completely?" I asked.

"Yes."

"When was this?"

"Over a year ago. If you want my opinion, it's 'cause Hassan got the feeling Mrs. Denton wanted more than an idle observer. She wanted a hit man."

"And you got that from the emails?"

"No," he said. "Not exactly. But Hassan's a pro. He's worked for some shady outfits that do this kind of thing—totally off the books. We don't even have an updated photo of the guy. In any case, what he's up to makes the CIA look like a church group. So he'd know better than to talk about a hit over email, or even by phone. I bet he got her a burner phone, fake email, the whole deal. We're never gonna find that paper trail."

Hux dropped his gaze to his hands, processing this information with the same disappointment I felt. In some ways, this new information was shaping up to be another dead end.

But at least we had a name.

"So you feel confident Hassan was acting as a hit man for Colleen Denton?" I asked Granger. "Is that your working theory?"

"Look, I didn't process the Denton scene. That was all you." He put his iPad down on the table and leveled his gaze at me. "What's *your* working theory?"

I was reluctant to say anything at the moment, especially to Granger. He wasn't an ally, at least not in my eyes.

Mercifully, Bodie interjected, "I can't use forensics to prove Hassan was in that room, sir. There were no prints or DNA to put him there."

"Of course there wasn't," Granger said. "He's a pro."

Bodie sank into his seat. "It's still useful information," I said, before turning back to Bodie. "Whose prints *did* you find?"

"Plenty. Both Dentons, Aria Privar, the housekeeper, various hotel staff . . . but they all had a reason to be in there."

"Anything from that photo on the wall?" I asked.

He shook his head. "No. That was clean."

"The bed?"

"DNA analysis is still pending there."

I sighed. "Okay, so we can't prove Hassan was in the room, but we also can't eliminate him as a suspect."

Granger said, "He's your guy, Harland. He's a professional killer, for Chrissakes. The jilted wife hired him to kill her husband, which he did."

"With a piece of glass? From a picture frame? Come on."

Granger puffed out his chin. "You want my opinion? Hassan was *so* good at this gig that he got flamboyant with it. Hell, maybe the lady wanted it done that way—messy, you know? Scare the girlfriend. Make a scene. Who the hell knows."

"We still haven't found the girlfriend."

"Well, that's your problem."

Thanks, I thought. *Anything to lighten your workload, eh?*

Hux massaged his kneecaps while Granger chugged a Styrofoam cup of black coffee and Bodie scanned through the files on his iPad. The other two members of Granger's team were essentially window dressings, since neither had said a word, but the one guy wore a perma-smirk on his face that grew every time Granger lobbed a not-so-subtle insult in my direction. The other one had no personality to speak of.

As the silence stretched on, Hux said, "So who put Hassan in that cellar, then?" He looked at Granger. "That *is* your problem, correct, sir?"

The junior agent's perma-smirk faded as Granger unfolded his legs and planted his feet on the floor. He looked a bit ruffled. "Look, I'm not gonna wait for Hassan to work through his PTSD, at which point he'll be more than happy to answer that question." He spoke with as much nonchalance as he could muster. "I'm signing this case out to you two, and you can ask him."

"You're giving the case to us?" I asked, trying to play it cool.

"The situation at the airport is highest priority right now. I don't have time to work this case. And you two, well, you've got nothing else to do except play in the woods."

That wasn't the least bit true, but I mustered my best diplomatic smile to keep tempers from flaring. "We'll take it. I was hoping for more of a neat little bow on top, but hey, you take what you can get, right?"

Granger mustered a smile of his own. "Look, you've got a black ops specialist for the Denton murder. As for Hassan, call that one accidental with accessory after the fact."

"How do you figure?"

Granger flicked a finger at one of his associates. Perma-Smirk read off his phone, "Magnetic-resonance imaging shows subdural hemorrhage secondary to occipital skull fracture." He looked up. "And his tox screen was positive for a bunch of stuff, as you know."

"I'd like a copy of those records, please," I said.

"He fell down some stairs," Granger huffed. "Call it accidental and move on; the wife had help putting him in the cellar after the fact."

"Move on?" I looked at him incredulously. "You just said someone drugged him."

"Could be, but you can't prove it, Agent Harland. You've got no witnesses, no security footage. The one thing you do have is a black ops hit man who fell down some stairs and did us all a favor. Nobody's gonna miss this guy, trust me."

Granger wanted this case off his docket, that much was clear. He was ready to hand the Denton homicide off to the prosecutor, too. This hand-off wasn't a blessing for us to work the cases on our own; it was Granger telling us to close them up quickly and move on.

I wondered if he was feeling pressure from someone else—an investor in the hotel, maybe. There was a lot at stake here, not just for the Pinnacles Grand but for the park itself, especially given the overcrowding issues at other parks in California. Pinnacles was supposed to off-load the masses flocking to Yosemite and Sequoia. The hotel, of course, was a critical part of that master plan. It could close its doors permanently if this homicide turned into a cold case.

"What about witnesses?" I asked. "Did you talk to the staff?"

"Dunaway got the whole staff together again last night and urged anyone with information to come forward. He also gave us a list of everyone who was registered as a guest on the 26th, and we contacted them all. I'd say we made about a hundred phone calls, talked to maybe fifty employees. No one saw or heard anything."

I was a little miffed that Granger hadn't told us about this employee gathering, not that I expected him to do us the courtesy. Hux and I had tried to get Dunaway to give us a guest list, which hadn't materialized either. Granger had that persuasive quality about him, I supposed. At least it would be in the file, in case Hux and I decided to track those people down ourselves.

For the most part, though, I was losing hope that we were going to uncover any useful witnesses. I knew the answer was in that file, though. It had to be. We had photos, forensic evidence, a prime suspect, and a narrative that was slowly coming together.

I just wasn't convinced we had the killer.

Yet.

"Anyway, we're done here," Granger said. "You should think carefully about what we talked about, Agent Harland." He pointed a nubby finger at me. "I've been at this a lot longer than you. When the gods smile down upon you, smile back."

I wasn't in the mood to smile back at him, so I looked over at Hux instead, as if to say, *I'm so done with this conversation.*

Hux followed my lead and stood up. "You better get going, then," he said to Granger. "I think I heard your chopper flying in."

Granger shuffled to his feet, dodging Hux's gaze to avoid engaging with an insult that he knew to be true. Granger's two assistants gathered up the iPads and random pieces of paper on the table and stuffed everything into a large duffle bag. Granger walked off with heavy strides, his hips sinking with the weight of each step. He wouldn't have fared too well on that four-and-a-half mile hike, not that he'd ever admit it to either one of us. *So be it,* I thought. *Do your job and forget the rest.*

Bodie looped his bag over his shoulder and pushed himself up from his chair. "Well, um . . ." he said, trailing off. "I'm sorry this wasn't a slam dunk forensically."

"Don't be sorry," I said. "That's just how it goes sometimes."

"The pool café was a mess," he said. "Tons of prints on various surfaces, lots of people coming and going. Like I said, the freezer itself was clean, though—so *that's* interesting."

"But the question is, how did Hassan—or whoever it was— get into the cellar? It wouldn't have been an easy lift for one person, and certainly not a woman."

Hux, who had been looking down the hallway next to the reception area, mused aloud, "What about *that?*"

I turned around. "What about what?"

We all got up and walked over to what was supposed to be a storage area for luggage, although it was empty at the moment. Among the standard luggage carts was a stainless-steel metal cart with what looked like a hydraulic foot pedal.

Bodie smiled. "That could work. Heck, it could be our missing piece."

I had never seen a piece of equipment like this, but I could guess what purpose it served. The cart was equipped with a small platform that could be elevated to a height of almost three feet from the looks of it. The hard part would be lifting the body onto the cart itself, which at its lowest setting was only six inches off the ground. Even *I* could do that. From there, it was just a matter of transporting the load to the café and dumping it into the cellar.

"Missing piece to what?" I asked Bodie, wondering what he meant by that.

"The freezer in the café had a scratch on the front of it—a tiny one, barely visible, but it was there. Probably metal on metal."

"Could we get a print off this?"

He frowned. "I bet it's been handled by a hundred people, at least," he said. "No one ever cleans these carts, especially when you're dealing with dozens of pieces of luggage every day. They're like faucet knobs or saltshakers—frequently handled, never cleaned."

Gross, I thought. He was right, though. We weren't going to get anything off the cart, but we might have found another piece of the puzzle. One sticking point for me in Cellar Man's murder was the question of how someone could have transported him to that location. Unfortunately, we weren't going to get another shot at Colleen Denton; her lawyer had made that much clear.

"So the cameras are a dead end," I said. "What about security personnel?"

"What about 'em?" Bodie asked.

"Did Granger talk to the security detail?"

"Not sure."

I listened briefly to the distant sound of a vacuum humming in the lobby. Most of the staff had vacated the premises along with the guests, but a skeleton crew was doing its best to keep the hotel in prime shape for when it reopened. "Let's go talk to him, then," I said. "He'll want to know the plan going forward anyway."

Nodding in agreement, Hux and Bodie followed me down the short hallway to Dunaway's office. I could tell Bodie wanted to firm up our dinner plans, but that would have to wait.

Hux knocked on the door. When no one answered, he knocked again.

At last, the door swung open. Dunaway coughed into his hand as he wrestled with his mask. "Yes?" He sounded equal parts flustered and congested. "I'm on an important call with the Board."

"I'm sorry," Hux asked. "We just wanted to know if we could talk to your security team."

Dunaway walked to the desk and muted the call. "I wouldn't call it a team," he said, coming back over to us. "We have two security guards on-site at all times, but the hotel doesn't employ them. They're an outside group we contract with."

"So you don't have a head of security?"

"No," he said, sighing. "It's part of my job description, among a thousand other things right now." He loosened his tie. "I'm sorry. I'm under a tremendous amount of stress with all that's going on. Agent Granger gave us the go-ahead to reopen, but we're in damage-control mode, as I'm sure you can understand."

"We do," Hux said, pleasant as ever. "Just one more question, though—what's the deal with your security cameras? Were any of them functioning on the night of the 26th?"

"It's been an ongoing issue, Mr. Huxley. I can show you my correspondence with the security company. They were supposed to have it online two weeks ago."

"Who's the company you contract with?" Hux asked.

"I'll give you their number as soon as I have a free moment." He turned to go back to his desk. "Is that all right with you, Mr. Huxley?"

"Yes, sir. Thanks."

The door closed with a soft click. Hux turned away from the door, leading us back down the hallway to the lobby. I couldn't help but think that he belonged out in the wilderness, confronting the toughest terrain that nature had to offer.

"What was that about?" I asked.

"I want to dig deeper into these security cameras," he said. "If even one of them was on . . ."

"It's a dead end," Bodie said. "Granger's team checked every camera on the property."

Hux shrugged, but I knew he wasn't about to let this go. When Hux had a plan, he stuck with it, no matter what. Bodie wasn't going to dissuade Hux with talk of Granger's team, but Bodie didn't know that. I was just glad we weren't talking about our date.

I checked my watch. It was a little after nine AM, which meant we had the better part of a day to search the hotel property again or hit the trail. Griffiths had finally called off the search, which remained a sad and frustrating loose end in our investigation, since it meant we were unlikely to find Aria Privar at this point. I knew Hux wanted to start from the beginning—trace her path from its origin, see where it led—but we didn't have time for that now.

"So what's your plan?" Bodie asked. "Are you guys calling it, too?"

Hux looked at me, waiting for my answer.

"Not quite yet," I said. "I'd like to stop by Peregrine one more time."

"What for?" Bodie asked. "We already turned the room over to the hotel; it's been cleaned, refurnished. The whole shebang. You're better off looking at the photos."

"I know," I said. "I just want to take one more look before we go."

"Then what?" Hux asked.

"Then we see if we can find Batman."

22

B ODIE WAS RIGHT; the Peregrine suite had been restored to its natural state, which meant new carpets, new paint, and a new glass frame on the wall to replace the one that had been used as a murder weapon. The painting inside was different, too. Gone was the shadow-ridden cave; in its place was a pleasant vista of the mountains surrounding Chalone Peak.

Huh, I thought, realizing in that moment that the cave photo that *used* to be on that wall reminded me a lot of the one that I had just been looking at in the Cox case: Balconies Cave.

I took out my iPad and scanned to the cold case files, suddenly curious to see if the subject of the painting from Peregrine matched the grainy crime scene photos from the Cox murders. Hux noticed that I was fumbling with my iPad and wandered over.

Bodie stayed out on the balcony, admiring the view despite the dreary weather. He once told me that after he'd processed a scene, he didn't like to go back. To him, it was like reading a book he'd already written: an unwelcome opportunity to question his own decisions.

"Look here," I said to Hux, showing him the collection of old photos from the Cox case. "This is Balconies Cave, as you know."

"Yup."

I clicked on the file from the Denton case that contained all of the photographs Hux had taken of the crime scene, starting with our first foray into the Peregrine suite. Hux had captured several close-up photos of the shattered frame and its broken glass. The painting nestled inside of it was almost an afterthought compared to the wreckage that encased it.

Now, though, I saw it in a new light. The cave that Marchand had painted was definitely a talus type, with its dusty, sepia-toned boulders and tepid light that penetrated the shadows. Beyond that, though, the boulders had no distinct markings or identifiable features. The only reason I recognized the cave itself was because the boulders were arranged in such a specific and familiar way, perched above a thin trail that sloped down to a flat patch of dirt. There was no doubt about it; the Marchand was an exact replica of the cave I had seen in crime scene photographs just days earlier.

Balconies Cave.

"Huh," Hux said, peering in for a closer look. "It's the exact same spot. No doubt about it."

"Could there be a connection to the Cox case?" I was almost afraid to ask the question since it felt like such a reach. There was always significant danger in trying to establish a link where none existed, but there was also something about the shattered painting in Denton's murder that struck me as intensely personal—and targeted.

Hux scrunched his brow. "What do we know about Marchand?"

"Nothing," I said. "I haven't had time to dig into him."

Bodie, hearing this, came back inside. "You need help?" he asked cheerfully.

"Could you run a quick search on someone for me?"

"Sure. Who you got?"

"Leon Marchand, the painter."

Bodie nodded as he slipped his bag off his shoulder and reached inside for his laptop. He put it on the desk and powered it on. Hux, meanwhile, whipped out his phone and produced an answer for me before Bodie could even get his internet browser pulled up.

"Marchand is a California native, specializes in landscapes," Hux said. He glanced over my shoulder at the side-by-side renderings of the caves. One was from the Peregrine suite, clearly painted with an expert hand, and the other was an old photo captured by a low-tech camera. But the locations were identical.

I turned to Bodie, who had sunken into a chair with his laptop. He seemed a little miffed that Hux had scooped him on the Marchand search. "There were no prints on the photograph or frame?" I asked Bodie, trying to soften the blow.

He brightened up a little bit. "*Nada*. But the glass itself was thicker than your standard art-glass variety. It almost looked pre-cut."

"Pre-cut?"

"I mean, the glass was shattered, but . . . I don't know. The pattern felt off. I just couldn't imagine why someone would precut glass in a frame . . ."

Hux, still on his phone, said, "Marchand has a website, but I'm not seeing a picture of him anywhere. Nothing on social media, either."

As Bodie and I waited for Hux to dig up information on the mysterious landscape painter, I studied the print that had replaced the one of Balconies Cave. It was clearly a Marchand, with his signature masterful colorwork infusing a twilit sky over the mountains. Sure enough, his name was there in the lower right corner. I wasn't sure what to make of the protective glass; to me, it looked like standard museum glass intended to minimize glare.

Still scrolling through his phone, Hux said, "So, bad news. According to Wikipedia, Marchand has a reputation as a secretive artist. Kind of like Banksy."

"What do you mean, 'secretive'?"

"It's part of his appeal. He doesn't do exhibits, events . . . nothing public-facing. He works with one art dealer, and she's never even given an interview."

I could see that Bodie hadn't yet given up his internet sleuthing, but I suspected it would take more than a Google search to get useful information about Marchand—which could be done, of course, but it would take time.

"We'll run his name through the system," I said. "At the very least, I'd like to talk to him."

"I'll work on it," Bodie volunteered, a little too eagerly.

"Are you sure?"

"I've got time," he said. "I want to solve this one as badly as you do."

I smiled at him. "Thanks, Bodie."

Acutely aware of the two men awaiting my direction, I looked back at the two renderings of Balconies Cave on my iPad screen. Despite the fact that thirty years had passed since the photo was taken, the subject matter hadn't changed at all. That was the incredible thing about nature; it could transform itself in an instant, or it could hold its form for millennia.

Hux stood next to me, shoulder to elbow, as it were, as we studied the images of Balconies Cave. One was grim, grainy, and sinister; the other possessed an alluring, almost mystical quality. It was incredible how the same location could evoke such different emotions. "How much do Marchand's works go for?" I asked Hux.

"*Lots*," he said as he pulled his phone back out. "Here's an article I found."

It was a recap of an art auction in Manhattan two years ago, where Marchand's largest landscapes had commanded high six figures. The paintings in Peregrine and Condor were all prints, but I wondered who had chosen them to display in the hotel. They were, admittedly, a lovely and fitting addition to the aesthetic.

Hux walked over to the window and put his hands on the sill. "Who decorates the rooms at places like this?" he asked.

"No idea," I said. "Probably an interior designer hired by the hotel."

He looked back at me. "You think Dunaway could give us a name?"

"It's worth a shot," I said. "If the painting played a role in the murder, it could really help to know who put it there. That person could probably tell us about the glass, too."

"Um, guys," Bodie interjected, "not to be a downer, but these Marchand paintings are everywhere here. They're in the lobby, the other rooms . . . even the fitness center." He typed on his laptop and swiveled the screen in our direction, which showed a little news bulletin from the NPS website highlighting artists in the park. "See here? This Marchand guy exclusively paints scenes from Pinnacles. It was the obvious choice for this hotel."

I sighed, realizing all at once that we had tumbled down a bit of a rabbit hole. Colleen Denton remained the *obvious* suspect. Our *best* suspect. Hell, she had even hired a hit man to kill her husband. I had to remind myself of that.

"Okay, let's get back to the victim," I said. "What's his connection to Marchand and Balconies Cave? *Is* there a connection? Or was the painting just collateral damage?"

Hux turned from the window to face me, a hint of mischief in his expression. I could tell he had been winding up to tell me something. "Maybe he's Batman," he said.

I held his gaze for a long moment—maybe a little too long. Even Bodie seemed to notice. He shifted in his seat.

"Denton was only forty-six," I said, breaking eye contact with Hux as I went to pull up the case file on my iPad. "That would make him sixteen at the time of the murder."

Hux wandered over to the bed and sat down. "It's still possible, though."

"Sure, but it's unlikely. Denton didn't have a criminal history, either."

"Mistaken identity, then," Hux said. "Maybe Cellar Man was Batman, and Chris Denton was just in the wrong place at the wrong time."

"I'm not buying that," I said. "This crime was too specific; it had passion behind it."

Bodie snorted, which made us both turn and look at him.

"Guys," Bodie said. "Bruce Wayne is Batman."

Hux responded with a benign scowl that made Bodie sink a little deeper into his chair. "I know that, buddy," he said. "It's a trail name."

Bodie cleared his throat. "What are you talking about, then?"

"It's a theory Hux has about the Cox case," I said. "The boy told authorities the 'bad man' did it, but Hux thinks maybe he meant 'Batman.'"

"So now we're looking for a guy in a cape?" Bodie sounded skeptical.

"It could be a trail name, like Hux said."

"What's a trail name?"

I glanced at Hux, who nodded at me, a signal for me to take this one. "Experienced hikers will sometimes use an alias while out on the trail," I said. "It's part of the culture. In a lot of circles, the trail names are so ingrained that you might never know your hiking buddy's real name. Maybe the Cox boy knew or recognized

'Batman,' but he wasn't able to describe him to detectives. They never grasped what he was trying to tell them."

"Hm." Bodie looked from me to Hux. "So, these names are just for fun?"

I nodded. "For the most part, yes."

"What's *your* trail name?" Bodie asked me, smirking.

"I don't have one."

"You should work on that. If anyone deserves one, it's you."

I smiled, blushing a little bit in spite of myself. Hux and I had talked a lot about trail names, but we had never gone so far as to bestow one on each other. "I'll give it some thought," I mumbled, aware of Hux's eyes on me.

"Okay, let's go back to the Cox case," Hux said as he got off the bed and went over to the chairs we'd arranged in a circle. He was the type that liked to think in motion. "I still think Batman is a viable lead. If we find him, or at least find out his real name, maybe it could help solve the Denton case."

Bodie cleared his throat. He was typing furiously.

"What's going on?" I asked.

"Well, I got Cellar Man's fingerprints from the hospital, and based on the prints I lifted from Peregrine, he was definitely in there at some point."

"When?"

"Hard to say." He glanced at Hux. "Sorry to debunk your Batman theory, but if Cellar Man was Mrs. Denton's hit man, well—the forensics would support that. You could argue that he went in there to kill Chris Denton, and then he slipped on the stairs getting out of there. Either that, or somebody pushed him. Aria Privar, maybe. Either way, we've got Cellar Man's prints putting him in that room."

Hux sighed. I could tell he was disappointed, but the forensics didn't lie. This was a brand new hotel, with a robust and attentive cleaning staff. Why else would Cellar Man's prints be in that room if not to execute a hired hit?

Bodie's phone buzzed in his pocket. "Oh shoot, that's Granger," he said. "I'll step out for a minute." He glanced at me on his way to the door. "Hey, Felicity, I got us a reservation by the way. Next Friday night, seven PM. A real nice Burmese place in San Francisco—you'll love it."

He grinned, but all I could manage was, "Great."

After Bodie was gone, Hux wandered over to the balcony window, which looked out over the expansive vista of mountains, sky, and bare earth. I tried to picture the volcanoes as they had existed millions of years ago, discharging their fiery violence on the mountainous terrain.

I stood next to him, resisting the urge to reach out and comfort him in some way. Our elbows touched, but that was it.

"The Cox case is still open," I said. "And Batman is still a good lead."

He turned to face me. "We don't have time to look into it, though."

"Sure we do. It's our job, Hux."

Hux allowed a small, grateful smile.

It was time to expand our search for a killer.

*   *   *

Bodie admitted that he wasn't in shape for a wilderness excursion, which meant that Hux and I were on our own. Bodie did, however, confirm our dinner date for the second time. I could tell he was excited about it, but I had mixed feelings for some reason.

"He's into you," Hux remarked as we made our way down the trail. Ollie, who had been waiting outdoors for a good long while, eagerly kept pace.

"Who?" I decided to play dumb to keep the peace. "Bodie?"

Hux shrugged. "Just thought you should know so you don't break the guy's heart."

The wind picked up, hinting at winter just around the corner. I thought briefly about changing the subject to the weather, but Hux would have called me out on such an obvious deflection. We couldn't avoid this subject forever.

"I'm just getting dinner with him, Hux," I said. "Relax."

"*Are* you seeing somebody?"

In all our time working together, Hux had never come right out and asked me such a pointed question about my personal life. It took me by surprise.

"I, well . . ." I looked at Ollie to save me, but he seemed intrigued by the question, too, almost like he thought it was overdue. He stared up at me with those wide, sensitive eyes.

"I've been on a few dates," I said. "Nothing serious."

As we crested a small ridge, I took my map out of my backpack and glanced at the route. The hotel trail was an easy and flat two-mile hike, but the Juniper Canyon Trail was more difficult. I was hoping we could make it to Balconies Cave in two hours, assuming the weather held.

Ollie was game. He had on his official NPS red harness, since dogs weren't allowed on any of the trails in Pinnacles, and I didn't want to attract the ire of conscious hikers.

"It's just that, well, Bodie doesn't seem like your type," Hux said.

I put my map away and soldiered on. "I'm not sure you know my type," I said, which Hux must have taken as a rebuke, because he tucked his head and walked on. I felt bad.

Fix it, Harland. Fix it before it gets awkward.

"Are *you* seeing someone?" I asked, which felt like the only question that I could possibly ask in that moment, since it was Hux who had taken a chance by bringing up a personal subject.

"Not really," he said.

"What's that supposed to mean? Are you back with Megan?"

He sighed. "Look, Harland, I shouldn't have asked about your dating life. It was inappropriate, and I'm sorry."

"It's okay," I mumbled.

For the next hour, we hiked in a breathless silence, tackling the trail's twists and turns as it snaked deeper into the wilderness. The sun shined bright overhead, casting its glare on the statuesque rocks that dotted the landscape. At one point, when a condor tore across the sky—a streak of black on a lofty blue—we all looked up to admire it, even Ollie.

As the last hours of morning waned, we spotted the hulking Machete Ridge looming over the trail. Glowing orange, the cliff attracted climbers state-wide, and a few of them were out there now, scaling the impressive rock. I knew we were close.

After hoofing it another quarter-mile into the canyon, we reached a footbridge where the trail diverged. Hux took out a piece of beef jerky and munched on it.

"That there to the left is the Balconies Cliffs Trail," Hux pointed out. "And to the right is the one that'll take us right through the cave."

"How far?"

"Point-four miles to get through the cave."

"Okay," I said. "Onward."

As we descended into the shadows that enveloped the trail, I felt myself being transported to that clear day in autumn 1994. It would have looked the same back then—identical, really, since these boulders had come to rest here thousands of years ago, and it could be thousands more before an earthquake or some other force unsettled them again.

The only difference was that back then, no one had seen the Cox family walk into the cave—no one except, perhaps, their killer. Had he taken this same route? Stalked them on this same trail? Felt the same hard-packed dirt under his feet, his footsteps muffled by the wind whistling through the boulders?

Today, there was no way to escape the other hikers, as the good weather had drawn them out, anxious to explore one of Pinnacles' most popular attractions. It was an easy hike, too, just a two-mile out-and-back from the parking lot at the Chaparral Trailhead.

Hux stopped at the metal gate marking the entrance to Balconies Cave.

"What's wrong?" I asked.

"Well, I'm just thinking about the plan here. I'm not sure the Pinnacles regulars are going to take the cave trail on a day like this; it's too crowded."

"What do you want to do, then?"

He pointed over his shoulder. "Go back to the footbridge."

I agreed that it made more sense to intercept hikers long before they reached the cave, so we backtracked to the bridge. Ollie whined a little, echoing my own sentiments, but it only took us ten minutes to get back to Hux's chosen spot.

By then, it was a little before noon, the sun high in the sky. For a lot of hikers, the cave would be an opportunity to rest a bit and enjoy some shade.

Hux took the lead on talking to people, while I sat down and had a quick bite. Ollie lay in the dirt beside me, content to warm himself in the sun. After I'd finished my lunch, I joined Hux on the footbridge, where we took stock of the people coming and going. For the most part, the crowd skewed younger, with hardly anyone over the age of fifty.

After an hour or so, with nothing to show for our efforts, I told Hux I wanted to change tact. "I'd like to explore the cave a bit," I said.

"Do you want me to come?"

"No, that's okay."

We agreed to meet on the other side of the cave, where the two trails converged. Despite the sun shining bright overhead, I felt a rising sense of dread heading back down into that canyon, almost like I was inhabiting Joy Cox's state of mind on that fateful day, as she ventured into a place that, unlike the rest of the park, was hidden from view. Had she picked up on a sinister force in her midst? Or was her *husband* that sinister force? It was a possibility, of course, and perhaps the most likely one based on the scant notes from the lead investigator at the time. *Possible murder-suicide*, the detective had written. *Natural scavengers consumed the remains.*

I didn't think so, though. It was the randomness and starkness of the violence in that cave that struck me in those photos, and it came over me now, as I walked the same trail that Joy Cox had ultimately died on. I felt my body shudder.

The other hikers were oblivious, of course, chatting as they made their way through the cave's natural obstacles. They didn't know that two people had died in these shadows, and that those two people had left a boy to forever wonder what had happened to his parents.

It made me sad. Angry, even. That boy deserved justice.

But had he taken it into his own hands?

I found the area of the cave that had once been a crime scene, although the blood was long gone now after thirty years of foot traffic and floods. I stood there a while anyway, though, with Ollie by my side, where we immersed ourselves in a deep and eerie silence. The *drip-drip* of errant rainwater echoed in the hollows of the cave.

After a while, we moved on, emerging on the other side of the cave where the trail made its way back up to the canyon, ending at the juncture with the Cliffs Trail. Hux was already there talking to a man in a ragged red T-shirt and dark pants. The salt-and-pepper-haired hiker wore a makeshift straw hat with a string that looped down around his chest. His hair was long and wild, his beard the color of rust. *The kind of man who has a trail name*, I thought.

I didn't approach, worried that the man might bolt if I did. After he had moved on, Hux spotted me and waved me on. Ollie took it as an invitation to bolt up the canyon, leaving me in the dust. I rubbed my sore back and made my way uphill with slow, plodding steps.

"You okay?" Hux asked.

"All good."

He nodded, leaving it there. "Well, that was Harley."

"That's his real name?"

"Harley-Davidson," he said. "Trail name. He's been known to ride in on a motorcycle."

"Huh. Does he know Batman?"

"Nope."

I let out a sigh, failing to hide my disappointment. "That's a bummer."

"Wait a minute, I'm not done," he said with a grin.

I felt a smile spread on my face. "Okay, let's hear it."

"He knows a homesteader up in the foothills that's lived there fifty years, knows pretty much every regular who's ever come through here."

"Where?"

"Not too far from here." He glanced at his watch. "I think we could be there by mid-afternoon if you're game."

"Does 'game' mean a suicidal pace?"

He laughed. "Nah. Somewhere between 'leisurely' and 'comfortable.'"

"Okay," I said. "Let's do it."

CHAPTER

23

NORTH OF BALCONIES Cave was the Old Pinnacles Trail, which looped around the northern fringes of the park before winding its way back down to the east entrance. According to Harley, the old homesteader's name was Levitt Cullen, and he lived on the West Chalone Creek a quarter-mile off the trail that passed by there. Harley didn't know specifics—he tended to avoid technology of all kinds, except his motorcycle—but he had described the location in such detail that Hux felt confident he could find it.

I didn't argue, even though my muscles were sore and the straps of my backpack were digging into my shoulders. For some reason, I still couldn't get the fit quite right. Having a child's size backpack had solved a lot of my problems, but these long treks were challenging no matter what. I tried to savor the beautiful weather, which buoyed my spirits and kept me going. Ollie's enthusiasm helped me to stay focused, too.

As the trail dipped into a pleasant grove of blue oaks, Hux pointed to the left—north, as it were, away from the heart of Pinnacles National Park, and further off the grid.

"This is the turn-off here," he said, indicating a narrow opening in the chaparral that couldn't have been more than a foot wide.

"Is that even a trail?"

He directed my attention to a crooked cottonwood tree on the other side of the trail, directly opposite the gap in the low-lying brush. "See that tree there?"

"Yep."

"That's the marker." He stepped off the main trail onto the narrow path of hard-packed dirt. "Let's go."

Because Hux was one of the best orienteers in the world, and especially so with Ollie by his side, I didn't hesitate. I wasn't sure I trusted Harley, but Hux had a good read on people, and this was our best chance at testing his theory. If Batman was a real person, it could inject new life into the Cox case. If he *wasn't*, then we could move on to other leads, other possibilities.

In my gut, though, I suspected that Hux was right, that the "bad man" was in fact an avid hiker who had traversed these trails in decades past. As we made our way down to the creek bed, I could see that the path we were on in fact hugged the creek for a good quarter-mile before suddenly disappearing.

Ollie started barking.

"We've got to cross here," Hux said. "It's up this way."

We splashed into the creek, which was running high due to the recent rains. The cold water soaked my hiking boots and socks, but I knew they would dry quickly in the sun. Once we were back on dry land, Hux picked up his pace. We climbed a steep hill, cresting a ridge that looked out over the impressive sprawl of Pinnacles' now-dormant volcanoes.

And there, nestled in a shady grove of cottonwood trees, was a small, log-cabin homestead with a slanted roof. Two rocking chairs occupied the humble front porch. The vegetation that surrounded the house was natural and overgrown, but the cabin itself had a fresh coat of paint. The California state flag out front glistened white and red.

Hux said, "What do you say? Should we just go ahead and knock?"

I nodded. "I'll put my badge on. You should do the same."

Looping our agent badges around our necks, we made our approach. A light wind rustled the high grass as we waded through it. When a shadow fell across our path, I looked up to see that a single cloud had passed in front of the sun.

We stepped up onto the porch together. Hux did the honors of knocking while Ollie sat on his haunches, still as a statue. The drapes rustled in one of the windows, which made me think we were being assessed by someone inside.

After a short wait, the door creaked open. To my surprise, a woman answered.

"Hello," she said, shifting her gaze from me to Hux. "May I help you?" Her voice was pleasant, almost delicate, which matched her appealing features that had gone soft with age. She looked about eighty, but a youthful eighty, with a slight frame and long white hair tied up in a bun. Her clothes were the practical kind, weathered but well cared for.

"Yes, hello, ma'am," I said, as I went to remove my hat. "I'm Felicity Harland, and this here is my partner, Ferdinand Huxley. We're with the Investigative Services Branch; our agency investigates crimes in national parks."

"I've heard of you," she said. "Please, come in."

Ollie stayed on the porch, but Hux and I went inside, taking stock of the homey interior that smelled faintly of leather and spice. There were thick fur rugs on the floor and checkered curtains framing the windows. Our host introduced herself as Jan Cullen, nee Comerford.

Hux and I sat on a rust-colored leather couch while she went off to make tea in the kitchen. We folded our hands and waited in silence for her to return. The cabin's intimate interior discouraged conversation that could easily be overheard.

When the woman came back, we thanked her for her hospitality and complimented her on her lovely home. She settled into an old wood chair by the hearth. Displayed on the mantle above her was a framed black-and-white photo of a young man in a military uniform.

I smiled placidly at her. "Ma'am, we're investigating a murder at the Pinnacles Grand Hotel, but we actually came here to ask you a few questions about a crime that occurred in Balconies Cave over thirty years ago now."

Her expression changed, morphing from warm curiosity into sudden pain. "Oh, yes," she said. "Leland and Joy Cox. What a terrible tragedy that was."

"You're familiar with what happened?"

"Of course. I was living here when it happened."

"Does anyone else live here, ma'am?" Hux asked.

She shook her head. "My husband died a number of years ago. It's just me now."

"I'm sorry," Hux and I said at the same time.

"Thank you," she said. "It's quiet here, but it isn't lonely. My family has owned this land for generations. We were part of the effort to make it accessible to everyone."

"You were quite successful," I said.

"Perhaps too successful, with that new hotel." She let out a rueful sigh. "I saw the NPS bulletin about the woman who went missing." She sipped her tea. "You know, I never thought the hotel was a good idea."

Hux nodded sympathetically. "Ma'am, are you familiar with any of the hikers in this area? I'm talking about the regulars—the ones who come through here often."

"Harley, you mean?"

"Is he the only one?"

"No," she said, chuckling. "But he's a character. There have been a number of them over the years, not that I ever learned their real names."

Hux put his hands inside his pockets and glanced at me out of the corner of his eye. "What about Batman?" he asked, making it sound almost like an afterthought.

She looked at him for a long moment, her pale blue eyes betraying nothing. Her brow twitched the slightest bit.

"I haven't heard that name in a long time," she said, finally.

I felt the wind go out of me, the way it tended to do when someone said something completely unexpected. Hux played it cool, too, but I could tell that he was doing his best to temper his excitement.

"But you do know him?" Hux asked.

"I *knew* him," she clarified. "This was a long time ago—decades ago, now. He was just a teenager when he came to live with us."

"He lived with you? For how long?"

"A few months." Her gaze wandered to the window, with its expansive view of the mountains in the distance. "He was a troubled boy, had no family. No home. He had been living on our land for weeks before Levitt invited him in."

"I'm sorry?" I asked, searching for clarification.

"Pardon me. Levitt was my husband."

"Ah."

"When was this?" Hux asked.

She looked down at her hands. *She doesn't want to say*, I thought. *She's hiding something.*

"A long time ago now."

"Ten years?" Hux asked. "Twenty?"

She looked up, her eyes glistening in the bright sunlight. For the first time, I could see the sadness in them. "It was 1994," she said.

24

OVER HOT TEA and biscuits, Jan Cullen told us about the boy who had come to live with her in the summer of '94. "He called himself Bruce Wayne," she said. "I never learned his real name, but then, I never learned much about him at all. When he came to live with us, it was clear to me that he was deeply troubled—on the brink of something terrible, it seemed to me. Levitt didn't think so. He thought that a few hot meals and a comfy bed would set him straight."

She put her tea down and gazed out the window. A large, elderly dog lay at her feet, its whiskers trembling as it snored through the long hours of the afternoon.

"The boy claimed he heard voices in the night—bail bondsmen coming for him, he said. I don't think he'd ever been in prison. He was only fifteen or sixteen, and he lacked the disposition of a hardened criminal." She sighed. "To this day, I don't know what was going on with him. I suspected a mental disorder of some kind, but I really don't know. He started acting erratically. There were strange behaviors." She dropped her voice to a whisper. "I became afraid."

"Is there a chance there were drugs involved?" Hux asked.

She shook her head. "I never found anything to that effect," she said. "I suppose it's possible, but back then, the other homesteaders were fiercely protective of their land. We didn't tolerate vagrants. The boy never left the property once he came to live with us. I'm not sure how he would have gotten any drugs, to be honest."

Hux leaned in with his elbows on his knees. "So what happened?"

"It was unfortunate," she said softly. "Levitt threw him out."

"Why?"

The old woman stirred her tea with a tiny silver spoon. The sound echoed in the small room. "He attacked me one night after dinner." She inhaled shakily. "He stabbed me in the arm with a knife." She glanced over at the old knives stacked on the counter, one of which, I was sure, had played a crucial role in this story.

"And your husband saved you?" Hux asked.

She frowned. "No, Mr. Huxley. Levitt wasn't home at the time. I managed to talk the boy down and kindly asked him to put the knife away."

Hux's neck reddened. "Got it."

"In hindsight, I should have called the rangers. But Levitt liked to handle such things privately, so that's what we did. He packed the boy's bags and sent him on his way." She touched the thin silver band on her finger. "I never saw him again."

I exchanged a glance with Hux, our silent signal to shift our strategy. "How long after he left did you hear about the Cox murders?"

"It was a few weeks later," she said. "I don't recall exactly. I thought about Bruce, quite honestly, but the police called it a murder-suicide."

"The case was never actually closed," I said. "It remains open as a double homicide."

Her trembling exhale filled the room. I watched her refill her teacup with shaky hands. "I didn't know that," she said.

"Do you know what happened to Bruce?"

"All I heard was that he had started using the name Batman and spent a good deal of time on the trails here. After one of the other homesteaders down by Chalone Peak chased him off his land with a shotgun, he disappeared for good."

"Did you ever try to find him?"

Another pause. "Levitt told me not to," she said. "He thought it would do more harm than good."

"But you tried anyway," Hux said gently.

She nodded. "I heard, some years later, that he had gotten his life together—that he had even started a business."

I swallowed hard.

"Do you know the name of it, by chance?"

Her blue eyes met mine. "It was a silly name," she said. "Chips & Trips."

25

"Am I vindicated?" Hux asked, his green eyes glistening in the tepid glow of dusk as we stepped off the front porch. His giddy enthusiasm brought a smile to my face.

"Just about," I said. "Assuming Chris Denton is Batman, then we may very well be able to link the two cases. The problem is, the FBI thinks his wife did it, and I can't see how she could be involved in the Cox case. For one thing, her company bio says she grew up in Switzerland."

Hux glanced at me out of the corner of his eye as he walked down toward the creek bed. "Yeah, but is that what *you* think? I mean, this case is ours, right? I don't think the wife did it."

"Why? Because you like the Batman theory better?" I wasn't trying to take Hux down a notch; I just wanted him to keep an open mind. Colleen Denton had openly expressed disgust for the victim, after all. She also had motive and opportunity. I wasn't ready to kick her to the curb as a suspect just yet—or Aria Privar, for that matter.

"Look, I hear you," Hux said. "We can't say for sure that Chris Denton is 'Batman,' or even that Batman killed Joy and Leland Cox back in 1994. But we've got a disturbed teenager living a couple miles from a crime scene, which makes me think we should at least try and track him down. I mean, we *know* Denton started that poker company."

"Yes, but it's still circumstantial," I said. "We need DNA evidence, which we don't have. The cold case file doesn't say that any blood was collected from the scene."

"Sounds like sloppy police work," Hux muttered.

"It was different then. Pinnacles wasn't even a National Park. They may have concluded they were never going to solve a 'no body' case in such a remote area, so they wrote it up as a murder-suicide and moved on—or tried to, anyway."

Hux stood at the edge of the creek, where he waited for me to catch up. The soothing sound of moving water always had a calming effect on me.

He turned and met my gaze. "Here's what I think: someone with a direct and personal connection to the Cox murders killed Chris Denton. It wasn't his wife, it wasn't Aria, and it wasn't the hit man."

"So who was it?"

Hux slipped his hands in his pockets. "I have some ideas."

"Look, I agree the connection to the Cox case is compelling," I said. "But we've still got Colleen Denton behaving badly in that hotel. Your theory throws Occam's razor out the window." I bent down and picked up a stone in the shallows of the creek. "Not to mention Cellar Man. How is *he* related to all this?"

Hux frowned at the mention of our John Doe. "Has he said anything yet?"

I shook my head. "Granger sent an agent to the hospital, but they still haven't been able to identify him. The drug cocktail really did a number on this guy; he can't recall anything."

Hux took the stone from my hand and ran his finger along its sharp edges. "I'm thinking this was a crime of vengeance, not a lover's spat. And in that case, I really think there's only one person who the killer could be."

The trees shuddered with a sudden gust of wind. I thought I saw another condor streak across the sky, but no, it was just a pack of turkey vultures. Something must have died in the wilderness, and there they were, coming home to roost.

I didn't want to utter the thought, but it had to be said.

"The Cox boy."

* * *

With dusk descending on the Central Valley, Hux and I took to
the trail with a renewed urgency. I tried to ignore the hunger roiling in my stomach, the fatigue wearing on my muscles. In some
ways, it wasn't that difficult. We had a solid lead on not just one,
but *three* unsolved murders. I wondered if Bodie had made any
progress on his end.

Unable to hold off any longer, I used my sat phone to text him
and waited for a response. When it didn't come right away, Hux
reminded me that we had to keep up the pace.

"I don't want to get stranded out here after dark," he said.
"You know how that goes."

I *did* know, all too well. In Hux's mind, hiking in darkness
through unfamiliar terrain was an unnecessary risk. He had done
it plenty of times, of course, but that didn't mean he relished the
experience. In these particular circumstances, I had to agree that
it wasn't worth taking the chance. Bodie was probably on the road
somewhere, heading back to San Jose.

The stars were out, the moon a ghastly yellow orb in a purplish
sky by the time we made it back to the Pinnacles Grand. Because
the hotel was still closed to guests, at least until the weekend, the
property was vacant: the pool devoid of swimmers, the restaurant
closed, the lobby lit by a single, lonesome table lamp.

The front doors, though, were unlocked, so we walked inside,
unsure what else to do since we had expected a little more activity.
It seemed odd, in a way, that the cleaning crews were nowhere to
be seen, especially with the hotel slated to reopen in the next day
or two. Granger had left quite a mess, especially down by the pool
area. From the lobby, I could see the café and the cabanas. Everything was still blocked off with police tape.

Hux turned to me. "Are we, um, not welcome here anymore?"

"It's starting to feel that way," I said, fending off a chill. "Where
is everyone?"

"Dunaway must still be here," Hux said. "You want to check
out his office?"

"Might as well."

We walked down the dimly lit hallway, which seemed darker
than I remembered without the daylight spilling in through the
lobby's windows. The hardwood floors creaked with our footsteps;
the only other sound was the distant hum of the air conditioner. I

thought I remembered hearing some pleasant background music when we'd first arrived here, but at the moment, there was only an eerie silence.

The door to Dunaway's office was closed, so Hux knocked with his usual authority. When a man of Hux's stature knocked, there was no ignoring it.

Seconds passed.

No answer.

My phone chirped with a new message. It was Bodie.

Leon Marchand appears to be an alias. No DoB or SSN. I got nothin.

I was disappointed, but not necessarily surprised. There would be plenty of time to investigate that aspect of the case, which could be done behind a desk. For now, though, I wanted to ask Dunaway some questions about Cellar Man. A thought had occurred to me on the hike back to the hotel that maybe the man in that hole had been Peregrine's original occupant, which could explain why his fingerprints had been found in the room. In that case, he might just be collateral damage—or something else. I texted Bodie:

Any update on Cellar Man?

No. Waiting on dental records/DNA to assist with ID.

Hux was about to knock a second time when we heard footsteps behind the door. Another painstaking few seconds passed before it creaked open.

Dunaway sighed when he saw us. He looked nothing like the polished hotelier who had greeted us days earlier. His hair was mussed, his tie askew. The copper-colored drink in his hand smelled like whiskey.

"You're back," he muttered.

"We're sorry to disturb you."

"No you're not." He turned to go back inside, but he left the door open for us to follow. Hux and I took the chairs we had occupied the first time we had talked to Dunaway in his office. Little had changed since then, except for the fact that his landline was unplugged.

Dunaway leveled his gaze at Hux and me, like he was waiting for us to speak. A fresh cup of coffee flanked Dunaway's laptop, but his mask was on, which seemed unnecessary. I waited for him to take it off so he could drink it, but he made no move to do so.

As Dunaway straightened a pile of papers and some pens, I noticed the painting mounted on the wall behind his desk, a sprawling panorama that all but reached from one corner to the other. It was stunning: a vast, whirling sky of white clouds and rosy gold sunlight that made the mountains beneath it look almost pedestrian.

I recognized the subject, too—another Pinnacles landscape, rendered in Marchand's signature style. While I had certainly come to recognize his work by now, this one in particular stood out. For one thing, it wasn't in a frame.

"Here to admire the artwork?" Dunaway asked wearily.

"Is that a Marchand?"

Dunaway straightened his shoulders. "Pardon?"

"Marchand did the paintings that were mounted on the walls in Peregrine and Condor," I said. "This one looks like one of his." I pushed myself up off my chair, gesturing to the captivating landscape on the wall behind him. "May I?"

"Go right ahead."

I walked up to it, compelled by the artist's skill in capturing nature's raw beauty at an incandescent time of day. Hux must have been confused by my sudden interest in yet another landscape painting, but something compelled me toward it. It was almost like the canvas possessed its own raw, undeniable power.

And then, it hit me.

It was an original, not a print.

An *unsigned* original.

"This is an original," I said, more to myself than to anyone else in the room.

"Pardon?"

"It's oil on canvas—an original."

"Is it now? I didn't put it there."

I backed up a step from the mammoth frame and searched the other corners—but no, there was no signature anywhere. Kevin used to dabble in the art world, and I remembered him telling me that some artists only signed their works for other people, in some cases as a marketing tool.

But if that was the case, then why wasn't this one signed? The larger-than-life sky, lit with ethereal colors that danced on the landscape, definitely fit with Marchand's style.

If that was true, though, then Dunaway had a six-figure piece of art hanging in his office. Maybe seven figures. Adding to the mystery was the fact that it was unsigned.

I began to doubt myself. After all, I was no art connoisseur. Maybe this wasn't a Marchand at all but just an impressive imitation.

Dunaway suddenly stood. "Can you excuse me a moment?" he asked. "I just received word from the kitchen staff that our head chef turned in his resignation."

"I'm sorry to hear that," I said.

"You know how it is," he said. "One domino falls, then the rest go quickly . . ." He slipped his laptop into his backpack and scooped it off the floor. It occurred to me that his backpack didn't fit his ensemble very well, but then again, some men didn't do shoulder bags.

With a curt nod at Hux, Dunaway left the room with his backpack slung over his shoulder. The door closed behind him with a quiet click.

Hux got out of his chair to have a closer look at the painting that had captivated my attention. "What's going on here, Harland?" he asked.

"What do you mean?"

"You spooked him."

I turned to face him. "Dunaway?"

"Did you see him grab his backpack? He's outta here."

"Why would he do that?"

Hux turned back to the painting. "His whole demeanor changed when you mentioned the painting. I could feel it. Something changed."

I had learned long ago never to dismiss Hux's concerns. "Should we go after him?"

Hux shifted his feet. In that moment, he seemed uncharacteristically unsure of himself. I found Dunaway's departure odd, too, but then again, he was dealing with an unprecedented disaster at his hotel. Maybe he needed his laptop to deal with whatever situation was going on in the kitchen.

Hux could read people, though; he'd been doing it in a professional capacity for years. His unease gave me pause.

"Hux, look—"

"Nah, it's probably just me." He settled his gaze on the painting while I tried to decide if it was worth pressing him a little bit. Maybe Hux was right. Maybe we should have refused to let Dunaway leave.

Before I could question my own decision-making in front of my partner, Hux said, "So, explain to me why this painting is so important."

"I didn't say it was important," I said. "I just realized sitting over there that this is an original. The ones in Peregrine and Condor were prints."

"And you think Marchand is the artist?"

"Well, that's the strange thing. It's unsigned."

"Could the signature be on the back?"

I attempted to pry the canvas off the wall with two of my fingers, but it hardly budged. "I'm not sure it's worth it. I'd hate to damage the painting. Plus, I imagine Dunaway would be annoyed."

"Why?"

"Well, I mean, this is his office."

"Yeah, but he said he didn't put it here." Hux pressed his fingers to an obscure corner of the work. Even from where I stood, I could see the thick, colorful brushstrokes rising off the canvas in waves, curls, and heaps. A work of this size and scope would have taken the artist years to complete; it was a masterpiece, really.

Hux took out his phone.

"What are you doing?" I asked.

"Googling Leon Marchand again."

"Don't bother. Bodie said it's an alias."

"I'll search the painting then. If it's one of his, the art dealer will have a record of the transaction on their website."

He typed onto his phone, scrolling through the results as fast as he could. I was way too short to look over his shoulder, so I stood by his elbow, watching him do it.

"It's not here," he said. "But the website is extremely thorough. It's got every painting he's ever done with dates, subject matter, sales records . . . the whole bit."

"So maybe it's not his."

Hux teasingly nudged my arm. "You're the art expert, Harland. You tell me."

"I'm no art expert, Hux. I just—it's hard to explain. This painting is trying to speak to me."

I thought Hux was going to rib me for sounding woo-woo, but he didn't. "Let's say it *is* an original. Why would Dunaway have a million-dollar painting in his office?"

As our eyes met, both of us debating that question in the amber glow of the desk lamp, a low-toned *beep* sounded in the distance. It wasn't quite the volume or pitch of a smoke alarm, but it did have that warning quality.

"What was that?" I wondered aloud.

As Hux went to part the shades so he could peer out the window, the lights went out. Acting fast, Hux put his phone on flashlight mode and shined it at me. We had left our backpacks in the lobby, along with our high-tech, high-powered flashlights. I had my cell phone, though, so I took it out of my pocket and turned on the flashlight. In doing so, I noticed that there was no signal; the Wi-Fi was out, too.

"This is weird," Hux remarked.

"Very weird." I walked briskly to the door. Oddly, it wouldn't budge.

Someone had locked us inside.

"The door's locked," I said.

"Not a problem," he said, nonchalant as ever. "I'll just break the window."

"But wait—is that a good idea? I'm pretty sure someone locked us in here."

Hux went over and scrutinized the lock on the door. Like all the rooms in the hotel, it was equipped with an electronic lock and a deadbolt. I remembered what Dunaway had said about a master key and made my way over to his desk to search for it.

To my dismay, all of the drawers were locked, and not with an old-school, lock-and-key mechanism, but with that same electronic keypad.

"You're right," Hux said.

"I'm right about what?"

"Somebody locked us in here, but they did it using their phone." He pointed to the lock on the door. "It flashed red right before the lights went out."

I glanced back at the painting on the wall, lit by the ghoulish glow of Hux's flashlight. The colors had changed, its shadowing more prominent. It wasn't just speaking to me anymore.

It was screaming at me.

Marchand had painted this with his own hand; I was sure of it now. The proof was in the brushstrokes, the dramatic interplay of light and shadow, the daring mix of colors. If he hadn't signed it or sold it or even displayed it for an appreciative audience, then that left only one explanation for why it was here:

James Dunaway himself had painted it.

He was the artist, the enigma: Leon Marchand.

But was he also a killer?

I tried, in those frantic moments in the darkness, to put the pieces together. First, there was the matter of motive. Leon Marchand, the painter, was obsessed with Pinnacles. One reason for that could be his parents' murder. *The Cox boy.*

Leland and Joy Cox's son would be thirty-four years old today. The man we knew as James Dunaway looked fortyish, but he could have been younger. His mask made it difficult to tell. *A mask that he wore pretty much constantly.*

Could it be?

Was *he* the sole surviving member of the Cox family?

Was this murder not about love or money, as Hux had theorized, but revenge?

As those questions raced through my mind, Hux broke into Dunaway's desk with the heel of his boot. He pulled out a plastic card—

A driver's license.

Whose photo matched that of the man in the San Jose hospital.

Cellar Man.

It was the name on the license, though, that made my stomach clench: James Dunaway.

I thought for a moment, careful to keep my emotions in check. Cellar Man's head injuries had left his face bruised and swollen. I couldn't be sure that it was him, but I strongly suspected as much. It was just a matter of time before Cellar Man himself or the wonders of forensic geneology confirmed the truth:

Cellar Man was the *real* James Dunaway.

In the eerie darkness, Hux and I stared at the unsmiling man staring back at us from a tiny piece of plastic. The real James

Dunaway was older than the grown-up Cox boy would have been: forty-two years of age, with brown hair and brown eyes. He was listed as five ten, 185 pounds. Stole-cold average in just about every way.

But the man *we* knew as James Dunaway was a little taller than that, and a little leaner. His hair was brown, styled in the same way as the man we had found in the cellar. His eyes were also brown, not that I had paid much attention to them. Overall, though, the two men had similar features. With some effort, I could see how one could be mistaken for the other.

Another fact, of course, was the mask. Dunaway had used it to his advantage, especially around his staff. It would have helped him pull off the con.

Now it made sense; our killer had been impersonating James Dunaway, the real hotel manager, since the Pinnacles Grand opened. The staff, somehow, hadn't noticed, probably in part because Dunaway—or rather, Marchand—had delegated all of his personnel-related tasks to Kelly Spier. His disguise was good—not great, but good enough.

Hux jabbed his elbow at the window and shattered the glass with a single blow. Within seconds, he had climbed out of the opening, ready to chase down a killer.

I figured he would want to take this one on by himself, but Hux jutted his hand through the broken window and grabbed mine. He hoisted me out while keeping an eye on our surroundings. The entire property was drenched in darkness, no lights on anywhere. It was as if nature had reclaimed the Pinnacles Grand Hotel, and we were at her mercy. I wasn't so worried about Mother Nature, though.

I was thinking about the Cox boy, who over the course of his troubled life had morphed into Leon Marchand, the painter—and who, at this point, seemed to have the means, motive, and opportunity to kill Christopher Denton, and to dispose of the hotel manager he had been impersonating. A double homicide thirty years in the making had inspired an elaborate murder scheme at the Pinnacles Grand Hotel. It wasn't practical or efficient, but it was personal as hell.

And sometimes that was the answer.

Why hadn't Marchand taken off after the murder, though? I wondered. *Why take the risk of waiting for a team of federal investigators to show up?*

The answer, I decided, had everything to do with the one witness we hadn't been able to find.

Aria Privar.

26

WITHOUT INTERNET, I had no way to access any incoming calls or messages on my cell phone, but my sat phone was still operational. The problem was that we'd left our backpacks in the lobby, and all the doors to the building were locked. Hux had no qualms about breaking down doors or shattering windows, but Marchand knew the hotel property far better than we did. He also had what Hux called the master key: his own cell phone.

"Everything is app-based," Hux reminded me as we hunkered down near the dumpsters. "It's all functional, too. That part about it not being up and running yet was a lie, but he didn't want anyone online until after he'd killed Denton and tidied up some loose ends."

"How about the cameras?"

Hux nodded. "My guess is he really did have to install them for insurance purposes, but he kept them offline. As the guy with the master key, he could do that."

I couldn't make out Hux's face in the darkness, but the note of frustration in his voice was unmistakable. We had let a killer slip out of our grasp, and now he was gone, lost to a wilderness that he knew better than anyone. Leon Marchand, after all, had painted every corner of Pinnacles, and he had done so with an artist's reverence.

I tilted my head toward the starry sky. The moon was but a yellow sliver, hardly any light coming from it at all. I didn't trust myself in the darkness, few people did. Marchand had taken his backpack with him, and I could only guess what was in there—a weapon, perhaps. Something to shoot us with if we came after him.

I wasn't willing to take that chance. Not now, not with every-thing that had happened in Sequoia and Gates of the Arctic and the Australian outback. The smarter play was to synthesize the evidence we had to nail Marchand later. He might not even make it out of the park. It was a four-and-a-half-mile trek to the parking lot, and from there, he had only one option: Highway 146. All we needed to ensnare him was a roadblock.

"We have to get back inside," I said. "I need my sat phone to call Vee."

"Vee? Why?"

"To set up a roadblock."

Hux nodded. "I like it."

Deciding that the threat of retaliation had passed, and that Marchand was probably prioritizing his own escape, Hux and I emerged from our hideout. Seeing that the coast was clear, we made our way back into the Pinnacles Grand hotel lobby. The doors were all locked, the windows sealed tight, so Hux resorted to what he had done before.

He broke in.

With our flashlights in hand, we grabbed our backpacks off the floor and hurried out again. There was something deeply unset-tling about a lobby without its lights on. The hotel and its sur-roundings had that creeping sense of abandonment, like the walls were closing in, or perhaps receding into nature. I could picture it a hundred years from now, vines dangling from the scratched and broken windows, dust heaped up in the corners.

For now, the future of the Pinnacles Grand was unknown, but there was no denying its ominous origin story. Assuming Leon Marchand was the orphaned Cox boy, then Denton's murder had been a lifetime project: a carefully curated attack that had taken years of planning. His obsession came through in the works he had painted, and in the violence he had inflicted on a slumbering man. To do it, he would have had to pull off a long con involving the real James Dunaway—a con that had ended not in death, but in a mysterious sort of captivity. *Had Marchand planned to free him when all was said and done? Were the two men working together?*

My sat phone alerted with an incoming call.

It was Bodie.

"Hey," I said, my voice echoing in the darkness. Hux was already on his way back out the door, which he had managed to unlock by breaking the glass. For the first time in my life, I felt like a genuine criminal.

"Hey," he said. "Are you okay? I tried your cell phone a couple times, but it's going straight to voicemail."

"We're, ah—we ran into some trouble at the hotel."

"Is everything all right?"

"Sort of. What's up?"

"Well, a couple things, actually." His voice threatened to cut out, but then came back through again. With a satellite phone, these kinds of periodic interruptions could happen. It depended on the topography of the land and the position of the satellite. With the Wi-Fi out, this was my only option.

"You still there?" he asked.

"Yep. Go ahead." Hux and I were back outside, using our flashlights to find our way onto the trail. The downside was that Marchand would be able to see us coming from a mile away, which made me uneasy. To get back to our vehicle, though, there was only one trail through the wilderness; if we didn't take it, we'd have to rely on a compass and Hux's bushwhacking skills.

"Two things," he said. "First, I did some more digging on Leon Marchand. It wasn't easy, and I stretched a couple laws, but I made it happen."

"Thank you for that," I said. "What did you find out?"

"It turns out the Cox boy was legally adopted weeks after the murder by Moira and Dean Leon. Marchand was Joy Cox's maiden name. Later in life, as he made his way in the art world, he took the name Leon Marchand."

I felt the wind go out of me. "So it's definitely him."

"Yup. Now, here's what I found out about this kid—and it's not good."

Hux was standing up ahead at the trailhead. I wanted to loop him into the conversation, but my satellite phone didn't have speaker capability, and in any case, I was worried about someone else being privy to this information.

Someone like Leon Marchand.

"Let's hear it," I said.

"Marchand ran away from home at fifteen and spent the next decade squatting in national parks in California. He was arrested a number of times for things like petty theft, vandalism—nothing major. But in his mid-twenties, the arrests stopped, right around the time he sold a painting for a good bit of money. His first."

"What was the subject?"

"So this is interesting. He's only ever painted one thing: Pinnacles. He made a name for himself, painting landscapes from all over the park."

This part of his history was already known to me, but I wanted to know how Marchand had become James Dunaway, the seasoned hotelier. It seemed like a strange course for his career to take, especially given his arrest record.

"So when did he get into hotel management?"

"Pardon?"

"Sorry," I said, realizing a little late that Bodie hadn't been there for our *a-ha* moment involving James Dunaway's driver's license. "We think Marchand has been impersonating James Dunaway to execute Denton's murder."

"How do you figure?"

"We have reason to believe that Denton was actually the man who murdered Marchand's parents in 1994."

Bodie gasped. "Are you serious?"

"It's complicated, but yes."

"Okay, but—I've got another wrinkle."

"What kind of wrinkle?"

"It's the second thing I wanted to tell you." By now, Hux had his head against my ear so that he could hear Bodie's voice as it came through the Iridium speakers. I didn't mind. He deserved to hear this information at the same moment I did.

Hux looked at me. I looked at him.

Then Bodie said, "Granger finally got something out of Cellar Man after repeated attempts to interview him."

"And?" I asked.

"No name yet, but we're working on that. What we do know is that our John Doe fell down a flight of stairs, which he thinks happened because he had taken some sleeping pills that night. In any case, he says he doesn't recall an altercation with anyone that may have precipitated the fall. No murderous intent or anything like that."

"Okay. What else?"

"Well, here's the kicker. This man actually knows Leon Marchand quite well, since they worked together during the hotel's development. The last thing he remembers is having dinner with him at the hotel restaurant the night before it opened."

A brief pause. Hux and I held our breaths.

"He said Marchand even gave him a painting to hang in his office—as a gift."

27

B EFORE I COULD ask Bodie any more details about the March-and-Dunaway connection, the call ended. My battery was running low, down to 10 percent, and I realized we might need that sliver of battery life to get us safely through the park at night.

A high-pitched scream echoed in the night: a coyote, sounded like, but it put my nerves on edge. Hux shivered in the space next to me.

"I say we go now," he said. "Marchand may be more dangerous than we thought. We have no idea what his intentions are."

"Do we really want to sneak up on him in the middle of the night, then?" I wondered aloud.

Hux wrestled a jacket over his shoulders while I zipped mine up. "What if we were wrong about Aria Privar?" he asked, a rare note of urgency in his voice. "What if he's holding her somewhere—like he was holding Dunaway?"

He had a point there. It didn't make sense that Marchand had stuck around after Denton's murder, especially if he was impersonating James Dunaway; there were just too many opportunities for the ruse to unravel. He must have known it was just a matter of time until it happened. I couldn't help but wonder if Aria Privar was the reason he had pushed his luck.

At the moment, though, we had no bead on her location, and no easy way to track her. Griffiths, an experienced park ranger, was convinced she had left the park days ago. At some point, we might have some luck with an all-points bulletin, but for now, Hux and I were on our own. Without the support of the Park Service, we faced an uphill battle.

As for finding a scent article or something else here to assist with the search, Marchand had probably taken Aria's luggage out of Condor, essentially eliminating any trace of her. In addition, he could have manipulated the room audits to cover his tracks. Why he had spared Dunaway, I didn't know, but it occurred to me that Aria might have been a witness to his murderous rampage. I couldn't imagine a scenario in which he had let her live.

Unless, of course, she had escaped. If that was the case, it could explain why Marchand had stuck around the hotel, relying on the Park Service for updates. As the hotel manager, he was privy to many of their communications, which gave him direct access to their search efforts. In recent years, the NPS had tried to keep the location of hospital transfers of rescued hikers confidential, but this type of information was relatively easy to obtain for people in the know.

I could tell by Hux's mood that he was thinking about the same scenario. He never liked giving up on a search, even weeks or months after the fact. I wanted to tell him that this wasn't on him; the park rangers had called off the search, while we were fulfilling our obligations in a murder investigation. We couldn't be in multiple places at once.

In the end, the events of the last week were moot. If Aria Privar was alive, and Marchand was waiting her out, we had to find her before he could execute the last part of his plan.

"Where do we go?" I asked Hux. "You're the expert."

"North on the hotel trail to Juniper Canyon," he said. "That's what I told Griffiths to do because I believe that's where Aria would have gone."

"But what if he's holding her somewhere, like you said?"

"Then we'll never find her," he said, his voice grim but matter-of-fact. "I'm saying we set our course based on the assumption she's hiding from him."

I nodded, relieved to see Ollie taking the lead, like he believed in the plan, too. He darted down the hotel trail while I made one last call to Deputy Vee.

"Agent Harland?" Vee sounded revved up on adrenaline. "What's the problem there?"

"I need a roadblock up on 146, west entrance."

"Oh, shit. Why?"

"We've got a killer on the move."

"Mrs. Denton's *back*?"

"No, it wasn't her. The killer is named Leon Marchand; he was impersonating Dunaway at the hotel. Long story—look, I need you to block the road ten miles south of the entrance and put out an all-points-bulletin on Dunaway's red Subaru. I've got the license plate here."

"Okay, hold up," she said. "I'll get a pen."

I tried to walk and talk, but at Hux's pace, it was a challenge to keep up. After Vee had vowed to coordinate the roadblock, I hung up. The silence made me feel safer, for some reason, even though I knew that Marchand had the advantage. Maybe he was watching us now, even.

With every step, I listened for the sound of gunshots, the whisper of footsteps on hard-packed dirt. I ignored the dull roar of pain in my lower back, the crushing weight of fatigue in my shoulders and hips. I kept pace with Hux because the situation demanded it.

This is your only chance to find her.

I knew we had reached the Juniper Canyon Trail by the glint of the trailhead sign that caught the beam of our flashlights. Hux glanced back at me as we turned onto the trail, heading north. I could see the question in his eyes: *Are you okay?*

"I'm good," I said. "Keep going."

I stumbled a few times, landed hard on my palms more than once, but Hux never faltered. We soldiered on, jogging the straightaways, taking care on the downhills to avoid injury. I tried to trust my body, even though it had failed me several times before.

When at least Hux's flashlight fell on the sign announcing the hotel parking area, I put my hands on my knees and heaved a few deep breaths to recover from our blistering pace. I also knew, as Hux did, that we had no time to rest. Every minute out there posed a risk.

There were only a couple vehicles in the parking lot, and one of them was ours. Denton's Jeep, I noticed, had already been impounded and towed away.

Hux shined his beam into the three other cars in the private hotel lot and was met with sleepy eyes and disgruntled voices in two of them. Neither license plate was registered to anyone who worked at the hotel; these were squatters, taking advantage of a secluded corner of the park.

For me, though, the real discovery was the *absence* of a red Subaru, the vehicle registered to James Dunaway. The Park Service had given us a list of all the staff vehicles and their license plates.

Marchand's getaway car was gone.

28

H UX LOOKED RELIEVED.
    "He doesn't have her," he said. "He wouldn't have driven out of here otherwise."

"Unless she was tied up in his car?"

He shook his head. "In that case, she'd be dead by now anyway."

Hux was right, especially with the scorching temperatures earlier in the week. I tried not to think about that possibility, although it was an outcome we couldn't have done anything about anyway. For now, the search for Aria was still on.

With my charger handy, I powered on my satellite phone and checked for any new messages. Vee had texted to let me know that the state police were coordinating with the Park Service and local police department to block 146 in both directions. So far, they hadn't intercepted anyone coming or going—which made sense, since it was well after dark and the park was closed.

Still, I was feeling optimistic that they were going to get him. There was only one road out of here. *Where else could he possibly go?*

Hux smelled faintly of sweat and juniper, his face ruddy with exertion. He reached for his canteen and took a healthy swig. "Did they get the roadblock up?" he asked.

"Yup. I'm just waiting for word from the team down there."

"Should we hit the trail? I say we go north—"

"Let's hold up a minute, Hux. I know you want to search for her, but what about Marchand?"

Ollie paced the small space between us. He must have sensed that our business here was unfinished and that Hux was dissatisfied with the outcome.

"You don't think the local police can handle him?"

"Do *you*?"

He swore under his breath, which told us both the answer to that question.

"So how'd he do it?" Hux mused aloud. "How the hell did a landscape artist impersonate a hotel manager so he could kill a guy?"

"Not just any guy, Hux. Chris Denton murdered his parents."

"I'm not disputing that, but it also sounds like Denton was a seriously disturbed teen. It could be he didn't even remember what happened in that cave."

"That doesn't make him innocent."

Hux nodded, but I could tell he had mixed feelings about Denton's state of mind at the time of the murder. "Well, he's dead now because Marchand silenced him," Hux said. "I'm not sure if that's justice or not. A sad case all around."

I leaned against the rear bumper of my Hyundai, comforted by its familiar contours and grateful for a chance to give my legs a break. Hux took another swig from his canteen.

"You seem conflicted," Hux said.

"I am. Marchand deserved justice for his parents' murders, and he never got it. So he took matters into his own hands."

"I thought you were against vigilante justice."

"I am, to some extent." I turned and met his gaze. "I understand why he went after Denton, even though it was wrong. This crime was intensely personal. More so, even, than a wife killing her philandering husband. He wanted it done his way. I think in some ways, he wanted *us* to know that he wanted justice done his way."

"What about the real James Dunaway, though? He didn't deserve what he got."

"He's not dead. It sounds like the fall wasn't part of the plan, but Marchand never intended to kill him. It's why he put him in that cellar—a cellar *he* had thorough knowledge of, with good airflow. Who knows, maybe it was part of some kind of deal they made—for the paintings, possibly. It was Aria Privar that put a crimp in his plans."

Hux fell silent at the mention of Aria. "And the hit man?"

"If there was one, he never made it to the hotel, just like Colleen said."

My sat phone started ringing. It was Deputy Vee.

"Eunice? Where are you?"

"Are you with Hux right now?"

"Yes, why?"

I heard her shout in the background, commanding people to put their phones down. "Sorry. We've got a big development here." She sucked in a breath. "We found the vehicle."

"Where?"

"In a ditch. Abandoned."

I rubbed my forehead while Hux drove, determined to keep my calm. "Is anyone in pursuit?"

"We don't have the resources, ma'am. Nobody here knows the terrain well enough to track down a guy on foot at this hour. We called the Park Service, SAR . . . and you guys."

"Any clue as to which direction he went?"

"No," she said. "I mean, he's got hundreds of images of Balconies Cave in his car, but I'm not sure that's a real lead."

I was in agreement there, but what else did we have? Hux's instincts had been telling him to go north, since Aria would have covered those trails on her way into the park. But what if she'd missed the turn-off toward the parking lot? The Juniper Canyon Trail intersected the Balconies Trail a mere 200 feet past the turn-off for the Chaparral Lot. Hiking at night, she easily could have missed it, at which point she might have followed the trail all the way to its destination.

Maybe Aria, disoriented in the darkness, had gone back to where it all began.

"We're going out there," I said, catching Hux's eye.

For the first time in hours, he smiled.

* * *

With our high-powered flashlights and knowledge of the terrain, our trek out to Balconies Cave felt more sure-footed than many hikes I'd done in the past, and more purposeful, too. We left our backpacks in the car and traveled light. Ollie followed at our heels.

It was only a half-mile to the cave, but long before that, Ollie started getting excited. He ran up ahead, barking into the darkness, alerting every creature to our presence. The coyotes howled back, challenging Ollie's claim over their domain. I looked up and peered at the vast night sky, speckled with starlight. The weather had cleared just in time for our final stretch.

When we reached the cave, Ollie sat on his haunches and whined. He pawed at the dirt outside the cave.

Hux crouched down beside him. "What's wrong, boy? What's going on with you?"

Ollie barked once at Hux's pocket.

"Sorry, bud. No treats today."

Ollie barked again. He was trying to tell us something, but we weren't getting the message. He got up on his hind legs and rubbed his snout on the back of Hux's pants.

"Either he's a big fan of my butt, or he wants something in my pocket," he said. "The thing is, it's empty."

"But it wasn't empty before. That's where you kept Aria Privar's driver's license."

Hux met my gaze as he coaxed Ollie to sit. I could tell that he had landed on an important realization, something that could turn this whole investigation on its head.

Aria Privar.

Could she be *here*?

29

As the hours passed, Aria lost track of day and night. At one point, it rained. The next day, the sun returned, illuminating the floor of the crevasse she had fallen into. She had no food, but the cave was damp, a natural reservoir for rain. She figured she could last a week or more.

At times, she heard voices, but she worried that it was him—that man, that lunatic, the Joker. That was what he called himself: the Joker. It was all so creepy and surreal. As the trauma receded and her memory returned, she realized that he wasn't a hit man at all.

He was Chris's mortal enemy.

Aria had gone back to Chris's room that night because she couldn't bear to be alone. She feared for his life, and hers, and she wanted to make this right. She had decided that for all her faults, Colleen Denton was still a rational human being. Maybe all they needed to do was sit down, the three of them, and talk it out.

And so, Aria, who had spent her whole life placating other people and meeting their demands, made her way back down to the Peregrine suite. It was the dead of night, the festive pool party long since over. The music had died down to an eerie silence.

The door was slightly ajar, but she figured that was just Chris being careless again. He'd leave a burner on, forget to turn the ignition off, stupid stuff like that. She couldn't recall him ever locking a door in his life. He was just, well, lazy that way.

Still, her instincts told her that hotel doors were supposed to lock automatically—weren't they? Why was this one open? She didn't even have to use her keycard to get in . . .

Then she heard noises inside—a grunt, a yell. It was Chris. She recognized his voice.

One part of her told her to run, but it was the other part—the loyal, faithful, empathic part—that took over, telling her to make sure he was okay.

And so, she peered inside, lightheaded with terror and dread. The first thing she noticed was the blood, streaks of crimson painting the walls. It was awful.

And there, on the floor, was Chris—facedown, struggling. The man on top of him wielded a blade in his gloved hand, and she screamed as he looped a tie around Chris's neck and pulled it tight. It was the same pale blue tie she'd gotten him for his birthday the year before.

As she watched a scene from her worst nightmares play out in front of her, she realized that her scream had caught the man's attention. He was wearing a mask—a grotesque, clown-like mask. Like a deranged comic book character.

Aria ran upstairs, back to the Condor suite, thinking she could hide there. She slammed the door shut and secured the deadbolt. For a while, everything was quiet. She picked at her cuticles and rocked back and forth, like a child.

Traumatized to the extent that she could barely move, Aria finally managed to pick up the phone. It was dead, no response at all. Almost like someone had programmed it that way . . .

Some time later, a knock came at the door. Aria thought about hiding in the closet but retreated to the balcony instead. She felt cornered, trapped. The vast night sky gave her hope. She couldn't take flight like a bird, but she could at least breathe in the open air . . .

Her one consolation was that the door was locked. She had checked it multiple times. These new hotels were secure, as safe as could be. Her room was safe. She was safe.

Until she wasn't.

The deadbolt slid open with a quiet click, like someone had actually programmed it to disengage. She had never seen anything like it before. How was it even possible that someone could open the deadbolt from the outside?

Did this person have a master key? *The thought was so ludicrous she almost laughed through her sobs, only to realize that she was completely outmatched.*

There was nothing she could do. Nowhere she could go.

The door creaked open. Aria stood, frozen in fear.

A man stepped into the room. It was him, Chris's killer, still wearing that terrifying mask.

Aria got off the chair. "Please don't hurt me," she begged. "I don't know you. I don't know what you want."

"Sometimes the Joker wins, you know. If he plays his cards right."

"I don't know what you're talking about, I really don't . . ."

"Of course you don't," the man said. "For most of my life, I didn't know, either. But I found him—the animal who killed my parents when I was a boy. You've been sleeping with a murderer, you know. He called himself Batman, once upon a time."

Aria shuddered as her knees threatened to give way. She knew, from her knowledge of anatomy and human physiology, that there was nothing she could do to outrun this man. The room was despairingly silent.

"I don't understand. Someone killed your parents?"

"Oh, yes. Batman. We met him out on the trail the day before. I thought he was cool, you know? A real Superhero . . . until he followed us into that cave."

Aria shuddered. "Are you going to kill me, too?" she asked him—quietly, softly. Her voice like a child's. She was guessing that it might resonate with him: this man, this demon, who had survived a childhood trauma. That was her hope, anyway.

She felt sorry for him.

Almost.

"I should," he said. "It would be the smart thing to do."

"And what then?" she asked. "Would that bring your parents back?" She couldn't fathom where her courage came from—maybe her past, maybe something else. Her own father, after all, had accused her of trying to kill him, an ugly lie that had almost ruined her life. She had recovered from that; she could recover from this.

His smile turned sad. "No."

"Then why not just let me go?"

His expression changed; his smile faded altogether. She had found the humanity inside of him, the common ground they could both stand on. *After all, she had parents, too. Watching this man unravel in front of her, she understood, finally, what she had gained from her relationship with her parents. It wasn't perfect—it wasn't even all that healthy, most of the time—but she had inherited from them her ambition, her drive, her strength.*

She was a survivor, too.

"Come over here," *he said, his voice cold. It pierced the air like a knife.*

He looked into her eyes.

Aria saw murderous intent in them, a man whose soul had been consumed by vengeance. He was never going to let her go.

Aria gripped the flashlight in her hand, one of the many "wilderness readiness" items the hotel provided. Its beam was bright and powerful, much better than the cheap plastic ones she'd grown up with in her household. It was also heavy.

Sweat bloomed under her arms and behind her neck. She could feel the prickle of goosebumps on her bare arms, her heart ramming her chest.

He came toward her—

And she hit him, hard, with the flashlight, connecting with his temple. The softest part of the skull, *she remembered.*

It was enough to stun him, to buy her time. She grabbed the flashlight and ran out onto the balcony, locking it behind her. Just below her was a ledge that she could easily jump onto without breaking a leg in the process. The hard part was getting there . . .

Somewhere behind her, she heard the balcony door splinter. She gripped the railing and pulled herself up and over. Aria had never been much of an athlete, but she wasn't afraid of heights. She dropped down to the ledge with a hard thump, *twisting her ankle as she landed. With a grunt, she slipped and slid down the rocky slope until she was hanging off a boulder with her arms outstretched, her legs dangling below. It was two o'clock in the morning, no one around to see or hear her. The path below was lit by the faintest of white lights, which was not ideal. She worried about being seen.*

She heard footsteps above, an angry grunt from whoever was up there. Her stomach clenched. What if he saw her? Would he shoot at her?

The flashlight slipped from her grasp as she let go of the eaves. Aria was tempted to leave it behind, but she nearly tripped on it as she ran toward the trees, and at the last second she bent down to pick it up. Behind her, she heard an ominous thud as someone landed on the roof she had just left, which meant she only had a few seconds head start.

It won't be enough, *she thought.*

Her heart was in her throat, her legs like putty as she ran. For all the hours she'd spent studying the sympathetic nervous system in medical school, it was only then that she understood what it felt like to be hunted by a predator in an environment that didn't suit her strengths at all. Death was imminent. She could taste it on her tongue.

As she was running, Aria almost tripped on something in the path in front of her—a dark, hairy, shapeless thing that had attracted the biggest birds she'd ever seen. Birds with bald pink heads that dripped blood when they looked up from their meal, their beady eyes reflecting the faint glow of the path's white lights. Aria stepped over the corpse, which enraged the birds as they took flight, cackling and cawing at the disturbance in the darkness. Aria used the distraction to flee off the path and into the brush, toward what she knew to be the trail to the Juniper Canyon Trailhead. She remembered seeing it earlier when they were hiking in.

She hoped that whoever was chasing her didn't know the park at all, that he wouldn't dare to venture out onto these trails in darkness. Aria didn't know the park either, but she had been on these trails once before, and that was good enough for her.

For a little while, Aria had escaped mortal danger—but then she heard footsteps again, a soft rustling in the still night air. She kept her flashlight off as she went deeper into the gulch, where the rainwaters collected in a small, mossy pond.

The air here was stale, the wind all but nonexistent. A dog with a half-decent nose would find her in a second.

Minutes passed.

Hours.

Everything was quiet.

Aria listened, but she heard nothing except the idle trickle of water, the distant chatter of nocturnal creatures.

When dawn was on the horizon, and a pair of hikers were making their way into the park's networks of trails, Aria finally extricated herself from her hiding place. She thought about going back to the hotel and calling for help, but something deep inside of her told her to stick to the original plan and hide out in the wilderness instead. She could ask these hikers if they had a phone, but what if they went back to the hotel and reported her location? Her pursuer wasn't likely to give up; he was probably canvassing the area for information. She was better off waiting for a park ranger to come along while she hid in the park's natural crevices.

Aria clenched her flashlight and scrambled over loose rock toward the trailhead. A part of her wondered if paranoia was setting in. After all, she hadn't seen the man since back at the hotel.

But she knew he was there.

She knew he was coming for her.

30

"OVER HERE!" Hux yelled.

I splashed through the puddles to where Hux and Ollie stood, the two of them peering down into a crevasse. Shining my flashlight into the gap, I saw what my partner had seen.

A woman, lying on the cave floor, not moving. Her long brown hair was matted to the rocks, her leg extended at an awkward angle. Her black cocktail dress was torn.

I called out to her.

"Aria! Aria!"

There was no response. Hux grabbed a rope and rappelled down because, well, Hux knew how to do such things. He always carried a thick rope and some bare-bones climbing equipment. His search-and-rescue training tended to come in handy at times like this.

Once he got to the bottom, he bent down by her head and felt for a pulse. My heart was in my throat as I waited for him to look up and give me the signal. I had to know if she was alive before I placed the call to search and rescue.

"She's alive!" Hux called out.

*　*　*

The MedEvac chopper arrived within the hour, but evacuating Aria Privar from the cave proved to be the real challenge. The paramedics took great care to get her secured on a spinal board since they couldn't tell if she had sustained a head or neck injury. These types of rescues took a while; the slightest wrong movement could cause paralysis or even death.

Hux and I convened with Vee and Niles Griffiths outside the cave, down near the footbridge. Even though it was almost eleven o'clock at night, the spotlights made it feel like the middle of the day in the canyon. Vee handed us two cups of coffee she had grabbed from the supplies tent.

"Nice work, you two," she said. "Do you guys ever sleep?"

"I do," I said. "Hux, not so much."

Hux smiled. "It's her fault," he said to Vee. "If she didn't work me so hard, maybe I would."

"Now that part's true," I said with a smirk.

I turned back to Vee. "What's the update on Marchand?"

"He hasn't been located," she said. "But he's out there on foot, so that limits his options."

"You're sure about that?"

"Oh, yeah. Highway 146 is the only way in or out, and we blocked it ten minutes after you called me. We've also got traffic cameras further down the road on both sides, and we haven't picked up anybody coming or going."

"He could hike out, though," I said. "The park isn't that big, and there are freeways to the east and west. All he'd need to do is coordinate a ride."

"It won't be easy in the daytime," Griffiths said. "We've got air cover coming in at dawn. Nowhere to hide."

I checked my watch. "So he's got seven hours till sunrise. That's plenty of time to hike out of here and hitch a ride."

Griffiths stared at his boots. Vee grunted.

Hux said, "He's been planning this for years. The only wild-card was Aria, and we found her before he did."

I couldn't help but think of Marchand's obsession with Balconies Cave, the photos and sketches he'd abandoned in his car. Perhaps Aria's rescue was the universe's way of telling us that some tragedies come full circle.

"You aren't worried about tracking him down?" Vee asked Hux, who, almost as a rule, never worried about tracking anyone down.

"Nope," he said.

"Why not?"

"Because his whole life is tied to this land," he said. "His family, his past, his work. He won't be able to leave it behind." Hux spoke like he had personal experience with the subject—which he did, as I knew from where he had chosen to live after his time in the military. Sequoia wasn't just an escape for him; it was home.

"So we wait for him to come back?" I asked, a little skeptical. "You're sure you don't want to do your Hux-signature and hunt him down?"

Hux shook his head. "Not this time. We just have to be ready for him when he comes home."

31

H UX WAS WRONG about Leon Marchand, as it turned out. The famed oil painter never returned to Pinnacles National Park.

He remained at large.

The real James Dunaway made a full recovery, and in two months' time, he took up his old post at the Pinnacles Grand, determined to revitalize the hotel's reputation and reinvigorate the staff. We spoke on the phone about his relationship with Leon Marchand.

"I don't think he ever intended to kill me," Dunaway said. "I had actually shown him the cellar weeks before when I was giving him a tour of the pool complex and the café. He was planning to do an elaborate tile project for the pool."

The cellar, he said, was actually part of the hotel's emergency response plan in case of an active shooter or other disaster. He couldn't remember how he had ended up inside, but he was confident that Marchand was planning to come back for him if he hadn't been found.

"What about all the technical stuff?" I asked him. "Marchand seemed to be very familiar with the hotel's technological capabilities."

"Yes, he was quite interested in that aspect of the job— especially the master key concept. I told him that having that degree of control made me uncomfortable."

What made Dunaway uncomfortable had likely given Marchand the confidence to pull off such an elaborate scheme in the age of internet surveillance. It became clear after the fact that Marchand had gone in and doctored the room audits, while also ensuring that we'd never have access to a single functioning security camera.

"You could have died in that cellar," I said. "You were lucky."

"But I *didn't* die," he said. "Certainly if he had wanted to kill me, he would have done it when he had the chance—don't you think?"

I wasn't sure what to think, although he had a point. Dunaway could have spoiled the whole scheme. After all, he was central to Marchand's con.

Before I could answer what sounded like a rhetorical question, Dunaway said, "Another thing I've though about . . . why else would he have given me one of his masterworks if I wasn't going to be around to enjoy it? Leon was passionate about art; he had commissioned that painting specifically for me after talking about our favorite areas of the park. I was very grateful."

In the end, we agreed that Marchand was a complicated man with complicated motives. Aria Privar, on the other hand, had very different opinion of the man that had killed her boyfriend. Two weeks after her ordeal, Aria agreed to sit down with me and Hux for a formal interview. We arranged to meet her at the FBI field office in San Francisco.

It was a raw, chilly day in November in the city by the bay, with a dreary gray rain pounding the pavement. I was waiting outside a grungy deli when Hux came around the corner wearing a heavy jacket and a navy wool hat. I'd seen him only a few days ago, but it felt like weeks had passed. In the urban jungle, he always looked like a slightly different person—more cosmopolitan, in a way. The dark pants and dress shoes, for instance; both were departures from his norm.

"No one told me that the FBI had a dress code," I said, smirking at him.

"What?" He glanced down nervously at his jacket and pants. "Am I too dressed up?"

"You're fine."

He sighed as he broke into a smile. "Look, I don't get out much."

"You got out last weekend," I said. "Remember?"

No matter the weather, Hux's green eyes seemed to shine through the gloom. I had dressed up a little, too, with my white sweater and dark jeans, and my hair had benefitted from some actual TLC that morning. I pushed a wayward strand behind my ear.

We stood there a while, neither of us sure what to say or where to go from here. As for "last weekend," Bodie had canceled our dinner reservation because of a work emergency, but he'd offered me the table at the restaurant—which, apparently, were impossible to get. I would have been fine with California Pizza Kitchen, but Bodie liked to impress.

"Take whoever you want," he'd said, doing his best to hide the disappointment in his voice. *"I won't be offended."*

I'd thought about going alone, but my sister had talked me out of it. Inviting Hux Huxley to a fancy dinner in downtown San Francisco for no obvious professional reason had posed some challenges, but in the end, we both knew it wasn't professional at all.

It was personal.

I just wasn't ready to talk about that yet.

"Let's be gentle with Aria Privar today," I said to Hux, who had taken to holding the door for everyone coming in and out of the deli. "I'm going to let her take the lead, for the most part. There will be time later for questions."

He nodded. "Sounds good to me."

Buffeting ourselves against the rain, we walked quickly down the block to headquarters. After a quick rendezvous with Granger, who gruffly commended our work on both Pinnacles cases, Hux and I met Aria in one of the interrogation rooms.

One of her legs was still in a full cast, but her cuts and bruises had healed. The three of us congregated around a plastic white table. The air coming out of the vents smelled like stale coffee and ramen noodles, and it made me relish my time in ISB.

The introductions were brief, the pleasantries non-existent. Aria had been through a lot, and I could tell that just being here had taken a lot out of her.

After Hux had gone out to get her a soda, Aria put an envelope on the table.

"He sent me this," she said.

The envelope had already been opened, and I could see a single piece of paper inside. When Hux returned moments later, I put on a pair of gloves and removed the contents. I wanted him to be there for the reveal, too.

The note was typed, the paper plain white. I'd send it to the lab for processing, but I also knew it wasn't going to matter.

I'm sorry for what I put you through, it read. *But the man you were with deserved to die. I feel no remorse for his death.*

It was signed, *Leon Marchand.*

I put the note back in the envelope and left it on the table. Aria dropped her chin to her chest, fighting back tears. I wondered who—or what—she was thinking about.

"We'll keep looking for him," Hux said. "We give you our word on that."

Aria picked at a divot in the table with her thumb. "I've cared for children like him," she said. Her voice was so soft I had to lean in to hear her. "Children who have seen and experienced terrible things; their trauma lives with them for years afterward." She wiped at her eyes. "In a weird way, I feel sorry for him."

Steadying her voice, she told us the story of her terrifying encounter with Leon Marchand—the murder she'd witnessed, her desperate attempt to negotiate with a killer. She said that after her frantic escape from Condor's balcony, she'd barely felt the ground under feet as she took to the trails that night.

It was only later, hours into her ordeal, that she realized one grave danger had morphed into another. A fear of retribution from Marchand had propelled her furious pace at first, but as the temperature dropped in the early morning hours, she started to worry about freezing to death. She didn't have a phone or any proper gear; she was running blindly into a vast unknown.

"I was trying to get back to the parking lot," she said, "but I was afraid to stay on the trail, so at some point I must have gotten off-course. I didn't have a map, or a phone . . . all I had was the stars, which I tried to follow north."

She reached for the Diet Coke Hux had brought in for her. "And then I saw the cave," she said. "I was so relieved at first. It was warmer in there than out in the open." She sipped the soda. "But I was so desperate to get in there and hide that I didn't see the crevasse; I fell right in."

"About twenty feet," Hux said. "That was quite a fall."

She nodded. "I felt my leg break, but the pain came later. I was just so terrified; I felt disconnected from my body, in a way."

Aria had actually fractured her pelvis, not just her femur. Now, just two weeks out from her surgeries, she used a walker to get around. I remembered those days during my own recovery: the anguish of unrelenting physical pain, the despair that things would never get better. For me, it had turned into an obsession. I was better, but I would never be whole again.

"Being down there, I felt like such a failure," she said. "I couldn't move—couldn't walk, couldn't climb out. At some point I realized that unless someone came looking for me, I was going to die in that cave. It was the most helpless I've felt in my life."

"You're not a failure," I said. "You survived."

She shook her head, something forlorn in her gaze. "Only because you found me."

Hux leveled his gaze at her. "No, Aria, because you didn't give up. You lasted five days out there on your own. That's an incredible display of willpower."

Meeting his eyes, she nodded. "Thank you. I mean, almost dying in that cave . . . it made me wonder what could have been."

"What do you mean?" I asked.

Her voice dropped to a whisper, which made the rattling HVAC system sound like a deafening roar.

"My life was kind of a mess," she said. "During my relationship with Chris, we were always being harassed by his crazy ex-wife. I was in residency, trying to prove something to my parents, probably also to myself . . ." Her shoulders sagged, but she quickly straightened them again. "I thought that if I could actually walk out of there on my own two feet, I might not necessarily have to go back. You know—fake my death or something. Start over." With some trepidation, she looked up. "Does that make any sense?"

"Yeah," Hux said. "It definitely does. But don't worry, Colleen isn't getting off scot-free. She'll do some jail time for harassment."

Aria nodded, placated by Hux's words. But hearing her talk about walking away from her life, only to inhabit a new one where she could put all her troubles in the rearview . . . and thinking about Leon Marchand, who had done just that . . .

It made me think of someone else.

It made me think of Kevin.

ACKNOWLEDGMENTS

OVER THE LAST ten years, my writing routine has changed dramatically. I used to write every day, at the same time, with my favorite sourdough bagel and a Diet Coke fueling every word. I was kind of precious about it.

Now, though, I'm only writing books because the people in my life give me the time and space to make it happen. Many thanks to my husband, Fletcher, who helps me break story ideas when I'm running on four hours of sleep. Thanks also to the amazing women who help care for our young kids when I'm at work or trying to get some writing time in. Our village is small but mighty, and I'm so grateful for their support.

I also want to acknowledge my wonderful literary agent, Beth Miller, and the entire team at Crooked Lane, for giving my stories a place to thrive.